SING A SONG
OF SIXPENCE

SING A SONG OF SIXPENCE

GARNET QUINN

Acknowledgments

WHILE WRITING IS a solitary occupation, bringing the results to readers is not. An editor is essential. Mine is Helen Cripe. She has the touch of angels, those with a sense of humor. This book is the better for it. Ann Mary Bishop is a whiz of a graphics designer whose covers add greatly to my endeavors. And all those wonderful readers who've eagerly asked "when is the next book coming out?" have kept me at it.

Cats Rule
But you knew that, didn't you?

SING A SONG OF SIXPENCE

CHAPTER ONE

S HERE KHAN LOOKED up as the bigger cat padded across the forest toward him on silent tufted paws. The Great One, as he was known hereabouts in North Central Maine, thought to himself as he chuckled—with no malice intended—that his wilder cousin looked like a feline designed by a committee. The large ears with their hairy tips thick and spiky sat on a broad head not unlike that of Henry Merriman's grandsire with his mutton-chop whiskers, a portrait Shere Khan had often seen hanging in Bethmom's back hall. His hindquarters were higher than his withers, which reminded Khan of that circus parade in Patten where a couple of mantoms became a cloth-covered horse. His tail was short and stubby and his paws—well, Bast Bespoke, his paws were easily as big as The Great One's own head! The old tom, no ordinary sized Maine Coon cat himself not far past his prime, sighed sadly. The coat on the huge Canadian lynx approaching him wasn't so long and silky as his own but it was thick, plush and very beautiful. Much to its owner's detriment. That pelt might mean the end of him. It was highly prized among humankind—but not with its original owner in it! And no amount of government legislation seemed to discourage the Ultimate Predator from coveting it. That the mantoms also seemed hellbent on destroying his ancient habitat didn't help either.

The handsome brown tabby tom with the blazing white teardrop in the middle of his forehead shook off such negative thoughts. Deep in the woods far from his normal haunts around Bethmom's Siberia Farm, he was about to greet an old friend, if one he only saw on rare occasions: Loki, the Canadian lynx. Normally the very disparate feline species would not interact. (And thank Bastet, nobody as yet had tried to make a house pet of him!) To Khan's vast relief and as Nature had intended, domestic felines were not on the lynx's menu for preferred dining. Their dinner of choice was the abundant snowshoe hare that also inhabited the same forests. Supply and demand, thought Shere Khan, grinning to himself. But as it is with most all creatures on the planet, sometimes life—and crises—make strange bedfellows. Like the fawn and the bobcat kitten who bonded closely when rescued from a raging wildfire out west and found themselves stashed together willy-nilly in the first place their rescuers could reach safely: a game warden's office. Khan often wondered how those two felt about each other when they grew up…

Loki and Shere Khan had crossed paths for the first time one cold afternoon in early spring as Khan was patrolling the outer perimeter of his territory. He didn't often come this way unless he'd been to see his kinsman, the red Maine Coon tom, Riddle, at Singletary's remotely situated farm far from any of the small inhabited places and crossroads of North Central Maine in the shadow of Mt. Katahdin. While he was out and about after such a visit, he had decided to check on some newly marked territory of a critter he didn't know. Shere Khan was always on the lookout for invaders, no matter what the species. He had just poked his head into an odiferous hollow log when he heard a terrible racket. Bumping his crown as he withdrew too quickly from the rotting timber, he shook his head and looked around for the source of the noise. It didn't take him long to find it. He winced at the pain in his noggin, stood up on his hindquarters like an edgy meerkat and, his curiosity getting the better of him, trotted toward the uproar.

A camouflaged steel cage-trap with a huge feline inside was rocking back and forth, its prisoner panicky and letting the world know about it. She'd evidently gone inside to the bait and couldn't get out. Her huge paws were just too clumsy to work the door. Her mate, still outside the trap, was prowling around it, trying to calm his consort and figure out how to get her free at the same time. They were evidently too busy dealing with their own predicament to worry about their smaller observer, standing poised at the edge of the small clearing.

For his part, Shere Khan wasn't real sure he ought to draw their attention, discretion being the better part of a whole skin as his sire, Minstrel, often said. To tell the truth, he'd never seen a lynx before, although he certainly knew what he was looking at in that clearing. This peripatetic Maine Coon was one of those rare creatures Ma Nature occasionally slides in amongst all her other creations to make monkeys of us all—in a manner of speaking. This huge very handsome brown tabby tom with large green eyes was not only highly intelligent but imbued with courage, finesse and quick-wittedness far beyond what ordinary mortals of any stripe might possess. Khan never thought of himself as the alpha cat but he most certainly was—and most all critters in his patch respected that.

He hopped up on an exposed boulder, quickly assessed the situation and waved his very luxuriant plumey white-tipped tail. "Hang on, Mistress," he said in a commanding voice. "I can't get you free. That trap door is too secure even for my clever paws. But I know somebody who can."

The Maine Coon strolled confidently up to the pair of lynx, secure in his mind that the big tom was more concerned with freeing his consort than in making a meal of *him*. The lynx turned in his direction quickly and looked at Shere Khan in surprise, his mate suddenly silent in response.

"What are you talking about, small cousin?" the huge wild feline barked, his wary gold eyes intent on The Great One. It was a look that would have shriveled a lesser cat—or a human being, for that matter. Stressed as he and his consort were, however, they'd clutch at any straws that might free the rather pregnant queen.

"I'm Shere Khan," the old Coon declared, "I'm sure you've noticed me and my kind hereabouts. Though I'm also sure we've never been properly introduced."

The big lynx looked abashed. Felines have always been ones to remember good manners in all interactions. It gave them time to assess any situation that might turn chancy. "I'm Loki," he said and, turning in the direction of the once more rocking cage, added, "This is my consort, Crya."

For her part, the big queen trapped in the cage quit struggling for a moment, rolled her eyes and gave the other two cats a disgusted look. "Will you two quit playing 'after-you-my-dear-Alphonse' and get me out of here!"

The two toms looked at each other.

"Hold your hisses, Mistress, as my young son, Star, would say." He turned and peered at Loki. "I'll be back shortly. And don't panic," he added with emphasis, "when you see a mantom with me. I'm going to fetch the game warden—a guardian for wild creatures, if you will—he'll have Mistress Crya out of there in Jig's time." He gave the pair a conspiratorial grin. "Then he'll go lookin' for that trapper and haul *him* off to a cage!"

"Not if I get to him first!" growled Loki, still prowling around his queen's prison.

Shere Khan sprinted through the woods towards the game warden's cabin/camp. He knew Chad Merryman was there; he'd seen his truck parked outside as he'd come that way. The mantom was an old acquaintance, who in the course of courting Khan's own mistress—if such a wandering feline as he could be said to have a mistress—had become a good and helpful friend on more than one occasion and in more than one crisis. Further, in their exploits together, the game warden had become finely tuned to the peculiarities of Bethmom's cats. Khan paused to catch his breath. "I'm getting too old for this," he said aloud to a curious squirrel high in the branches of the oak above his head. The squirrel kept a discreet silence. One didn't mess with Maine Coons. They could climb trees almost as good as he could.

The Great One started up again. A thought struck him, something that had been nagging at him. That cage trap back there. From what he'd seen of the vicious poachers and trappers hereabouts, they mostly used snares and those deadly steel-jawed leg traps. This cage trap was attached to a chain and the chain was secured to a wooden stake that looked very much like a strip of those wooden stretcher frames that Chad Merryman used to keep his painting canvas taut when he was playing wildlife artist. The big brown tom, his snowy white ruff swinging back and forth around his neck as he ran, stopped abruptly in his tracks. *Surely Chad hadn't set this trap? He wouldn't do that—would he? No way!* He threw off that thought and scrambled through some low hanging branches close to the game warden's campsite where the mantom retreated when he wanted to paint, read or just charge his batteries, given the stresses and vicissitudes of his profession. Most rural folk in Upper Maine kept small cabins like Merryman's, often at some little distance from their domiciles. An oxymoron perhaps, as "home" might often be little more than that primitive cabin in the back woods, which they most often referred to as their "camps."

Coming into the clearing, Shere Khan leaped up on the rickety porch just as the game warden came around the corner of the cabin with a canister of propane gas for his cooktop, his cat Smudge, a former street cat from New York City, bounding along happily in front of him. Chad's other cat, Sweeper, had elected to stay behind in Chad's apartment as he was still recovering from an injury received during an escape in that City, when he and Khan had teamed up with the wily old street cat to escape what one could almost call catpoachers, after which Smudge was brought back to Maine with the gang, homelessness for him a thing of the past. The silver and white mackerel tabby neuter with the notched ear and a smudge of black across his nose, no longer grubby, slat thin and scruffy, had taken to the North Woods like a loon to Millinocket Lake.

Yo, Shere Khan, what brings you here? You're a bit far from home, aren't you?

The two cats touched noses. *I've been to visit Riddle at Singletary's,* Khan explained, *but no time to talk now. Explain later.*

"RheoowwW!" He exclaimed loudly as Merryman put foot to porch step. *Quickly, Chad, the lynx need your help!* He reached out one big furry extra-toed paw and snagged the man's trouser leg, looking up at the game warden with appeal. Surprised to see him, particularly in this state of agitation, Chad put down the canister of propane.

"What's with you, old son?" He started to kneel down and run his hands over the big tom to see if perhaps he was injured.

Khan repeated himself. *Quickly, Chad, before the trapper comes back.*

"Rhiow!" he howled again, leaping off the porch and running to the edge of the clearing. There he paused, looking back over his shoulder at the game warden with a concerned gaze. To give urgency to his stance, he stood up squirrel-like on his hind legs and pawed the air, as if to indicate, "this way, hurry!"

Chad, not at all concerned what his co-workers might think seeing him traipse off after one of Beth's Coons, hesitated only long enough to shove the canister inside and lock his cabin door. Pocketing the key, he stepped off the porch and with Smudge on his heels, strode across the clearing after Shere Khan.

It being early spring, the birches and other deciduous trees weren't yet in leaf. But the hemlocks and slender conical spruces made the going a bit hazardous for a tall man. The deer path was there but whippy branches had to be flung out of one's face. For all that, the game warden had no difficulty following the white-tipped high flying banner of his guide and no reluctance to do so. Presently, they came to an open space where the resident deer—and moose perhaps—had bedded down of an evening, leaving the ground soft and bare. Chad stopped and gazed at the illegal black, spray painted cage trap next to a tree at the edge of this "deer yard" with an obviously pregnant Canadian lynx inside. He realized instantly why the trapper had used this method of trapping instead of the usual crippling leg traps. He wanted the kittens to sell to the hated wildlife farms where, for a fee, visiting gunman could play Mighty Hunter, killing indiscriminately and showing off such rare if secretly trapped creatures mounted on their game room walls. Chad was of the opinion that this was a fate more wished for on the hunters than the hunted. To his mind, killing wild animals could only be labeled real "sport" when the deer were armed with Uzis.

He paused in the center of the clearing. One lynx, obviously a big tom, gazed back at him as he stood motionless beside the trap. From inside the device, the smaller of the two wild creatures crouched down, eyes large with apprehension, wary of the game warden. Shere Khan bounded over to the cage and stood beside the bigger cat. Smudge, so recently transplanted from city to countryside, hunkered down where he was behind the man. Like all felines over millennia, he'd *wait*. It was a trait that had served his ancestors well and Smudge, never having seen a cat—let alone two—so huge, with paws as big as his head, well, he'd stay where he was until he felt certain he himself wasn't on their menu for lunch.

"Damn," muttered the game warden, "Trapping you big fellas is illegal as hell—" He chewed on his lip for a moment, assessing the situation. There was no doubt in his mind that the first order of business was to free the queen. But he also had great respect for the claws on those big feet and he wasn't at all sure both cats wouldn't attack him as he set about opening the trap door. Most wild animals would run from humans—unless they felt cornered. And this beautiful pair was certainly boxed in.

Before he could make up his mind how best to deal with the problem, he realized two things. The big lynx outside the cage was neither hostile nor frightened. He merely stood his ground. Obviously, that was his mate inside. Then he realized Shere Khan, that wily old Coon, was standing beside the bigger tom with only the tip of his tail making lazy circles as if the two of them had been making conversation at an afternoon tea party.

"Well, Khan, old son, if you're not afraid of the big fella, I don't reckon there's any reason for me to be."

Not wanting to make any moves that would spook Khan's wilder cousins, he approached the cage circumspectly. Slowly, he reached down and freed the trap's door, softly talking nonsense all the time as the lynx watched him. He carefully raised the metal door and stepped back out of the way. Secretly, he was filled with elation on seeing for himself—though the presence of such rare cats had been rumored—a pair of the Canadian lynx here on his own patch. Such majestic creatures they were! He could only watch in wonder.

The big queen looked up at him, raised a paw tentatively and then, seeing the mantom's benign stance, she bounded out of the trap, touched noses with her consort and the two big cats quickly vanished into the thick brush, their camouflaging pelts making them seem to suddenly disappear into the ether.

Merryman smiled and looked down at Shere Khan as Smudge slowly came up behind them. The old tom sat down, raised a paw and casually washed an ear. *All in a day's work*, the gesture said.

"Khan, you are somthin' else!" He declared laughing as he kicked loose the stake which had held the cage secure, inspected the contraption, folded it up, his lips pursed in thought and carried it back the way they had come.

"Greedy trappers!" he declared vehemently as he strode along with his two furry companions, "are just as bad as poachers. And this one sure had his nerve, setting an illegal trap so close to my camp." Elated at finding concrete proof that the lynx were really about in Penobscot County, he was going to go back to town and put the fear of God in the local poachers and trappers—one way or another.

A smile crossed Shere Khan's face at the memory of this episode, his first meeting with Loki. That had been a bit of luck for all of them—save the trapper—back in the early spring. Chad walked on air for weeks over the encounter. Crya had escaped the trap and Khan had become acquainted with allies he might never have come across otherwise. Now he casually went forth to meet the bigger cat in the high summer sunshine, the events going on back at Siberia Farm of no real importance to him. Humans taking consorts? So what else is new?

He'd known all along that the game warden would make his move sooner or later. Beth had turned, it seemed to him, as giddy as a young queen at her first cat show. He'd visit with Loki for a spell and with any luck, he'd get back to Siberia Farm in time to share the leftovers from the wedding feast.

CHAPTER TWO

"WHERE'S CHAD?" GASTON MICHAUD fidgeted. He straightened his tie, stretching his neck in an unaccustomed collar that pinched, and looked inquiringly at his wife, Martha, standing beside him. She was fiddling with the corsage of tuberoses and baby's breath that graced her shoulder. All the windows of the Moosery, a rebuilt old barn next to Siberia Farm which served as a community center, were wide open and a lovely summer breeze nudged the tuberoses, wafting sweet scent over her. At her husband's question, she frowned and looked round for Beth. It was early yet but the building was already busy with friends and neighbors readying things for the wedding banquet and eager wedding guests who were arriving. She'd last seen the bride-to-be in the ladies' room applying makeup, a most unfamiliar chore for Herself, Beth being normally about as interested in makeup as Madame, her Maine Coon matriarch. Quickly, Martha caught sight of her now standing a few feet away, nervously smoothing out her skirt.

She, too, was frowning, lost in thought, looking out a window of the Moosery, her bouquet of lilies-of-the-valley and stephanotis on the window ledge beside her. *Where's Chad indeed*, Beth murmured to herself, having heard Gaston's question. *Surely he wouldn't be late for his own wedding. Surely the deer and the moose and the beavers and those new—maybe—residents which so elated him, the rare Canadian*

Lynx, could spare him long enough for him to get married...The bride-to-be shook herself and gazed heavenward. What wild insanity prompted me to say yes to a man whose job is about as safe and boring as a sail-plane in a hurricane? Game wardens have an iffier time of it than policemen... and policemen, at least, usually have backup. Moose could hardly be called up as deputies... She sighed and looked again toward the empty road to the Moosery. She knew there had to be a good reason for his tardiness but that didn't make her any less anxious.

Somehow, Beth's preparations for her wedding had not impressed themselves on the cats at MerryMaines cattery up the hill at the old farmhouse. They were aware of much to-ing and fro-ing among Beth, Cheryl, Martha, Chad's mom and other ladies in the community but that there was soon to be a change in Siberia Farm's inhabitants, they really hadn't noticed all that much. Well, it was expected: their sleek very fey little blue Korat seeress Bhu Fan had told them all that, but so? The cats had watched as a group of Beth's quilter friends were spending a lot more time in her loft sewing room above the old barn floor that served as the cattery. A lot of joshing and laughter interrupting whatever they were working on resounded to the cats below. But after Bhu Fan's prediction, it was business as usual "below stairs". The sleek blue very royal Korat was busy keeping order in her feline kingdom, the doings of humankind of no great interest—so long as there were no crises. Her Highness always rose to the challenge in a crisis.

Madame du Maine, their tortoiseshell matriarch who lived principally in the old farmhouse, also kept an eye on things but she was busy instructing her half grown offspring, Magic and Moonrise, in the mores expected of show cat queens, with a bit of help from that old pro, Beowulf, who now that he was neutered, shared the house with them, Hawkeye, Bhu's favorite peasant and often, the Korat princess herself. Thus it was, when things really began to heat up in the Moosery and Chad let the cat out of the bag, so to speak, on the big event's eve by bringing most of his own bag and baggage into the old house (except for his wedding suit, which his superstitious mother had requested he put on at his apartment), the cats were only mildly surprised and none of them paid much attention.

Nevertheless, when Beth, with the aid of friends, tried on a real dress, all ivory silk and lace and showed off a few unusual purchases of more silk and lace, Bhu Fan began to get the idea that maybe this taking a consort among humankind was a bit more interesting than she had surmised. Certainly its ceremony would need her royal person to preside over things. And really, she should have access to all that silky, filmy fabric for a nest afterwards. It was only her due.

Out in the forest at some little distance from Siberia Farm on that particular day, however, and unmindful of the suspense at the Moosery with its missing bridegroom, Shere Khan and Loki renewed their friendship. The Great One didn't really care for crowds of humankind anyway. No matter how careful he might be in a crowd, someone was bound to step on his tail.

"You've a new litter of kits, have you?" Shere Khan remarked as Loki, having reached the log where Khan was lying, sat down beside him. The light summer breeze had the birches shimmering, their leaves dancing like tinsel on a Christmas tree. Sunshine danced among shadows across the deer yard. Counting back to their encounter with the trapped Crya in the early spring, Khan figured that the kittens must be about three months old now. And summertime for kitlings was sheer joy; they'd have the world by the tail. He looked expectantly at his big cousin.

"Yeah," growled Loki, who took his parenting very seriously, "four of 'em. And a knuckle-headed bunch they are. Got the attention span of a gnat." He shifted his stance as a hemlock branch slapped him across his shoulders.

Shere Khan chuckled. "Yeah, that's about right. Kits are just too curious about everything that flutters across their path to concentrate on learning anything." Khan peered around. "Where are they, anyway?"

"Crya's teaching 'em to fish—over by the beaver pond." Loki looked glum. "Might as well teach a hare to fly—and there aren't enough of *them* around to keep little bellies full this summer." He gave Shere Khan a long look. "But I'd rather they learned to fish than hang out at the garbage dump over there by that black evil-smelling roadway to the timberyard." He snorted. "It's just not fittin'; that scrounging in the garbage; my cousin, Brinna, calls it 'dumpster diving'. Blah!"

He nodded his head in an easterly direction. "They're down by the pond where it flows into the creek the beavers have dammed. Water's not so high now, so the creek's slowed a bit. Do you know the place? It's not far."

"Yeah," replied Shere Khan. "The game warden—remember him?—he's been keeping track of the beaver kits. Some sort of survey for his, what do they call it? The fish 'n game depart-ment." The Great One looked wise and grinned broadly. "I daresay he's there today, though. He's getting married."

"Married?" Loki looked taken aback." What's that? Some kinda treatment for some dreaded mantom disease?"

"Well, I suppose you might call it that; he's taking Bethmom for his consort." Shere Khan chuckled low in his throat. "Mantoms make a big thing of it." He licked his paw negligently.

"Well," Loki replied, giving his fellow tom a knowing look. "Let's hope *his* consort doesn't have the same troublemaking curiosity mine does." Loki was no doubt recalling the baited cage trap as he reached around and bit at his flank. A proud expression crossed his face as he sat back up. "Let's go see how the fisherkits are making out."

When the beaver pond came into view, a strange scene was playing out in front of the two felines as they hovered silently in the brush at woods' edge. Crya and the kits were nowhere to be seen. The two toms squinted in the bright sunlight reflecting off the pond, poised where they were, frozen in their tracks.

The game warden, in deep concentration, was standing near the reeds at water's edge by the beaver dam folding up his clipboard and glancing at his watch. He appeared to be leaving, unaware that another figure was sneaking up behind him with a large broken tree branch in his hand. Before the cats could react, the game warden's assailant struck him on the back of the head and as his victim fell forward, the would-be trapper bent over to push his head under water.

But by now, Loki had caught his scent. "The Cager!!" he roared as he leaped forward. "That's the dogdung who caught Crya in that trap!"

"This is not like Chad, Beth," her matron of honor, Cheryl Smith stated with fervor, coming up to stand beside her and Martha. "He's just not the kind of guy who would leave his bride at the church house door—or the Moosery either." Beth's best friend, clad for once in a real dress and, unhappily feeling the constraints of pantyhose, waved her small bouquet around. "Do you suppose there's been an accident?" She peered from the Moosery kitchen door at all Beth's friends and neighbors and Chad's family gathered near the tall stands of candelabra in front of the fireplace, over which a huge pair of moose antlers gave benediction to the gathering below. Were the wedding guests getting restless and growing concerned, too? A slight movement from above caught Cheryl's eye and she looked up.

A slim fuzzy red tail was hanging down from behind one side of the thick cradle of the moose rack where it hung over the fireplace. Cheryl poked at Beth and pointed in the direction of the huge bone-colored rack. A humorous diversion might take her mind off her missing bridegroom for a bit.

"What? Who—?"

Beth shook her head and strode straight into the big hall and looked up, her hands on her hips. At the sound of such purposeful footfalls and the sudden lack of sound from all the guests standing around chatting, a small head appeared between two of the points on the moose antlers and looked downward wide-eyed, whiskers twitching.

"Posey! You imp! How did you get up there?" Beth said sternly, trying her best not to grin. "You come down here this minute!"

As Loki crashed through the brush, Chad's attacker looked up and awkwardly attempted to rise from where he had bent over the prone figure of the game warden. Halfway to his feet, he was caught on his right shoulder by a flying fury who knocked him off balance and sank sharp teeth into his ear, all the while making a fearsome racket. As the poacher attempted to fight him off, Crya came leaping forward from her hiding place and sprang onto his back. As the two lynx savaged their former tormentor, Shere Khan tried to drag the unconscious Chad Merryman from the now roiling muddy pond. But the man was too much of a dead weight.

Loki! Crya! I need help! He cried from between clinched teeth.

The two wild cats, who normally would neither attack nor assist, but would shy away from any such close contact with humankind, left the game warden's assailant and leaped to help Shere Khan pull Chad Merryman from the water. Their erstwhile victim, the trapper, his shirt in tatters, his trousers ripped, scrambled to his feet and crashed noisily through the woods, leaving a bloody trail behind him, swearing roundly as he went.

Merryman, revived by the cold water, groggily raised his head from where it had come to rest on his outstretched arms and shook himself. Realizing he was being dragged backwards from the broken reeds at pondside, he twisted around to see who had come to his rescue. A lesser man would have thought himself hallucinating at what he saw. Chad just blinked and, realizing what had just happened to him, scanned his surroundings for his attacker. All he heard was the distant start-up of a vehicle badly in need of a new muffler. He relaxed, not wanting to have been caught napping a second time. Where had his assailant come from anyway?

Loki and Crya and Shere Khan had his belt in their teeth and were using powerful shoulder muscles to drag him away from drowning. Four lynx kits had his pant legs and sock tops in their teeth and were lending a paw. However, when the lynx family realized he had come to himself, they leaped away and, with a departing salute to Shere Khan, disappeared into the woods with their offspring scrambling along behind.

Merryman sat up and looked around again, shaking his dripping head. Whoever had attacked him, he was long gone now. Thank God for small favors. Not far aside lay a couple of beaver traps where his assailant must have dropped them. Slowly it came to him that he must have showed up with his clipboard at a most inopportune time for the would-be trapper who evidently didn't have the patience to wait for him to leave. Damn. Were beaver pelts important enough to a trapper to kill the game warden for them? He gazed at Shere Khan standing four-square beside him, shaking muddy paws.

"Well now, old buddy, I'm not sure how you engineered my rescue but I don't doubt for one moment that you did—and who'd believe *that* back at the office?" The game warden felt the back of his head. "Lucky for me that log was rotten." He got to his feet slowly, his head throbbing like thunder. Carefully, he rubbed his hair from back to front, trying to get rid of all the muddy pond water and bits of bark from the rotten branch.

"Rhiow!" exclaimed Shere Khan, looking pointedly in the direction of the beaver lodge. Three small heads and two larger ones had broken the water's surface and were paddling frantically in the direction of their dam where Chad's fall had dislodged some of its underpinnings. "Sorry, guys," he said with a faint smile as he got to his feet. "I really didn't do it on purpose." The game warden backed away from pond's edge, took off his wet shirt and wrung it out. Putting it back on to cover his shivering body, he glanced down at his companion.

"Dammit, Khan, it looks like I'm going to be late for my own wedding! That'll teach me to think I can expand time. And if I ever lay my hands on that trapper—" The man shook his head angrily, picked up his clipboard from where it had fallen against one of the trap chains and brushed it off. The mud would soon dry and with any luck, he'd be able to find his notes legible. He reached for the traps as well. Did they hold fingerprints? Well, maybe. Anyway, he'd impound the traps. Again, he glanced at his watch. Scorch it! He'd better hurry!

Smudge, who had again been asleep on the seat of Chad's truck when he'd set out to make some notes on the beaver kits, came furtively into the clearing, once again Tail-end Charlie. He stood for a moment watching his boss. The old fellow wouldn't have backed off from a cat fight in more familiar territory; he who had seen plenty of violence in his time. What transpired *between* mantoms, however, never bothered him so much—unless he got caught in the cross-fire or the fight involved his own human. It was clear now, though, that Chad was okay and didn't need his help. He turned his thoughts to the departed wild felines. A cat the size of the Canadian lynx was something else altogether different. He'd seen them back in the spring, of course, but not at such close range—even their kits were as big as he! Smudge faced The Great One.

You sure have some weird friends, Khan, he remarked as the two cats followed the striding game warden up the path that led to the overgrown logging track where Chad had left his truck. *Who was that mantom who attacked Chad?* The two cats hopped up on the seat as Merryman dropped the beaver traps into his truck bed and quickly opened the door for them.

He's a poacher, Smudge... One we've crossed paths with before. He threw away Zandra's kitlings once (but we rescued them) and tried to burn down Chad's camp last winter. A nasty piece of work, as they say on Simon's TV.

The two cats stretched out on the seat and tried to get comfortably balanced as the truck bumped over the ruts and potholes while the game warden drove with more urgency than usual.

I don't think this time Chad ever got a good look at him. Or he'd sure know who to go looking for once we get back to town. Khan chuckled. *But I have an idea that our game warden has other plans for the moment... 'n he's going to be even later gettin' there cuz he's got to stop at the apartment to pick up his good clothes. Somehow I don't see him taking a consort lookin' like he does now... I think he's got some explaining to do to Bethmom about how he thought he could count beavers and get hitched all in the same day...*

Smudge smirked knowingly. *What's that old saying about "out of the fryin' pan into the fire?"*

CHAPTER THREE

"HERE COMES CHAD'S TRUCK!" Cheryl cried from the front door of the Moosery, swinging around to face all the guests in the big hall. She looked around to make sure Beth heard her. Seeing the broad relieved smile on the bride's face, she knew Beth had understood as she came out of the building and started down the steps. Other guests crowded the doorway behind her as Chad got out of his truck, his shirt still damp and dirty, his hair disheveled, a Valpak containing clean clothes slung over one shoulder. The sight of her bridegroom in such a state stopped Beth Merriman in her tracks. *Surely he hadn't forgotten today's event? What in the world had happened to him?*

Having taken time only to stop and grab his wedding clothes at the apartment, Chad himself was a bit nonplussed to see the well dressed crowd all round the doorway. How to explain that he thought he had time to do a little research before it was time for him to arrive for the wedding? Would anybody understand that a man could get wedding jitters and try to distract himself for awhile? And, boy howdy, what a distraction it had been! He hesitated as the wedding guests gazed in confusion at his messy state. The game warden sighed and, seeing Beth poised on the bottom step, started forward again. There was no help for it. He'd explain his misadventure all in good time when more important matters were tended to. First things first: he had to play his part in the Main Event. He smiled sheepishly at his bride-to-be as he walked toward the building.

Beth took in that abashed grin and shook her head in exasperation. She knew Chad Merryman. He had no doubt been out playing with the beavers again and fell in the pond. How often had she heard him wish for four more hours in each day and another pair of hands? She had to say something and with forty people looking on, whatever she said would cause him embarrassment. But she couldn't help herself.

" What on earth happened to you? Are you okay, Chad? Don't tell me you fell in the beaver pond—today of all days?" Beth put her hands to her face and drew in a deep breath as she walked along beside him; at this point she didn't know whether to laugh or cry. Whatever had befallen Chad, it most likely had to do with his job. Didn't it always? Irrelevantly, her attention was drawn to Merryman's cats, Smudge and Sweeper, tagging along behind the game warden, tails to the perpendicular. Clean as a whistle they were; obviously they'd played no part in his mishap. Before her intended could make any response to Beth's questions, however, Cheryl came down the steps and took charge.

"Chad, go get yourself a shower in the visitors' rooms downstairs. Gaston, herd everybody back into the big hall and alert the pastor." Hiding a smile, she added, "We'll wait." Quickly leaning over, Beth's matron of honor bent down and scooped up the unintended four-footed groomsmen. "I'll take these guys to the cattery." She gave the guests crowded on the top steps a big smile. "By the time I get back, maybe we can get this show on the road."

As she tossed the cats onto the front seat of her vehicle, she added over her shoulder, laughing, "With any luck, Chad will clean up real nice." She glanced pointedly at the motionless game warden. "And Beth will still marry you if you don't—but you're not getting away from here until we have the whole story about how it is that you and your furry bachelor friends here got led astray."

In all the excitement of the bridegroom's rather unusual entrance, nobody noticed Khan, the third feline member of the arriving party, who furtively made his way, belly low to the ground, around the side of Merryman's truck, under the other parked vehicles by the door and into the old barn's understory where motel-like rooms were maintained for guests, hikers and tourists who visited this area of North Central Maine close by Baxter State Park. Khan was not about to let himself be shut up in Beth's cattery. Not yet. Somebody, after all, was going to be needed to render a report of this rather fancy affair of taking a consort, no matter how inconsequential he might have made of it himself. He was sure—and make no mistake about it—the furry Princess Bhu Fan, MerryMaines' resident royal Korat would want chapter and verse, no matter how insignificant the detail. Females of *all* species, he considered, would probably want all the details of frills and fancy dress. He suspected *that* interest was hard-wired. And almost losing one of the participants to the beavers, on this day of all days, would greatly interest the male inhabitants of MerryMaines, he was certain. Particularly the intervention and help of those unlikely guerillas, Loki and Crya.

Bhu Fan's ears were no doubt burning but if she had any real inkling of Shere Khan's thoughts, she was ignoring them. Once she realized the magnitude of this marriage for the inhabitants of her little kingdom, she was clearly annoyed. Bhu Fan licked at her shoulder compulsively. Royalty was not used to being excluded from Grand Events. A princess of such ancient lineage expected to preside over such fetes. Not shut up in the cattery with these glorified barn cats. Well, to be fair, one could hardly call Madame du Maine by such a derisive epithet. And she was there sequestered in the cattery, too. But all the same, Bhu Fan resented being left out of the big ceremonial doings taking place in the Moosery. That she might not have realized until the last moment just how important this ceremony was going to be, she brushed aside that fact as a mere oversight on somebody's part. (Certainly not *hers*.) Whatever. It was embarrassing; she was losing face with all the Coons, tarted-up barn cats or not.

Then suddenly, it appeared things were back to normal. Well, almost. Cheryl Smith waltzed into the cattery again (after her initial trip with Smudge and Sweeper), her silk dress swishing around her ankles, all swirls of rose and aqua, a tulip glass of champagne in one hand and a very disgruntled Posey in the other, an amused Shere Khan on her heels. Following along behind was Martha Michaud carrying two large platters of dainty finger sandwiches, aromatic with chicken and turkey. She set the platters in the middle of the floor, dropped some of the goodies in the enclosures belonging to the toms, Rio and Simon, while Cheryl sat Posey down with a scratch between the ears. The two ladies then departed, still in high good humor, chatting away to themselves. Weddings seemed to have that effect on the female of the human species, thought Shere Khan, as he helped himself to the buffet.

After this rare feast, Bhu Fan, still annoyed at missing the festivities in the Moosery, looked sharply at Posey, who was at the moment keeping a very discreet silence. The little Korat then favored Shere Khan with a glance. That Himself had been present was simply not something Bhu would question. The Great One's exalted status precluded any second-guessing. Even from her.

"I'd appreciate a report now, Sire, if you don't mind."

It was clear to The Great One—and certainly to all the other inhabitants of the cattery who had endured the irritation of the disgruntled aristocrat for the whole of the afternoon—that Bhu Fan was thoroughly displeased. She might be the smallest member of the cattery clan but she was also its most intense and demanding, the two matriarchs, Madame du Maine and Silver Sonnet notwithstanding. For all she was a spay *and* a Korat!

Shere Khan's favorite son, Hawkeye, had rescued Bhu Fan from a raging Penobscot River some two years past when a would-be thief had pitched her carrier aside during his escape from a roadside rest area. The carrier had popped open upon landing and a very frightened Korat had grabbed for the nearest refuge, which, alas for her, turned out to be a large dead tree caught up in an eddy of the flooded river. When it broke free and got caught up in the deluge, Bhu Fan found herself riding a juggernaut. Luckily for her, Hawkeye had snatched her up onto an overhanging tree trunk and brought her home to Bethmom. Life at MerryMaines Cattery on Siberia Farm had never been the same since.

It wasn't that Bhu Fan, displaying all the hyper energy and inquisitiveness of her breed, was disruptive and a troublemaker. Far from it. The little Korat had exhibited a great deal of courage and concern for what she secretively labeled "the shaggy locals." Her favorite peasant, as she referred to him, was her rescuer and mentor in all things Maine Coon: Hawkeye. She was also fey: a seeress—or the closest thing to it. She'd helped raise various kitlings and even bested a very large and predatory owl intent on making a meal of Madame du Maine. Alas, with all the good and interesting facets of the green-eyed Korat, she was also very blue-blooded, haughty royalty, with all the attendant expectations of her class. That the festivities concerning Bethmom and Chad had taken place without her blessing and royal presence was just an unbearable loss of face. Unthinkable. How was she to hold her head up among her subjects after such a manifest slight to her royal person??

Before Shere Khan could respond to Bhu Fan's command, however softly it was uttered, another corner was heard from. Kazandra's red imp of a kitling was unable to contain himself any longer. "Well, it's a done deal," Posey exclaimed as he strutted across the floor like a cat trailing canary feathers behind him. "The game warden is now a gen-u-ine member of the clan."

The half-grown red classic tabby kit stretched out on the floor beside Shere Khan and his younger ink-black son, Jet Star. The Great One laughed appreciatively at Riddle and Zandra's offspring. That had been some acrobatic descent he'd made down the fireplace stones from the moose rack during the wedding ceremony before he'd lost his grip. He wouldn't be at MerryMaines much longer. Soon he'd be leaving for Betty Ingram's Coonscradle Cattery to help her build her new lines on the late Marge Brennerman's very unusual "Viking Reds", a rare odd red and lilac classic coloring pattern in the Maine Coon which that canny breeder had marketed to "The Beautiful People" for $2500 a pop before her death. *Might as well let young Poseidon have his day in the sun before he leaves,* Khan grimaced to himself. Posey and his siblings had sure had a rough start in life, having been pitched in a ditch by that mean snot, Styles. Thank Bast, Hawkeye and Bhu Fan had come to their rescue before it was too late. He himself had been the one to reunite a frantically searching Kazandra with her kitlings. At the sound of a stern but motherly voice, Khan's attention was brought back to the here and now.

"Posey," his dam, Kazandra, admonished, "what are you talking about?"

Bhu Fan had stopped her irritated pacing and skewered the kitling with a laser eye. "You got to see all that ritual down in Moosery while we—I—were shut up here in Cattery? And just what made you so privileged?"

Posey hunkered down and squirmed under the Korat's imperial glare.

"Aw, Boo, ease up." Hawkeye, who'd been pumping his sire and Star for information, strolled over to his little blue sidekick, royal or not, swishing his long feathery tail across her chest. "Posey almost ended up skewered on the moose rack over the fire hole in the Moosery."

Bhu Fan turned her full attention on Hawk. "What?"

"Posey and Star were playing I-can-do-anything-better'n-you in the Moosery this morning before Martha 'n all came to fix it up for the mating match-up. "Star—" And here Hawkeye turned his own stern visage on his smaller sibling's hunched-up trying-to-be-inconspicuous form, "—dared him to climb up the rocks around the fire hole to sit on that old moose rack up there."

Star, who'd egged on the smaller kitten on more than one occasion, used those extra-toed paws of his to scratch at the old pine boards as if he hoped they'd open up and swallow him whole. He didn't dare look at his dam, Madame du Maine, certainly not Posey's momcat, Zandra, and he'd really tear up the floor to avoid censure from his sire, who, at the moment, was keeping very quiet.

Bhu Fan, for all her imperial hauteur, was not without keen perception—or pity. Hawkeye and The Great One exchanged amused glances as she defused the humiliation of Shere Khan's young poly-pawed son.

"So, Star--Posey, who should know better, accepted your dare, climbed up fireplace and then, one assumes, couldn't get down?" She paused, a twinkle coming into her large sea green eyes. "Then what?"

The half grown black tom drew a deep breath. "I went looking for somebody to get him down. But everybody was running here 'n there, with armloads of flowers 'n folding chairs 'n trays of food for the fridge 'n nobody was paying any attention to me." Star looked contrite. "Then Bethmom 'n Cherylmom came in all gussied up like there was about to be a party 'n the next thing I knew, Martha scooped me up and I was dropped in here."

"Leaving Posey high and dry on moose rack—right?" Bhu Fan turned her attention to the small red and lilac tom kitten who was very studiously picking between his toes as if he'd just descended triumphantly from Mt. Katahdin and needed to spiff himself up for his turn in front of the cameras and microphones of the media.

Posey," asked her royal highness, "how did you get down?"

"Oh," the insouciant kitling replied, "after Bethmom discovered me up there, she sent Gaston for a step-thing...but then Chad came with Shere Khan 'n Smudge 'n Sweeper 'n everybody got all excited 'n—" Posey looked downcast. "Everybody forgot about me." He sighed and then brightened, adding, "So I got to watch all that foof-eraw in front of the fire hole where Bethmom and Chad talked all solemn-like and repeated lotsa big words 'n then everybody laughed 'n cheered and—" Posey paused, embarrassed—"and I needed to use the litterbox and I was afraid I'd fall so I hollered at Shere Khan who'd been watching from the catwalk along the side of the big hall." The red tom kitten wasn't sure how his discourse was being received and fell silent, looking intently at the floor.

"Actually," inserted Shere Khan, "young sprout did very well." The Great One's big green eyes twinkled. "Necessity and, er, dis-comfort being what they are. Posey backed off the moose rack and carefully felt his way down those nubby old stones, slowly, of course, while everybody's attention was centered on Bethmom and Chad." The old tom paused in his narration, "However, not being all that experienced a climber...he slipped just about mantom-height from the floor."

Kazandra's eyes grew large and fearful as all Shere Khan's audi-ence sucked in its collective breath.

"About that time, Chad caught sight of him, ran to the rock wall before I could get there and grabbed him." Khan laughed out loud. "'Course the kitling clung to him like a cockle-burr; Gaston said something about Posey making a fine boutonniere and they handed off our red imp and Cherylmom brought us up here." The Great One favored his consort, Madame, with a conspiratorial glance. "I reck-on they didn't want a bunch of us felines sneaking out to the camp tonight—"

"—Mating rituals being what they are among humankind," re-marked Silver Sonnet, MerryMaine's newest recruit, who had been listening to this narrative with great interest. "I can understand that." The big silver queen, whom Cherylmom called a Mae West kinda girl, laughed slyly and rolled her large green-gold eyes. "Wouldn't it be somethin' if we all sneaked out to Chad's camp tonight, climbed up on the roof and serenaded the newlyweds?"

Sonnet got up and, leaving her audience to wonder where she learned it, did a burlesque queen bump-and-grind dance across the floor "—Roll me o-*ver* in the clo-*ver*, roll me o-*ver*, lay me down—" she sang in her clear soprano as all the grownups bunny-thumped the floor appreciatively and all the kitlings looked confused. Even Bhu Fan, who was not a fan of the uninhibited ex-show girl, laughed along with all the others.

It had been quite a day.

CHAPTER FOUR

"STAR, YOU LITTLE DEVIL, get your nose out of my dessert!" With that, Beth Merryman grabbed the black half grown kitten who had quietly inserted himself into her lap while her attention was focused on the book she was reading, at the same time eating a concoction she'd invented herself of cottage cheese, whipped topping, lemon Jello, crushed pineapple and pecans in a graham cracker crust. It was quick and easy to make, easy, too, on the calories, and she had more than enough pot lickers to help with the cleanup, most of whom waited very politely to be invited to help themselves when she finished. Alas, this state of affairs did sometimes pose problems with a certain persistent party black of coat and quick of tongue. She gave the kitten a baleful look and gently placed him on the floor. Within a nanosecond, he was back again. Kittens don't discourage easily. Goat-headed, her friend Cheryl called them: and spring-loaded. Beth rolled her eyes heavenward.

"Star, I have to admit, I will be glad to see you off to your new home in England—where Wisteria will find it very difficult to return you once she realizes what a little pest you are." She scowled in mock irritation as she once more picked up the pushy kitten and put him down. "You are a real pain in the tush, little man."

Jet Star looked at Bethmom owlishly as she sat him once more on the floor of the old kitchen. He knew very well she didn't mean a word she was saying. But he also knew he'd do well to lick the whipped cream off his whiskers and go find Hawkeye and his shadow, Bhu Fan. Before Chad came in and washed his face for him with that big rough-textured dishrag. The game warden ran a tight ship—if with a certain benevolence toward the newlyweds' combined feline population.

Even so, Star had mixed feelings about what Bethmom had just said about his prospects over on the other side of the big ocean; leaving MerryMaines was bad enough, England, he felt was just not *it*... Originally, he was to go to Denmark to live with a lady who had been to Maine on a number of occasions to visit with Bethmom and all her friends. The half grown tom suddenly felt very sad. Moll had died, Bethmom told him, of a particularly virulent form of cancer. The kitten wasn't all too sure about death and what it meant but he had heard Hawkeye and Bhu Fan and all the other Maine Coons in the cattery talking about their friend's going to the Rainbow Bridge and somehow he knew they'd never see her again. And that filled him with dismay. Pretty smiling Moll had a way of softly clucking to him as she held him in her arms, belly up, all the while tickling his tummy and crooning to him in Danish. While he was sorry about Moll, once that trip was off, he thought he'd dodged the bullet, figuring he was going to get to stay at home with his siblings and big brother Hawkeye, who was his idol. But then he heard another phone conversation that stuck him right back in the doldrums. He couldn't win for losing.

"Wisteria Cate at CumbriaCoons Cattery in the Lake District of Northern England called this morning, Cheryl, all the way from a place named Wiskdale Without—if you can believe that...One has to wonder: Wiskdale Without—what? Yes, I know...England does have some weird place names...Yeah, she's a delightful lady and an excellent breeder.... I've been to her cattery and I can tell you, not to use a cliché or anything, I could eat Yorkshire pudding right off the cattery floors..." At this point, Star hadn't been paying all that much attention, concentrating as he was on Bhu's trolling tail as she crouched by the back door chittering at all the birds flitting about over the meadow. His head came up, though, when he heard his name mentioned.

"Yep, she'd like to have Star; she loves the blacks and there aren't that many of them in England…And since I'm taking Hawkeye and Bhu Fan along on our wedding trip, adding a kitten is no problem, well—no more problem than simply filling all their mind-numbing requirements for entry in the UK. Lordy! They are so hung up on keeping rabies out…In this day and age, you'd think—"

That conversation still stuck in his mind, Star looked at Bethmom as she got up from the table, put her book aside and took her dirty dishes to the sink. He couldn't recall the rest of what Bethmom had said but it was no matter. The part he heard was bad enough. England! If he had to go somewhere, why couldn't it be to Cherylmom's cattery in Wesley or all the way down to sunny Florida and Hollymom?

When he related this treachery to Hawkeye and Bhu Fan, his big brother had grinned impishly. "Cheer up, Star. At least they speak the same language—and I understand the folks there are such great animal lovers they let 'em into cafes and even set water bowls on the sidewalks outside of stores 'n things." Hawkeye lifted a paw and scowled at a bit of litter caught between his toes. "I met a Brit at a cat show once who said most of the catteries over there have their own gardens where they can run about to please themselves."

The sleek handsome coal-black offspring of Shere Khan and Madame was not placated. The British Isles were 3000 miles from home. He knew this. He'd looked over Bethmom's shoulders while she was surfing the 'Net, making hers and Chad's travel itinerary. He recalled, too, Cherylmom's laughter when Beth told her their plans. The mistress of Snowmaines Cattery had stopped by on her way to a cat show down in Bangor.

"I don't believe you, Beth Merriman, going on your honeymoon with three cats! All I can say is Chad Merryman is a mighty tolerant soul—and are you going to convert, I wonder?"

When Beth had looked a bit nonplussed and asked, "Convert? What are you talking about, Cheryl?"

"Your names," Cheryl responded, still chuckling. "Are you going to stay Merriman with an 'i'—or convert to Merryman with a 'y'?"

At this, Beth joined in with her friend's amusement. Beth's late husband, Henry, and her new husband, Chad, had been cousins. But because of a family rift some two hundred years in the past where Henry's family were rebels and Chad's were loyalists, Chad's great-great grandfather had changed the spelling of the family name and there it had stayed. Even though Henry's and Chad's great-grandfathers had long since reconciled and worked their farms together.

All this, of course, was Greek to Star. All he understood of the matter he had gleaned from his two future traveling companions; Hawkeye and Bhu Fan, who were, he felt, no help at all, looking forward to the trip as they were.

Bhu Fan and Hawkeye were going along because, having become famous on TV and the internet for their exploits in New York City at the time of the big Animal-Rights-Militia raid on the cat show at the Garden and their subsequent abduction, adroit escape and return to Bethmom and Cheryl, they'd been invited to strut their stuff at the Birmingham, England first annual Maine Coon Classic...and if truth be known—although their mistress was not about to admit to it—Beth did not dare leave them behind. If there were ever two cats who could stir up a crisis, let alone a pot, it was that pair. Hawkeye was a polydactyl like Shere Khan and little brother Star, which meant he had extra toes. Only in *his* case, extra toes meant "thumbs", and very clever thumbs at that. There was no place that big brown rascal couldn't get into if he was of a mind to do so. And in the doing, Bhu Fan would be right there egging him on.

Shere Khan was invited as well but Beth had begged off on Khan as he was, if not really elderly, an old and independent tom whose territory around Siberia Farm he would not leave to chance—or newcomers. Because of Bhu Fan's attachment to Hawkeye though she was not a Coon, Beth decided to take her in his place. She would grieve if left behind at home and this way, at least, Beth could keep an eye on the very haughty and royal Korat who never hesitated to let anyone know of her aristocratic status. And since Starry would be going to his new cattery as a show cat and future sire, well, she'd just take the whole kit and kaboodle at the same time. Chad didn't mind when she told him of her plans. "The more the merrier," was his comment, as he grinned slyly at his pun.

The senior game warden of Penobscot County, Chad Merryman, wouldn't have minded taking along a *pterodactyl*, let alone a polydactyl, if it was what Beth wanted. He'd been fond of her ever since his cousin Henry brought her home as his bride. During those years he could only enjoy her company when the two of them had visited with his folks or taken part in the winter revels of homemade music and square dancing during long Maine winters. Nor had he made a move after Henry was killed in a freak accident, except to be there if she needed him, the Merrymans being a close-knit family. If she ever indicated that her interest in him was more than cousinly, he would certainly have come a'courtin'. But being basically a shy man, at least where females were concerned, he bided his time. And as luck would have it, that time came and Chad was too elated with his success to worry about anything so important to his bride as her furry housemates. If Beth wanted them along, then he would see to it that her expectations came to fruition.

Star was not so sanguine. It was all right for Hawkeye and Boo to look forward to this trip. After all, they were going to get to come back to Siberia Farm and the cattery. But his journey was one way. Sink or swim. Unless Fate and the Feline Goddess Bastet decided otherwise, he was stuck. And his demeanor was all too obvious.

"Aw, Starry," said Hawkeye as he gave his whiskers a good straightening, "Look at it this way. You're going to CumbriaCoons to be Catemom's new sire. You'll have your choice of queens, you'll get to strut yer stuff for visitors and from what they tell me, their lamb chops and beef-n-kidney pie are Four Star cat fare."

Star favored his older brother with a jaundiced eye. While any feline half-way conscious knew what made kittens, he was not yet old enough for it to be of any interest to him. He much preferred following along with Hawk and Boo, chasing his siblings, playing king of the cat tree and chowing down, *particularly* chowing down. While he watched his sisters, Moonrise and Magic, flirt with the toms in the cattery, he thought their putting on the wiles a bit silly. Girl stuff. He much preferred to stretch out alongside his sire, Shere Khan, on the old farmhouse back porch, and listen to his tales of life in the North Woods, his war stories and his adventures chasing off the car thieves who tried to stash a truck-load of Corvettes in the old Hartman barn, Bhu Fan's besting Momma owl, and Khan's journey with Hawkeye to Singletary's farm to find the elusive red tom,

Riddle. Life at MerryMaines Cattery was good and he had no desire to leave it. When it came time to go, he wondered, would Shere Khan take him off to a safe place in the woods like he'd offered to do for Bhu Fan when it looked like her larcenous former owner was going to come reclaim her?

Like it is with all the very young, no matter what the species, such thoughts are transparent as water on a lily pad. Madame du Maine, his dam, knew exactly what was going through her offspring's mind, as did his sire. But in the way of felines since time out of mind, it fell to the matriarch to set her kitling straight. And that's the way it came down. Star was going to CumbriaCoons and that was *that*. Growing up was never easy. But necessary all the same.

Beth Merryman, having shed the "I" with silent apologies to her late spouse, sat with her new husband at the old porcelain-topped table in the kitchen at Siberia Farm. They had already decided Henry's home place was better for them than Chad's apartment. Beth liked her in-laws but living in their pocket with her cattery some miles away was just not the ideal solution to their residential requirements, particularly with fickle Maine winters. There had been no hard feelings and now she sat, watching Chad fondly, paper and pencil at hand. The game warden lounged in his chair across from her, grinning happily, his coffee mug held up so he wouldn't look as foolish as he thought a new bridegroom must. Hawk, Bhu Fan, Beowulf, and Starry were lined up on the counter behind him like blackbirds on a high wire, tails wrapped tightly across front paws, motionless. Sweeper had found leaping to any height a bit painful ever since he was struck by that monster vehicle in the city and Smudge, who was not all that enamored with heights anyway, preferred to keep his paws firmly on the ground. He sat in his new fleece-lined basket next to Sweeper's by the cold fireplace, his eyes half closed. Of all the cats in the room only Bhu Fan felt apprehensive. While she was glad that she wasn't being left behind on this trip about which Bethmom was busy writing down all the details, she'd already come half-way round the world and it had *not* been a pleasant experience.

"You're worrying something, sweetheart, what's on your mind?" Beth, having just removed breakfast dishes from the table, gazed at Chad. Glancing around at the cats, she thought they all appeared to be waiting for something. But what? Surely the guys were used to Chad's presence by now.

"Actually, honey, I was merely wool-gathering over the irony of it all." Without consciously thinking about it, the game warden rubbed the back of his head. A lump was still there, the only unpleasant reminder of his wedding day, what? This past weekend? He found he still had memory gaps.

"Irony?" Beth laughed, if a bit tentatively.

A perceptive bridegroom reached over and patted her hand. "I'm not having any regrets, my love, if that's what I've unintentionally inferred." He gave his bride a tender boyish smile. "No. I talked to Dad this morning while you were doing cattery chores..." Her husband took off in another direction.

"You know I was in the north end of the county up there at the beaver pond when I got whacked—"

"Yes," she interrupted, cocking her head. "It's where you said you'd sighted Canadian lynx lately."

"Well, actually, I sighted them then." He didn't elaborate, unsure she'd believer his accounting of events. "What I was going to say is that tract of timber, some 1500 acres of it where I was doing the statistics on the beavers, if you can believe it, has been in my family for nine generations." He grinned ruefully. "Nothing like getting clobbered in your own backyard."

"This has to do with your dad's phone call, doesn't it?" Beth wasn't about to dwell on Chad's encounter with his assailant. She narrowed her eyes, thinking. "And that's about what Gaston told Martha who told me yesterday that the timber bandits were about to start clear-cutting up there even though they're not supposed to—"

Chad nodded, always amazed at the bits and pieces of information his bride picked up. He lifted Sweeps into his lap gently and started working on a cocklebur he had felt when he ran his hand down the old boy's tail.

"Time for a history lesson?"

"I'm listening." Beth grinned at the beatific expression on Sweeper's face.

Chad laughed gleefully at some mental image only he could see. "You know how this part of northern Maine is sandwiched between parts of Canada on both sides?" He gave Beth a sly glance. "In view of the way both the French and British coveted this hump of territory, I always think of it as our cheeky Maine mooning both parties."

Beth could barely contain herself at the picture this presented to her. "Ooooh," she gloated, "I like that!"

"It was a vast territory, honey, and with its wealth—*vast* wealth of timber, farmland and furs (and furs were a very important commodity in those early days)—it was certainly worth a fight or two to stake a claim and hold onto."

"But what chance did individual Americans or 'rebels', if you will, have in hanging onto land they settled way-the-hell-and-gone up here??"

"Well, actually, they did—in spite of the odds. Believe it or not, even Massachusetts (with the aid of various greedy entities at one point) made Maine a colony *of a colony* belonging to Massachusetts... but I digress... claimed a large hunk of this territory at one time, with claims, patents and royal charters from a couple of belligerent kings, various lords-and-dukes, flying in all directions. And 'Americans,' you know, were both rebels *and* royalists. They built their homesteads, farmed, cut their timber, collected furs—anything to make a living. And they were damned determined to let nobody move them off what they considered theirs—no matter which country claimed hegemony."

"So where did the Merrymans come into all this? They have a dog in this fight? Surely, they had no militia of their own."

"No, but I guess you could say they had *possession* and later (I'm not sure of the timeline here but it gives you an idea of how coveted our extensive forests were), that wild bunch downstate in Bangor was playing 'musical timber' all over the place while the Merrymans and other families were hanging on up here by the skin of their teeth, fending off everybody...often poor as church mice, mostly Scotch-Irish stock, but already tenacious as hell. Their attitude was they weren't going to be run off their land again. And nobody was giving *their* timber away."

Beth glowered. "I don't follow—"

"Remember the story about the tulip mania in Holland in, oh—1634 or thereabouts?"

"Oh, yes. Everybody turned into speculators, bidding vast unimaginable amounts of money for tulip bulbs, for heaven's sake—until the bubble burst."

"Well, imagine that kind of frenzy going on in Bangor about a century later over timber instead of tulips."

"Lordy."

"Oh, yes." Chad paused to take a sip of coffee and then triumphantly removed the burr from Sweeper's plumey tail.

"Surely, the Merrymans weren't involved with that rowdy bunch."

"No, they weren't. Capt. James' family descendents were hunkered down up here on his settlement of like-minded royalists merely trying to hang onto the land grant they had for loyal service to the king…until the treaty of 1843 gave it to them outright. All the while fending off the timber companies—who were darn near as bad as the French and British militias!" Chad sighed. "There was much more but you'd have to read Colin Woodward's book, *The Lobster Coast,* to appreciate the chaos that wreaked havoc in our beloved territory."

"Whew!" Beth laughed, "I remember your telling me about Capt. James and his brothers being divided by the Revolutionary War into rebels and royalists."

"Well, the descendents of those brothers, of whom my dad is the last one, still own that particular 1500 acres of forest timber."

"Oh Chad! *That's* what your Dad called you about so early this morning."

"Yep." Her husband turned grim.

"But how can they cut your family's timber? And what will become of its beavers and those new resident Lynx and all the other wildlife?"

"Well, the problem is…the pages of the county's deed book where that piece of property is recorded and also, I might add, the tax assessor's files as well, disappeared at some point and nobody is admitting when—or how. And while Dad has faithfully paid taxes, he has no written proof that 1500 acres belongs to us."

Beth sucked in her breath. "And now the timber company has decided to move in." She put her chin in her hands, "Oh, dear...Can't your Dad get a lawyer?"

"Against corporate big bucks? Well, don't fret over it, honey. Dad will come up with something. He's a crafty old devil. I just thought it was ironic, as I said, to have been banged on the head by an illegal trapper on the one hand and the more subtle timber barons on the other..." Chad grinned ruefully at his wife. "And nothing is likely to take place before we get back from England. So where are we on that?"

Beth, though distracted and distressed by the rapacious timber cutters, brought him up to date on their travel requirements and tapped her pencil against her teeth. "Have we covered everything? Can you think of anything else, Chad, we need to see to before we leave?"

"You've got all the necessary papers for us—like passports? The cats' health and rabies certificates?"

Beth nodded her head and then blushed guiltily.

The game warden was nothing if not a very insightful man. He smiled over his coffee mug, that errant lock of dark hair falling across his forehead. "What are you not telling me?"

His bride tucked her head, sighed and then waved her pencil nervously. "Would you mind if we took four cats instead of three?"

Chad Merryman put down his mug and laughed out loud. "What are you and Cheryl plotting now?"

Beth looked at the cats lined up on the counter and took a deep breath. Hawk and Bhu looked at each other. Star's mouth dropped open and he gulped. Did this mean he wasn't going to be left over there all by himself? And if that was the case, who—?

"Cheryl got a call from Wisteria a few days ago. She asked her if she had a female unrelated to Starry that she could let her have, one who could meet all the shipping requirements. It seems her grand champion has proved infertile and her other tom has gone missing." Beth peered closely at her husband to gauge how he was taking this.

"Of course, it would have to be a cat almost grown, what with the mandated 6 months quarantine in its own cattery, who fits all of DE-FRA's requirements."

"DEFRA? What the devil is DEFRA anyway?"

Beth sighed and scowled. "DEFRA stands for the UK's Department of Environment, Food and Rural Affairs—which is going around one's elbow to get to one's thumb to say: Ag department! Well, you know how unbending the Brits are about keeping rabies out of England." She sighed again. "Sure makes things expensive on the breeders over there—except maybe for horses: feline imports have to have rabies vaccinations, then 21 days later their rabies titer blood drawn so they're assured the vaccinations did their job; microchip; the six months quarantine here; and then that last minute worming!" A look of dismay crossed her face. "And I don't imagine *that's* too comfortable during a 12 hour incarceration in a pet carrier. No matter how big it is!"

Chad waved his hands. "I know all that, honey." He grinned. "I see what you've had to do with our crew. I just didn't know what the darned acronym stood for. But the question is: who does Cheryl have that meets that mountain of paperwork—and has six months under her belt since that rabies titer? That's hardly routine cattery work."

"A breeder over there who wanted one of her queens had to back out as she'd been served with divorce papers. So Cheryl does have a qualified critter." Beth gnashed her teeth. "With all the ills in this world which they blithely pass over, why do they have to nail mere cat and dog breeders to the wall with their over-the-top requirements for import?"

"Beth, honey, off the soap box. You're preaching to the converted." Chad suddenly laughed. "From what I've learned from the Scottish Wildlife Trust I'm going to be working with while we're there, the beavers they're re-introducing to Great Britain have had to waltz through the same darn procedure."

Somewhat mollified, Beth smiled impishly at her husband and shrugged her shoulders. "That's your department, darlin'."

"Yeah, I know: you love me. Just don't forget who's paying the air fare for us. That invitation from the Wildlife Trust was providential, wouldn't you say?" He returned her smile and raised his mug to his lips again. "So I repeat my question: Who're we taking along for Cheryl?"

"Angel...Remember? That little silver show queen who was part of the gang that went missing in New York City."

At this statement, Star almost groaned out loud. *Angel! Bast Bespoke.* How could he suffer any *more* misfortune? *Angel.* Mouse balls! What had he done to deserve *this*? The young black tom looked up at Hawkeye with a sunken heart and growled.

Hawk reached down and gave his younger brother a lick on the ear, having read him perfectly. *What's wrong with Angel, Bro? She's about as pretty a maiden queen as a squirt like you could ask for—*

She's, she's so full of herself it's a wonder there's room at Snowmaines for anybody else. She comes over here and prances around telling the kitlings if they're lucky, they might grow up to be a star on TV just like her... Starry shifted from his position on the counter, hopped down and paced slowly over to the water bowl. *Yukk!* He spat out as he went.

Hawkeye and his dam exchanged a long look. Madame du Maine, who had been having a wash near the back door, smiled knowingly. *Methinks he doth protest too much.*

Yeah, agreed her older son. *I'd bet a pork chop to a pepper pod she's given him short shrift somewhere along the line.*

Oh, yes, volunteered Bhu Fan from her observation post on the counter, *Angel told him last visit he needed to grow up if she was to take him seriously.*

CHAPTER FIVE

H AWKEYE, BHU FAN, STAR and Angel stood at the edge of Wisteria Cate's cattery garden overlooking Lake Windermere, gazing at the towering fells on the far side of the glistening water, eyes large with wonder. Unlike the tree-covered mountains clustered around Mt. Katahdin, that northern terminus of the Appalachian Trail, England's Cumbrian fells were mostly covered with tall grasses, bare rock, scree, gorse and bracken. And the drystone walls that divided them into impossible pastures galloped up, down and across their slopes without any regard for tidiness, or it would appear, gravity. Herdwick sheep grazed in these vertical paddocks unconcerned with their terrain or the hikers who appeared to take delight in bounding over difficult traverses around them. Hawkeye had never seen so many people scrambling upward for the sheer joy of it. But calling mountains "fells" was going to take some getting used to.

On this bright summer day where Northern England butts up against the Scottish border, the four cats were simply grateful they had survived the long trip to Boston's airport, survived the noisy airplane trip in cargo for interminable hours, survived the rough handling of the DEFRA vets, survived the train trip north still locked up in carriers and had come, at long last to their destination. Yet now for all of being free to wander about and stretch themselves, if truth be known, they found themselves greatly intimidated by the overpowering immensity of their surroundings. Lake Windermere, in front of them, being England's longest, sparkled like a handful of crystals left there by the last ancient ice sheet. And in some places, was almost a mile wide. Farms and villages on the far side of the lake at the foot of the fells were so tiny as to appear like miniatures on a Christmas model train display. Ducking down as if to avoid, like Henny Penny, a falling sky, they retreated warily to their hostess' cattery. As with so many such establishments in Great Britain, the cattery's gardens were not only fenced but covered over with wire and slats as well. No pieces of storybook sky were likely to bump them in the noggin. Nevertheless, Hawk, Bhu, Starry and Angel retreated through the cat flap into the big common room with great relief.

"Wow!" exploded Star, shaking his head and letting out his breath in dismay. "This place is just too big!"

Hawkeye, ever one to put things in perspective, replied, "Oh, I expect you'll get used to it, Squirt. That garden seems to have all kinds of interesting things: pond, waterfall, flowers, big sunning rocks...I'll bet there are even mice out there." He looked around the spotless big open room at the enclosures along the far wall where various queens, some with kitlings, some not, were gazing back at him with interest. There were cat walks like those at MerryMaines, fleece lined nest boxes, toys and television in the common room. Returning his smiling gaze to Star, he added, "You're gonna be the senior tom here, Starry! You need to get a grip!"

Star gave his brother a grumpy look. "They talk different," he complained, "I can't understand half of what they say."

It was clear that this polydactyl son of Shere Khan was not yet reconciled to his exile. Hawkeye sighed to himself, removed a papery clematis blossom from his tail and wondered how he could make his little brother's transition easier. How would their sire go about it? He'd have to think on that for awhile.

"What I'd give to see just one ol' moose wading through that big old pond out there," Star muttered, still feeling homesick as he sank down on his paws.

"Well, Starry," suggested Angel, who was in no way homesick, "look on those fluffy sheep things with the matchstick legs as miniature moose—" She giggled at the mental image of such.

Bhu Fan, sitting nearby having a wash, chortled. "Some of shaggy, funny-looking brown cows we saw on way here are almost as big as moose, Starry."

Star wasn't mollified nor did he like being teased. He changed the subject. "Where have Bethmom and Chad gotten to?"

"I'm not sure but I think it's somewhere just north of here in—Scotland?—that has to do with that beaver resettling project that Chad's here for...Catemom drove them. Bethmom and Chad haven't gotten used to driving on the wrong side of the road yet." If Hawkeye were to admit it, he'd been a bit disoriented himself as they drove along the motorways. "They were going sightseeing, too. I overheard Chad say there were places here left over from time out of mind they want to visit, places where big stones stand straight up in circles—"

"Why would anybody want to look at ugly big ol' rocks?" put in Star. It was clear to his feline family that this young tom was not going to have anything positive to say about his new country. Not yet anyway.

Bhu Fan went off in a different direction as was the prerogative of royalty. "Cultures here, some of them," she pontificated, "were almost old as Far East ones." She sat up and licked a paw, looking smug. "Only humankind *here* lived in mud hovels and wore—ugh—animal skins while *my* peoples in Orient wore silks and were living in palaces."

The two youngsters peered at the little Korat, questions dancing in their eyes. Even Star was interested. Hawk, however, was not put off. "Yeah, well, a lot of my ancestors came from here," he admitted, trying to visualize mantoms running around in animal pelts instead of trousers or jeans. He sat in thoughtful silence for a moment. "Minstrel, The Great One's sire, said Viking raiders brought felines from the desert and mountains of the Inland Sea to this frozen northway and foggy isles before they sailed the big ocean." He looked at Bhu Fan slyly with half closed eyes. "That big pond out there was originally called *Wynandremer:* 'Vinandr's Lake' which takes its name from early Norse settlers…No doubt they found a few pretty queens here living around those mud huts…Their mantoms may have lived rough but they were conquerors—whatever they wrapped themselves in to keep warm. And their felines were a mix of more'n one kind or another from all those different places." He delivered the *coup de grâce*: "Which probably accounts for their growing bigger than your skinny little Orientals, Boo."

"So? Then how come they're having to bring cats like Starry *back* over here now?" rebutted Bhu Fan, annoyed that her peasant should express himself so well. *She* was supposed to be the erudite one. She cut her eyes at her peasant slave. He was a sly one. Just when she thought she'd put him in his place, he'd surprise her with some observation she'd not thought of.

Before this discourse could continue and further embarrass the haughty Korat, the door to the cattery opened and in strolled a smiling Wisteria, followed by Bethmom and Chad. The cats looked up in expectation.

They all liked Bethmom's English friend. She was a shorter version of Cherylmom, Hawk decided. She looked a bit like that fairy godmother in the video thingie he'd watched with Bethmom one night many moons ago when he was a mere kitling. *Cindy-something.* He recalled that Madame and Gracie hadn't liked it because the mice had such big parts and there was an evil cat named Lucifer… But before he could go any further in his ruminations, Catemom, as they'd taken to calling her since "Wisteria" was such a catly mouthful, picked him up and set him on her grooming table.

"This chappie, I think, needs a proper show bath, Beth, don't you think, before we take him and his mate there to the cat show? Bhu doesn't, I don't think, being short-haired but he's a bit tatty. Our longhairs tend to get that way in the garden. Hawkeye is really a lovely boy; it's a shame he could never have been shown." She held up Hawk's outsized paw and inspected it, tickling him between his pads as she did so. "Maybe Hawkeye and Star can change a few closed minds about that." She shook her graying curls in exasperation. "Coon breeders either love the polys or hate them. As if extra toes are some kind of disfigurement." She snorted to herself. "Mitten paws are no more a malformation that folder ears or hairless bodies like some I could name!"

As Beth came over to the table to examine her handsome big neuter and Chad excused himself to do some reading, Star and Angel exchanged glances. Upon finding themselves in alien territory, former adversaries often became allies. It appeared that such was the case with these two kitlings. Angel giggled. *Catemom sure talks a lot, doesn't she?*

Yeah, he admitted. *She does go on a bit.* He paused and pulled his feathery tail around for a close inspection. If Hawkeye had blossoms in his tail, most likely he did, too. *But I like her. I don't know what she's sayin' half the time but she's nice. Smells like some of those flowers out in the garden.* He looked thoughtful. *An' there's no hard kibble in this cattery; it's all real food!*

Angel bristled. *But it was good kibble at MerryMaines, Starry. I didn't see you going without. Bethmom fed us very well—*

Okay, Okay, admitted her companion, *I just meant the grub is good here.* Star looked contrite. He just didn't seem to be able to get anything right. But if he and Angel were going to stay here, he was smart enough to know he needed to be in her good graces. Something caught his eye across the room. Bhu Fan was on the move.

She was walking over to one of the enclosures where a luxuriantly coated big blue queen with a pretty spotless white bib lounged on a thickly fleeced sheepskin. She noticed that while the queens' quarters here were narrow, the space was long, adorned with everything a cat could wish and had a flap opening on the far end to an outside run. The cattery apartments might not be so spacious as they were at MerryMaines but then she doubted that the whole of Great Britain had as much room in it as the state of Maine. That was just a guess, of course. The little Korat had covered half a world but geography was not her strong suit. Royalty had underlings to tend to that sort of information. Well, they were *supposed* to at any rate.

Bhu Fan sat down, wrapped her whippy tail around her paws and assumed, albeit with difficulty, what she felt was a non-confrontational posture. The velvety blue queen, whose name was Violet, looked at the little Korat with interest but said nothing.

The silence stretched out.

You've come from America, haven't you? Violet finally broke the impasse as Bhu Fan hoped she would. She'd been counting on the queen's curiosity.

Yes, the little Korat replied. *I am Bhu of House of Fan. From MerryMaines—*

You're no Maine Coon, Violet interrupted. *What are you doing here? And what are you anyway? I don't mean to be rude,* she amended, waving her tail; *just curious.*

Bhu Fan drew herself up, trying not to let her irritation as such probing questions show. *I am Si-Siwat princess from palace in Bangkok. I am here on royal visit.* She was well aware that the word *royal* was deeply imbedded in the English psyche, whether humankind or feline.

Oh, Violet gasped, her liquid gold eyes growing large. *I thought all Siamese were skinny little things: tan with smudgy-brown faces and huge bat ears.*

Those creatures, Bhu Fan declared with distain, *are Siamese... moggies.* Bhu's dam had once had an encounter with the British Ambassador's moggie at a garden party in Phu Ket. Moggies, she'd told her daughter, were the British equivalent of common street cats. Or if one wanted to be politically correct: random *bred* cats and those, her dam emphasized, included those smudgy-faced felines. And here was Bhu's chance to set the record straight where it counted— at the source, the British having been the first importers of such cats in the mistaken idea that *they* were the royal cats of Siam.

So are all—Si-Sssswat — Violet was having trouble with her s's—*blue like you and I?*

Mostly, but there are few among us known as lilac, Bhu replied and, taking pity on her new acquaintance, added, *we are also known as Korat, which comes a little easier to one's speech.*

Violet nodded mutely, curious about the dainty visitor in front of her boudoir. *So have you visited our castles yet, Your Highness?*

Bhu swelled up with pride. Finally, she felt, she was getting the proper deference that royalty was entitled to. At the mention of castles, though, she grew a bit confused. *Castle; what means "castle"?*

Castle, Violet repeated, *A castle is where our royals live.*

Oh, Bhu's eyes lit up, *you mean palaces—*

Yes, replied Violet as she shifted around on her sheepskin, revealing a trio of tiny blue kitlings about seven weeks old. *Castles like Blenheim, Buckingham, Windsor, Muncaster…and Muncaster is not far from here. My mistress took me there once. They have owls. A whole aviary of owls…All kinds of owls.*

Bhu Fan shuddered. She had never forgotten her encounter with Momma Owl, who had nearly made a meal of her and Madame. She changed the subject quickly. Castles she would learn about later. And about owls, nothing at all. What was important here and now was knowing where the power structure lay.

Tell me please, Violet, who is matriarch of your cattery?

Oh, that would be the Countess: Cottia of the Iceni. Violet sat up very straight, displacing irate kittens from their nursing. *She is descended from that tribe's felines.* The big blue queen hastened to resettle her own tribe.

Iceni?

Oh, yes. The tribe of our first humankind queen: Boadicea.

The little Korat was not interested in humankind queens. She had enough competition among felines. *And just where can I find this Countess Cottia?*

Before Violet could answer this question, Catemom had padded up behind Bhu Fan and swept her off her paws. "Come along, ducky, we're off to Birmingham for your Command Performance."

The little blue Korat gripped Catemom's shoulder tightly and wondered if there was a castle she might investigate in Birmingham. A palace, she hoped fervently, with no owls.

CHAPTER SIX

A ND SUCH WAS THE case: no owls lurked about the big conference center in Birmingham, although they visited no castles either. There'd been plenty of cats, though, along with exhibitors and visitors who spoke, as Starry had said, in strange but very musical tongues. Bethmom and her feline celebrities had been well received and Hawk's display of polydactyl virtuosity brought forth many cheers and whistles. The registry officials might distain them and forbid their members to show them but just as it was at home, the so-called mitten cats were very popular with cat lovers and if it had been possible, Hawk was sure he would have been swamped with autograph seekers. It had been an exhilarating if exhausting day after which they'd taken a break in Alvechurch at the Old Rectory Bed and Breakfast while Bethmom and Catemom took in a play at the Royal Shakespeare in Stratford-Upon-Avon. Now they were feeling a bit more relaxed on the wrong side of the roads as they chugged toward the Lake District and Wisteria's Rose Cottage.

"What did you think of our English Coons, Beth?" Wisteria asked as she looked to the right at the roundabout. Beth, who was still habitually looking in the wrong direction for oncoming traffic, smiled and shook her head.

"If I didn't know better, I'd say yours are bigger and brawnier than ours overall." She teased her companion. "Must be all the fish and chips you all eat."

Wisteria laughed and eased off onto the A6. "Steak and Yorkshire pudding, too," she added…"what did you think of Zoltan?"

"Zoltan? Which one was he?"

That big black and white intact male of Julie's…he's one of my Freddie's sons."

Beth looked sharply at Wisteria. Something in her voice stuck a very sad note. "Freddie? Do you still have him? I thought you had no intact males in the cattery at present."

"I don't." The driver glanced wistfully at her seatmate. "Freddie was CumbriaCoons Prince of CastleRigg; the biggest most handsome black and white tom you can imagine. My whole heart—"

Beth hesitated. She didn't want to bring up a sad subject. But perhaps her friend needed to talk about it. "Did something bad happen to Freddie, Wisteria?"

"I don't know, love…he simply disappeared. One day he was in the cattery and the next day he was gone. I found a big hole in the garden fence that morning but if he went exploring, he wouldn't have gone far. Freddie was a stay-at-home sort of cat."

"I had one of my studcats stolen once, Wisteria, could that have happened to Freddie?" Beth would not have added that "tomcat" was synonymous with "wandering opportunist", to phrase it modestly, and "intact males" as the Brits most usually called them, did tend to go where the girls were.

"Not bloody likely," Wisteria declared forcefully. "As you see, my cattery is a bit isolated, nothing but sheep farmers thereabouts and hikers (we English are inveterate walkers) and I don't see one of them carrying him off. Freddie was a big, heavy cat…my house is not all that easy to find…it's just not the sort of place where a thief would go looking for a show cat. And Freddie's markings are very distinctive. He had a black mask across his eyes—somewhat like your raccoons are marked. All white otherwise except for black patches on his shoulders and flanks. Very unusual boy, Freddie was," Wisteria repeated sadly. "Quite famous among our Maine Coon lovers."

"I'm sure you asked round about, posted notice on the internet, let vets in the Lake District all know?"

"Um, um, oh, yes. But cats are not the main interest here. Tourists come to the Lake District mostly to see Border collies, the Herdwick sheep, our ancient breed of shaggy cattle, go rock climbing, sail the lakes, fish, walk…Cats are mostly taken for granted here. Most of my kitten buyers come from the south: Lancaster, Manchester, the Cotswolds, London or the continent…Basically, around the lakes and fells, tourists are catered to and draw the most interest." Wisteria changed the subject. It was evidently a very painful one for her. "Tomorrow after we get back to Rose Cottage, we'll go sightseeing, too. I want to take you and Chad up to Hardknott Pass and the old Roman fort—and then we'll go see my old friend Paul at Fellshadow Farm."

Silence fell on the car's occupants. There didn't seem to be anything else one could say about the lost Freddie and tomorrow's sightseeing would speak for itself. Hawkeye and Bhu Fan, though, had taken a great interest in Wisteria's account of her lost tom. Cats might not be the main interest among the Lake District's tourists and residents but they certainly were to a pair of feline sleuths like Hawkeye and Bhu Fan.

The little Korat chewed on a whisker as she lolled up against Hawkeye's big furry flank. Something was stirring in her brain. Unfocused, she murmured to her seatmate. *Freddie's not gone to Rainbow Bridge, Hawkeye, he's out here somewhere…I hear laughter…and clinking sounds…and loud thumps…smell sharp odors…*

Yeah, well, Boo, that's all good and well but we're out of our territory now. How are we gonna get cut loose and go looking for Wisteria's lost tom? And even if we did, what's to keep us from getting lost??

Bhu Fan licked a paw and drew it slowly across one ear. *I not know, Peasant—not yet. But Bastet will send us in right direction…I hope. All is dark right now.* The little blue Korat straightened her whiskers and stiffened. *Starry and Angel!* She sat up suddenly and shook her head. *I hate it when head goes all fuzzy like that!*

What about Starry and Angel, Hawk asked, suddenly alarmed.

I not know. But I have dreadful feeling they're about to get themselves into a boatload of trouble. Just like Freddie!

Hawk never got a chance to interrogate Bhu Fan about the wayward pair of half-grown kits. Wisteria had started to speak in the front seat and Bhu Fan was not one to miss a word of humankind conversation—or comment on it.

"Before we get home, Beth, I'd like to stop in Kendal. There's a place there I think you'd enjoy. The Age Concern Warehouse—funny name, isn't it? Actually a big old flea market (I think you call them)—I need some more feed bowls for the cattery." Wisteria glanced at her seatmate to see if she was interested.

"Great. I love to prowl through such places." She looked over her shoulder at her cats spread out on the back seat, loose for once as Her Majesty had complained bitterly about long confinement in a carrier. When Bhu Fan was annoyed, that Oriental rusty tin-can of a voice didn't bear listening to. It was easier just to give in to her demands. After all, she wasn't going anywhere.

As Beth turned her attention back to the scenery in front of them, enjoying the mix of period picturesque architecture of the old market town of Kendal nestled in the Cumbrian fells, Wisteria pulled up and parked in front of a rather large weary-looking building which had certainly started out in life as a warehouse, busy though it obviously was. People were coming and going, mostly with armloads of clothes. And they were not, for the most part, people who looked like they couldn't afford to shop at Marks and Spencer's or Fortnam's. *But hey*, Beth thought smiling to herself, *everybody loves a bargain!*

As the two women got out of the car, Bhu Fan leaped to the ground, a curious Hawkeye right behind her.

"Bhu, you pushy broad, come back here—"

"Oh, let her go, Beth. We don't get all chapped about our animals. They're welcome most everywhere." Wisteria opened the entrance door for her visitor and the cats. "I rather think if those two rascals caught a mouse, we'd most likely get a discount."

Beth laughed and looked about her at the narrow aisles, piled high on both sides with a myriad of goods: books, glassware, crockery, clothes, bedding, furniture. Even bicycles. Which shouldn't have surprised her, bikes being an honorable alternate form of transportation in the British Isles. Oddly, the high-ceilinged building, careworn though it might be, did not have a musty odor nor were those expected flea market twins, dust and disrepair, evident anywhere. Things might be stacked up in a jumble but from their condition, she could only surmise, the goods on offer moved quickly and were not without quality. She smiled: although that old-fashioned pushchair right out of Edward Gorey's gloomy illustrations just might be there for awhile.

Beth browsed the book shelves, happy to find a copy of Paul Gallico's *The Silent Miaow*, which she'd long since lost and *Blitzcat* by Robert Westall, another treasure she'd loaned out and never gotten back. She quickly grabbed the books, circling around to see where her cats had gotten to as Wisteria rejoined her with an armload of crockery for the cattery.

"Bhu? Hawk?" she called, trying not to raise her voice in her concern for their whereabouts.

"Rhiow!" responded the small blue Korat, leaping to a stack of piled up old blankets and quilts in a dim corner of the warehouse, Hawk jumping up beside her, waving his plumey battle flag of a tail.

As the two women approached, the cat began pawing through a stack of quilts and then, to everyone's great surprise, burrowed underneath and wormed her way to the middle, causing much laughter among Beth, Wisteria and a couple of browsers. Wisteria set her bowls on a nearby antique piecrust table. Beth, always intrigued by old quilts, put her books down beside them and reached out to the stack of old bedding.

"Bhu, you silly twit! What are you up to?"

Yeah, Boo, what you after? Hawkeye had climbed up on a stack of pillows on an adjacent shelf so as not to impede the tunneling Korat. He shook his head in exasperation. With Her Royal Highness, one just never knew.

"Rhiow-murumph," came the muffled response.

Beth and Wisteria grinned at each other and began carefully folding back the stack of quilts one by one, making comments as they did so.

"Toe-snaggers," Beth murmured as she examined the top ones.

'Um, um, yes," responded her companion, "those quilting stitches are a bit long, aren't they? You'd really have to keep toenails clipped short to avoid getting tangled up in one of those." She giggled as she helped her visitor inspect the flea market offerings. Most of these old quilts, Beth decided, were fit only for wrapping furniture when one was, as Wisteria said, "moving house". Others were merely serviceable patchwork or mundane designs. Some were of colors that did little more than assault the eye. But then Bhu Fan was revealed, stretched out like a sultan's dream on the quilt of her choice.

This one, Bethmom, she crowed, *this one is important. This one is going home with us!*

"Beth, what is that cat talking about?"

"Who knows?" Beth responded in a distracted voice. She was at once seized with wonder at the quilt Bhu Fan was lying on. She ran delicate fingers over it carefully, reverently, whistling to herself.

Wisteria, too, was taking a very close look at the double-bed sized quilt. It was made of a homespun ivory muslin, appliquéd with ruched, that is to say: pleated and stuffed roses in a perhaps primitive yet highly stylized and well made appliquéd pattern. Instantly, Beth realized something else, she who had made a study of antique quilts from the Deep South to New England. The green of the leaves surrounding the roses had faded on some to blue and to yellow on others. That could only be the result of the old homemade two-step green dye! Which meant this quilt was most likely made (in the United States, at any rate) before 1845. That was about when a green dye became commercially available. Before that time, quilters made the color green by mixing blue and yellow dyes. And in recognizing this, she also had a very firm feeling that this quilt, even though it was buried beneath other offerings in an old warehouse in Kendal, Cumbria, was an American made quilt.

Beth and Wisteria looked at each other. Both of them were experienced quilters. Both of them knew what they were looking at: an antique jewel of textile art. "If it could only talk!" marveled Wisteria.

Beth turned up one corner of the quilt. Someone had stitched a small six-inch square in one corner like a label. Only, to the women's disappointment, it wasn't a label. It was, as far as Beth could tell, part of a page from a child's nursery rhyme book copied out in cross-stitch. Covering a hole in the quilt perhaps? That wouldn't be an unusual occurrence in an old quilt.

Wisteria ran her hands over the backing as Bhu Fan and Hawkeye stood over them watching closely. "Curious, isn't it?" she commented.

"Yes," agreed Beth. "The quilt is mostly quilted with lovely tiny, tiny running stitches in the old Princess Feather pattern—except for this quarter where it's tied instead. Now why on earth would anyone ruin a lovely quilt by poking yarn through it at intervals and tying it merely in knots to keep the batt from shifting between front and back?"

"That is strange, isn't it? I think maybe the quilting stitches on this part broke or rotted—after all it *is* at least 200 years old—and someone repaired it by quickly tying it instead of taking the time to re-quilt it. And I'd wager *that* wasn't done by the original quilter!"

Beth made up her mind. "Well, no biggie—and price no object." She grinned broadly, carefully taking up the precious bed covering. "I can re-quilt that. This old girl is going home with me!"

Bhu Fan and Hawkeye leaped gracefully to the floor, Bhu Fan, to her companion's consternation, chortling to herself as their little procession made its way to the cashier.

What in Bastet's name, Boo, is so important about an old blanket? I mean, I wouldn't mind having it to line a nest box for the kitlings but, shoot, Bethmom can find old bed-stuff like that at home. She doesn't need to have to haul it across an ocean.

Bhu Fan peered at him dismissively over her shoulder. *I thought it was pretty. Like the one Bethmom has in her quilting loft on top of cattery, the one she and Cherylmom made out of that soft silky stuff for Bethmom's wedding.*

Hawkeye grumbled. *Bethmom catch you prowling around her quilting stuff, she'll have your badge, hat, ass and spats—*

Don't be vulgar, Peasant! I know what I'm about!

Hawkeye sighed as he followed his happy humans out to the car. He didn't doubt it for a moment.

CHAPTER SEVEN

S HERE KHAN GAVE HIS whiskers one last adjustment and looked out over the hills and pastures toward the Moosery. He sat beside Smudge on Beth's back porch. If he were to admit it to himself, he missed his rascally offspring, Star and Hawkeye, not to mention Angel and Bhu Fan—Bethmom and Chad as well. Not that Martha Michaud wasn't faithful in looking after everybody in their absence. Still, he was enjoying the quiet interlude. He was getting a bit old, he sighed, to be running all over the countryside, chasing after Riddle, Zandra's red consort, and keeping Chad out of harm's way. He smiled at that. Loki and Crya had certainly been johnny-on-the-spot with the game warden's last mishap. As Smudge suddenly sat up, he brought his attention back to the old shorthaired neuter. The street cat had swiveled his head suddenly to the east in the direction of Ketler's apple orchard on the far side of Siberia Farm's rolling pastures.

"What's—*that*?" he whispered, as if the huge hulk in the distance strolling nonchalantly toward the cedar swamp could hear him.

"Oh," acknowledged The Great One, smiling, "that's our resident moose." Shere Khan turned to Smudge. "We call him Shaggy. A poacher shot him last fall and he hid out in the Moosery to heal up before it was rebuilt…he's not a bad sort…minds his own business." He chuckled. "Has a weakness for apples."

Khan stretched out on the old pine porch boards worn smooth by generations of Merrimans and closed his eyes. Smudge nodded his head absently, satisfied.

"I'll sure be glad when Bethmom and Chad get home. It's just too quiet around here." The old silver and white tiger with the notched ear and smudged nose gazed at his companion with a rueful grin. "I'm used to things happenin'; interestin' stuff to watch, cats and critters to chase—" He mused to himself, "the noise of garbage cans as they clank down the pavement, the rather picturesque language the mantoms use when they chase after them—"

The big tom chortled. "Be careful what you ask for, old friend. The gods of felinity might send us more'n we could handle." Shere Khan mimicked a dumb country boy actor he'd watched on Simon's TV. "Lak—whaddaya do if ol' Shaggy come a'stormin' up on Bethmom's back porch 'n Miz Marthy hadda git after him wi' her broom?"

Smudge appreciated the joke—if the patois was a bit foreign to him. Things might be slow but the morning's sunshine sure felt pleasant on a furry pelt. They stretched out and fell asleep, the former street cat dreaming of loose moose being chased with a broom, while Shere Khan wondered as he drifted off if his humans' honeymoon was proving to be everything they had hoped for…and would they bring him some of that York-shure pudding he'd heard them talk about?

✡ ✡ ✡

"Oooh!" gasped Beth Merryman, as their slow moving Taurus tilted upward to a stomach-churning degree. As if that weren't enough, the road on which they were inching along was only wide enough for one vehicle. But carrying two-way traffic! Beth took a deep breath and forced herself to relax. At least there were pull-outs every quarter mile or so, enabling cars to pass each other. She was sure they were on the backside of nowhere but for all that, traffic was heavy—in both directions. Then she wondered: *is* there a backside of nowhere on this small island? Well, "small", she supposed was a misnomer. It all depended on what you were used to. And keeping her mind busy just might take it off the tight curves and tall embankments they had to funnel through occasionally as they worked their way slowly upwards toward Hardknott, one of the highest passes in England.

She thought she heard snickering from behind her. Looking over her shoulder, she was about to make a rude remark to her husband when Wisteria glanced at her and spoke up.

"My friend, Paul Mellish lives at Fellshadow Farm in the valley just north of Hardknott—we'll be heading there next." Wisteria returned her attention (to Chad's immense relief) to her driving.

"Just think, Beth. Roman soldiers had to make frequent marches from down there at Ambleside by the north edge of the lake above the Furness Fells through Wrynose Pass, up this track to their fort at Hardknott Pass—and one at that with the mind-numbing name of Mediobogdum. And in all kinds of weather. It's a couple of hours by car. Imagine what it must have been like on foot!"

Chad, who was sitting on the back seat beside the carrier wherein lounged that unconcerned pair of travelers, Hawk and Bhu Fan, said nothing. He was busy marveling at the hikers and bicyclists swarming about on this rare sunny day on the fells. How anybody would voluntarily *pedal* up this grade or even *walk* it had to have some sort of death wish. *And who are we to talk*, he admonished himself, gazing up ahead where the all-but-vertical zigzagging roadway looked about as navigable as Jack's beanstalk. At Wisteria's comments, he started thinking about those poor wretches in their armor, heavy helmets, shields and spears, in sandals yet—with the wind stinging bare knees--and other body parts. He shuddered and stared at the cats. Traversing such Godawful terrain would certainly be a lot easier if you could walk on four feet instead of two and something you certainly wouldn't do just for the fun of it. Not then, not now... Bhu Fan looked up at him and he had the uncanny notion that she knew exactly what he was thinking. He shook himself and grinned conspiratorially at the little Korat.

Wisteria carefully nosed the car over the summit. For heart-stopping moments, they saw nothing in front of them but blue sky and then, as the car nosed downward, they could see in the hazy distance the Irish Sea and the village of Eskdale below them, all so green as to appear tinted like an old-fashioned postcard. It was, trite though it might sound, a breathtaking and timeless vista. Well worth the scary drive getting there. Well, maybe.

"Eeeee," exclaimed Beth again as Chad laughed (after all, he was in the backseat) from behind her. The going down was even worse than the coming up. The road snaked along what seemed impossibly narrow 90-degree turns with no guard rails to lend heart's ease. Only a few huge boulders leaning drunkenly in one direction or another along the way to stop a vehicle if brakes failed. Chad bethought himself on a huge pinball machine. You could only hope one of those boulders would stop your wayward descent down the grade. He realized he was pressing hard on an imaginary brake pedal from the back seat and shifted in his seat. He'd swear Hawkeye was laughing at him.

Beth did her best to relax. She didn't doubt that Wisteria had ferried many visitors along this precipitous route before. She concentrated on the remains of the Roman fort—*Mediobogdum*, for heaven's sake—below them to the right. The stone-littered bounds marched over the uneven terrain in a pattern that might have marked off a large encampment, squarish but not precisely so. It couldn't have been. The ground was too uneven and lumpy. A small burn no more than a couple of feet wide trickled like molten silver along its course from high up in the rocks down along one of the fort's outside walls.

They weren't far below the summit now. The athletic Herdwick sheep grazed lazily along the verges and inside the fort's perimeter. More craggy boulders poked up through long grasses here and there as if some giant—Jack's, perhaps? —had planted them there to provide himself with a foothold or two. A few stunted trees leaned away from the sea.

"Of course," Wisteria explained, "in the time of the Roman occupation, there would not only have been soldiers up here keeping an eye on things, particularly any attack from the sea, but all sorts of Celtic tribesmen who set up stalls along the outside walls to sell their wares to their conquerors, along with the camp followers' huts (called *vicus*) for the women. I picture it as a regular good-sized community. All sorts of people milling about, dogs scavenging, cats prowling for mice, women strutting about with an eye to making a few obols, ponies bearing packs of firewood and all the things a garrison of solders would need to maintain some sort of standard of living...there were certainly not enough trees up here to heat the water for the baths. And the Romans did dearly love their baths. It would have been a busy, thriving place—for all the difficulty of getting up here. But what else did they know? It was the only transportation they had: feet and hooves." Their hostess pulled her car adroitly off the narrow roadway onto a space wide enough for maybe four vehicles beside the fort. And just as she did, the car's engine sputtered and died. Nobody spoke for a full minute.

"Oh, dear, I forgot to fill the tank before we left Ambleside." In the stunned silence that followed, the three of them had very vivid pictures in mind of what might have transpired had the tank run dry only minutes past. Ever one to be upbeat, Wisteria exclaimed as they all got out of the car, "No need to worry, love, someone will come along and help us out."

The three of them glanced back up at the summit, the two Americans a bit weak in the knees. There were neither hikers nor bikers on this side of the pass at the moment but a Range Rover was coming toward them, wending its way very carefully around the hair-raising curves. Chad went around to their vehicle's bonnet and lifted it. As the universal sign of car trouble, it had the desired effect. The approaching SUV stopped on the road behind their car. The driver's window descended. "I say, you're having difficulties, are you?"

Wisteria smiled at the driver and walked over to speak to him. In a few minutes, she returned and directed her comments to the game warden.

"Chad, this chap says he'll give you a lift into Eskdale where there's a petrol station. He thinks they'll fill a can for you and give you a ride back up here."

The game warden nodded smiling, touched Beth briefly on the shoulder, walked to the waiting vehicle and was soon on his way, talking easily with the driver.

"We may have a bit of a wait," Wisteria said as they watched the Range Rover fade into the distance as it disappeared around

another curve all but standing on its nose, "Would you like to explore the fort?"

Beth tied a silk scarf around her head and nodded. They had, after all, avoided disaster. "It's certainly a place that stirs the imagination. Hard to believe it was once almost a small town up here among
the rocks and crags...Would it be okay to let Hawkeye and Bhu out
of their carrier?"

"I don't see why not," Wisteria said as she donned a furry cap.
"I wouldn't want to deprive them of a splendid tale to tell when they
get back home. In my fantasy life, I see cats as great storytellers—
would you agree?"

"I wouldn't doubt it for a minute." Beth responded, laughing as
she reached into the back seat and unlatched the big carrier. The two
cats scrambled out and leaped to the ground—and just as quickly
bounced up onto the nearest slate wall. "Wait!" commanded Beth,
reaching into her bag. "Bhu, you're going to freeze your tail off up
here." So saying, she picked up a wiggling Korat and slipped a small
red knit sweater over her head. At that point she gazed at the small
cat's feet and grimaced. "No wonder you and Hawk were so quick to
jump up on the wall. The ground here is sure soft and muddy." Bhu
Fan looked at Beth in annoyance and started shaking her paws one
by one. *You could have warned us!* Sometimes a disgruntled meow
says it all.

Hawkeye laughed, although he, too, stood on the wall shaking
mud from his big hairy feet. *Well, look at it this way, Boo; you could
have stayed in the car and missed out on communing with the sheep. Or
talked them out of a bit of fleece for booties...*

The Korat princess ignored her companion, shook herself so as
to get comfortable in her sweater and ambled along the stones as
Wisteria and Beth set out to explore Mediobogdum, Hawkeye, still
amused, following along behind, the little burn that trickled along
beside them making its own watery music. When they reached the
back wall, Beth gazed down over the sheer drop-off of some two
hundred feet, her stomach lurching. In an attempt to offset her diz-
ziness, she tried to figure out how far that escarpment was in meters.
No matter, she righted herself and looked at the large farm below
in the swale, its stone paddocks dotted with cattle. It seemed to sit

peacefully close by a tiny road that clung precariously to the terrain of the fell on the other side of a narrow valley, itself scored with the ubiquitous drystone walls, running willy-nilly in all directions. Or so it appeared to Beth. The way some of them clambered vertically up fellside, she couldn't imagine sheep or anything else grazing inside them.

She turned around. From up here, one could see in all directions. This made the selection of such a site certainly valid for the conquerors—if very hard on the constitution of its inhabitants. If the unruly Britons attacked the fort from the pass, they could quickly be routed before they got close enough to do any real damage. And if they came from any other direction, the same applied. She shook her head, trying to picture such violent scenes. It was difficult to think of the British Empire as once no more than an odd collection of isolated primitive tribesmen under the yoke of Rome.

"E-Oow!" She heard behind her. Wisteria spun around, too. Bhu and Hawk were racing toward them at full tilt, hair along their backs standing straight up. More ominous noise and movement arrested the two women and centered their gaze to the upward side of the fell where it loomed over the pass and its roadway. A huge decahedron of a boulder, sunlight reflecting off its ten uneven surfaces, was wrenching itself from its water-soaked earthly moorings, scattering smaller rocky adherents in all directions. Slowly, it was tipping sideways. As the two women and the cats watched in fascinated disbelief, the soft ground gave way as the tiny burn, which had probably been undermining the boulder on its downhill side for quite some time, ate at the soft dirt around it and spilled mud and debris out over the grass in all directions.

Suddenly, gravity got the upper hand. The boulder broke free, screeching like a thousand rusty hinges and tumbled down along the side of the encampment, gathering speed as it went. Beth and Wisteria were in no danger from their stance some feet away on the upper edge of the fort but it was a riveting experience nevertheless. The large orb of granite, following the path of the burn which acted as a trough for it, bounced over a ridge, which acted as a brake to its rotating tumble and came to rest beside their vehicle where it sat placidly unaware of any danger. Both women heaved a deep sigh of relief, picturing their transportation with a large irate elephant sitting on top if it. The sudden silence was awesome. Beth Merryman shook her head in wonder. That boulder had been deposited up above and locked in place during the last ice age 10,000 years ago when a glacial sheet covering the Northern Hemisphere was miles deep. Now it had been moved once more. And by nothing more dangerous than a tiny freshet of water.

The little group looked back uphill to where the monster had wrenched itself free. On a lesser outcropping beside the shallow hole it left, sat a huge cat, a small rodent in its mouth. It, too, appeared to have been frozen in place by its near miss. Hawk and Bhu Fan galloped up the incline toward the furry hunter.

Are you okay? Hawk called. *Was anybody else with you?* The big Maine Coon, with Bhu right behind him, skidded to a halt on the slick grass below where the stranger sat mesmerized, his eyes large with dismay.

The longhaired cat, at least on a speaking acquaintance with Maine Coon ancestry, white except for a few red patches here and there and a red mask across his eyes, came to himself, dropped his catch at his feet, squinted and looked down at the newcomers. "Um, yes, I'm okay. Just out hunting…there was a cache of mice that tunneled all about that big rock…" His voice trailed off as he peered down at the road where the boulder now sat immobile in the middle of a crowd of people who seemed to have materialized out of nowhere. It was even taller than the men circling it, who gazed upward in wonder.

"I'm Tatty Bumpkin," the red and white splotched neuter said. "I live at the farm down below." He hesitated. "You lot talk funny. You're not from around here, are you?" The cat looked a bit abashed as if regretting his nosiness. Unlike dogs, cats are well defined by their reserve. Even among their own kind.

Hawk, who had been looking toward the road where Beth, Wisteria, Chad and their rescuer stood talking to other travelers who had been drawn to the granite behemoth now reposing where it had dug out a gouge the size of Wisteria's Taurus, nodded his head. As long as his humans were safe, Hawkeye could relax.

"Yeah, we're just visiting." He answered absentmindedly. "Out for a spot of sightseeing—as Catemom would say." He chortled. Hawk did love some of her expressions. He couldn't wait to get home and try some of them out on his sire.

"Catemom?"

"That's what we call her. Bethmom calls her Wisteria."

"Right-O! Wisteria…I couldn't make her out from here." Again Tatty Bumpkin looked abashed. "I'm a bit close-sighted." He looked down at the dead mouse at his feet and nudged it with a paw. "I can't even see these little blighters until I'm right on top of 'em."

He gazed back toward the roadway. "My sire came from Wisty's cattery." He laughed. "My dam was out on the lake fishing with Old Woolly Socks (that's what we call our guv'nor) and they stopped in over there for a cup of tea with Wisty—the guv's a bit sweet on her. Anyway, my sire, mum tells me, took a fancy to her. And she to him, if she'd admit it." Tatty Bumpkin chuckled and shook his head. "I don't know how he managed it, he bein' some good way from up here but not too long after, he came callin'. The guv was a bit surprised when we kits showed up…I don't think he ever figured out who da was. None of us was black and white like him. We was all red 'n white like mum—"

"Bhu! Hawk! Where are you?" Beth swung around, looking anxiously for her cats. Seeing them, she hesitated, "And who's that you have with you?" She cocked her head and shaded her eyes.

Looking uphill, Wisteria squinted at the two cats sitting on the boulder: Hawkeye and—of course—Paul's Tatty Bumpkin. She identified the strange cat to Beth as her friend started toward the pair.

At the sound of Bethmom's voice calling from a distance, Hawk turned around. Where was Boo? He cast about for his small companion. A splash of red sweater caught his eye. Bhu Fan was crouched down, poised at the edge of the little burn a few feet away. The boulder had gouged a wide hole there and the water was noisily spreading out to fill up the space. Bhu Fan was evidently looking at something in the stream. She touched her paw to the surface and quickly drew it back. That water was icy! Hawk jumped down and, followed by a curious Tatty Bumpkin, joined the little Korat at the new bank of the stream. *What's up, Boo?* He asked, not seeing anything of great interest in the shallow rivulet.

Very, very old, responded Bhu Fan cryptically.

Before she could elaborate, Beth Merryman had reached the curious trio. She looked down to see what held their attention, sucked in a breath, squatted down and reached into the water, hissing involuntarily at its frigid temperature. As Chad and Wisteria, themselves curious, came up and stood over her.

"What's going on, honey?"

Beth shivered and wordlessly held up her hand. It contained a clump of muddy but well defined scarred, newly-glittering coins and a few tiny pieces of broken pottery.

CHAPTER EIGHT

"I F WE CLIMB UP on the wooden floaty thing and go to the far end, Star, we can see all those busy little fishies much better...I'll bet I could even snag one with my paw—"

The young black tom snorted. "Huh! More likely you'd lean too far outta that boat and fall in." Star grinned at the prospect. "And wouldn't that make a sloppy mess of your pretty coat?" The young cat absentmindedly looked up and down the shoreline of Lake Windermere. There was no one and no other animal in sight. Except for the ever-present sheep dotted here and there high up on the fells.

Momentarily deterred, Angel looked at Star thoughtfully, sat down at water's edge and sighed. "Aren't you bored, too, Starry? When's Bethmom, Catemom and everybody comin' back? How come they didn't take us? They took Hawk and Boo... Where'd all this water come from? Is it an inland sea like where our ancestors came from? Why do all those queens in Catemom's cattery have to be so snotty? Our queens aren't like that. What's with all those funny woolly things that look like Bethmom's goats but aren't?"

"Angel!" Star declared sternly. "You'd talk the ears off a brass owl. You wanted to come down here to the big pond 'n I opened up that hole in the fence for you. Bethmom isn't going to be pleased if she comes back and finds us missing. I don't know where they went after the big cat show. They just came back with a bunch of stuff they were laughing about—armloads of it—and next thing I knew, they were off again, taking Chad with 'em. Somethin' about 'sight-seein'". The little silver torbie's fellow escapee was getting a bit nervous. "Now c'mon, you've seen the fish up close and personal; let's git back up to Catemom's garden." He added with emphasis, "If you weren't so stuck up yourself, maybe that blue 'n white queen Violet, would talk to you. She talked to Boo and she has some pretty little kitlings. C'mon, let's go."

Angel laid her ears back, slapped at Star and hopped up in the boat that was lightly mired in the wet gravel at water's edge. "Foo on you, ol' stick-in-the-mud!"

With that, having hopped over planks wedged between gunwales piled all about with fishing gear and oars, the young queen sprinted to the far stern where she could watch the fish. Her movements set the small craft rocking but so intent was she on achieving her destination that she didn't notice. Searching for the sight of silvery salmon fry, she leaned over the stern, setting it in motion side to side. A gust of wind helped the rocking boat loosen its grip in the gravel.

"Angel!" cried Starry, "Get out of there. The boat's moving. Pretty soon you'll have to swim. C'mon." The black tom saw Angel turn around and race for the prow, which inadvertently sent the small fishing boat further out into the water.

"Starry!" she cried, now thoroughly frightened, "I can't swim!"

Star knew that she *could* swim; most creatures can if needs must. But he also realized she was too panicked to try. And he couldn't leave her to her fate. With a prodigious running leap, the young tom sailed through the air and managed to sink his claws into the pointed wooden prow as it slipped away from its gravel bed. The breeze pushed the craft along out into Lake Windermere with its small stowaways as Star, scrambling for purchase, managed to climb into the boat.

Now isn't this a pretty kettle of fish? He thought to himself as he joined a thoroughly contrite silver torbie amidships, shaking droplets of water from the tip of his plumey tail.

"What're we gonna do, Starry?" She whimpered. "We're going farther and farther away from the rocks and pebbles." The young queen hunkered down in the pile of fishing gear and canvas and started to cry.

"Hush up, Angel!" commanded Star. "You didn't give up and cry when you were lost in the big city, did you?"

Angel turned large teary eyes on the young black tom. "No," she muttered, "but Shere Khan was there…n' Hawk…'n Boo an'—"

Star sat up straight and puffed out his chest. "Did I stay at water's edge? Did I leave you to your stupid rocking-the-boat? Did I let you float out here all by yourself?" The young tom clamped his mouth tight. He was, if he admitted it to himself, as frightened as Angel. But letting it show would only make matters worse.

Angel started to say something and changed her mind. She took a deep breath and bent to nervously composure-grooming her left shoulder. While she didn't care to admit it, Star might not be his sire or Hawk or Boo—but really, he hadn't abandoned her. Without another word, she hunkered down and looked away from her companion.

Star gazed at her. He knew she was trying to save face. There was no reason to further admonish her. He looked about him. After all, there was no real danger. At least he hoped not. No reason for the boat to overturn and dump them in that cold water. Angel opened her eyes and the two of them watched as Catemom's garden receded farther and farther away from them and the dark menacing fells on the other side of the lake, loomed ever larger. Angel scrunched down into a tight little ball and shivered. What was going to happen to them? She closed her eyes tightly and tried not to think.

Star, who had ventured carefully to the prow, the wind and water action having turned the small craft around, took a deep breath. With any luck, the wind and waves would push them ashore. Somewhere. He retreated to where Angel was curled up and hunkered down beside her. They'd just have to wait and see—and trust Bastet. What was it Shere Khan had said that day they were coming back from Muller's barn and stopped to get out of the rain—when the wounded moose was between them and escape from the understory of the old barn?

"Wait," Khan had said. "We wait. Something will change: the king may die, the horse may die, or the horse may learn to sing."

Khan was quoting from the old story he'd told Star and his siblings when they were mere kitlings. It was a cautionary tale about a storybook king who wanted his horse to sing. He commanded his manservant to teach the horse to do this—and if he didn't succeed in two years' time, the servant would lose his head. In despair, the servant had consulted his wise old cat. This venerable shaman had advised him to *wait.* "Who knows?" He counseled, "the king may die, the horse may die—or the horse may learn to sing." Starry fervently hoped so.

"Boy!" exclaimed Beth to her weary companions. "That rollicking adventure was not on the itinerary, was it, Wisteria? Do you always have such drama when Americans come visiting?" She took off her muddy boots, one hand on Chad's shoulder, left them on a mat by the front door and followed her hostess down the hall.

Wisteria shook her head, smiled with relief and sprawled in an easy chair in her pleasant sitting room. Surrounded by bookcases and shelves holding not only a large collection of books but a varied array of cat figurines, beveled glass windows lending all the colors of the spectrum to the walls with reflected sunlight, the room had a curiously timeless quality to it, as if the books had been read and reread and the figures lovingly collected for decades. Over the fireplace was a large painting of the fells surrounding the Castle Rigg stone circle at Keswick. A collection of small framed photographs anchored the mantle beneath it. It was so very English that Beth longed to take it home with her. Wisteria had even found a small stained glass panel of Rennie McIntosh *art nouveau* vibrant scarlet roses which she'd hung just inside the front window that looked out over the lake.

After a moment, Wisteria drew breath. "I'll put on the kettle, shall I? You two prefer coffee, I believe? I've got some of that excellent Netherlands blend—though I can't pronounce its name. The Dutch insert 'w's' in the weirdest places, almost as if it were a vowel…" She chuckled. "I shouldn't wonder: the Welsh are just as bad…"

Her two visitors nodded agreement and followed their hostess into the kitchen. Countess Cottia, from her cushion on a rocking chair by another fireplace, rose up and stretched. CumbriaCoons' matriarch, like Madame du Maine, wore her badge of office in her attitude. As imperial as Bhu Fan, she was an amber-eyed Maine Coon the color of ripe apricots; "cameo" in the standard book, with a ruff as bright as the fells in winter. Or as her offspring were fond of saying: the Herdwick lambs in spring.

"Raoul!" she uttered softly, by way of greetings to Hawkeye and the small blue Korat as they came into the room on the heels of their humans. *What did you think of Boggytown?*

Boggytown? echoed Hawk as he watched Bhu wrestle with her red sweater. The two cats settled themselves on the rag rug in front of the fireplace as Beth knelt down and relieved Bhu of her woolly wrapping. Bhu Fan looked at her gratefully and waited for Cottia to enlighten them.

Boggytown, yes, repeated Cottia. *That's what our kind always called it. My gran told me her great-gran came from a farm below there and her gran had all kinds of tales to tell about Boggytown. So many moons in the past, warlike foreigners wore shiny skirts that clanked and fierce native-born tribesmen painted themselves blue.* Cottia, who loved to lecture, assumed a proud stance in her chair, one a bit incongruous with the tatty patchwork cushion on which she was sitting. *That was before we big long-pelted cats sailed to America with the Vikings. Can you imagine: they didn't even have* litterboxes *in those far off times...*

Primitive, murmured the Korat dismissively.

Mayhaps, agreed Cottia, not taking offense. Where humankind and their civilization was concerned, the cats were rather indifferent. Cottia chuckled as the ever fastidious Korat set about cleaning her velvet paws, so recently encumbered with mud from felinekind's aptly named long-ago settlement up in the fells.

I see Boggytown hasn't changed.

What?

It stays rather wet up there; what with lots of rain and mist banging up again the fells. Keeping paws dry was always a problem. She laughed again at some memory only she could see. *Or so my gran told me. She said, 'the mud we will always have with us.' I know the rightness of that because of Old Woolly Socks.*

Seeing the confused look on her audience's faces, she explained. *Every time Old Woolly Socks has come to call (Wisty calls him Paul) she has him leave his boots at the door. They are sooo mud-caked!* The matriarch relaxed back into her cushion and smiled. *He lives up there behind the fort... He always brings us fish. Lovely mantom, old Woolly Socks. But I hope Wisty never takes him as her consort.*

Oh? Bhu Fan was thinking of the jolly mantom who showed up just as they were leaving the old fort at Hardknott Pass. He reminded her a bit of Bethmom's carpenter, Gaston. A largish mantom, unusually graceful on his feet with a very pleasant face. The little blue Korat nodded her head. *I rather like him myself. Why shouldn't she take him as consort?*

You met him? The large cameo queen pulled at an errant whisker. *Well, the last place we'd want to live* (the Countess Cottia, of course, meaning the CumbriaCoons inhabitants) *is up there under Hardknott fell on Old Woolly Socks' farm in the shadow of all those ancient ghosts. And it's so far away; hours and hours shut up in a wicker carrying basket. I know, Wisty took me there once to show Old Woolly Socks my kitlings.* She shook herself. *That place is spooky. You should hear the tales old Francis tells about our kind in the days when the foreign mantoms inhabited that big stone fort.* Cottia circled round on her cushion. It had a hard knot of something in one corner. *Mantoms already here didn't like them at all.* She paused. *Which made things very difficult for our kind, who were just trying to get along and keep decent fare before their kitlings. Sir Francis says their shades are still up there.*

Then they did have cats? put in Bhu Fan, who really couldn't get all that interested in warlike mantoms or their ghosts either. Unless, of course, they had cats among them. She'd not forgotten her dam's tale of the Korat hero Rattanakiri and the Siamese conquerors of Cambodia in the days of a younger world. He, who having vanquished the giant rats from the *wats* of Angkor, rode back to Bangkok on the horse of their chieftain and became the queen's favorite. Bhu Fan was certain he was among her revered ancestors. Conversation at the table interrupted her thoughts.

"Who would have thought, Wisteria, that somebody almost *two thousand* years ago would have buried a cache of coins outside the walls of that fort?" Beth looked at her two tablemates. "—And then *we'd* come along and find them so many centuries later?" Wonder filled her voice. "It's kind of like being caught in a time warp."

Chad laughed softly. "Well, sweetheart, don't let your imagination run away with you…if it's all the same to you, I wouldn't care to change places with them. Not for all the coins of that realm." He shook himself. "That is one haunted, desolate place up there. Like something out of Tolkien." He looked off in the distance, thinking of *The Lord Of The Rings*. The women nodded in agreement. Wisteria brought them back to the present, getting up to go to the whistling kettle. "More coffee?"

"Please," responded her two guests.

Beth frowned. "What happens now, Wisteria, about the coins, I mean? Who owns them?" She helped herself to the sugar and her hostess' thick Jersey double cream, spooning a large helping from a dainty bowl—something else she'd like to take home with her. *Well, I probably will* she admonished herself sadly, *if only on my hips.*

"Oh, the local authorities will sort it out." Wisteria paused to gather her thoughts, looking out the window at the dark outline of towering fells rising beside her cottage. A shooting star arced across the velvet night and shimmered briefly in the mirrored surface of the lake before it winked out as she went about setting out their supper.

"First they'll have to determine in whose bureaucratic hands the decision falls. Then deal with it…Is it the Lake District's National Park blokes? The local county council? Is it public land—or does that particular little patch belong to Fellshadow Farm?"

"I daresay," interjected Chad, "they'll award you and Beth anything for finding that treasure hoard since the wayward boulder did all the work." He grinned and looked around for the little Korat. "—And it *was* Bhu Fan who actually discovered them—not that she'd have any desire to spend her reward, although that would fund an awful lot of 'nip." Her Highness gazed at him from hooded eyes, smirking as she did so.

As the laughter died away, Wisteria looked, well, wistful. "I do hope that spot of land belongs to Paul. Fellshadow Farm is a real drain on him. Farmers bear a heavy burden these days. The place isn't all that easy to get to and his farm store (something so many of our farmers have reverted to in order to make ends meet) barely breaks even." She shook her head slowly as the three of them ate their supper, "although his eggs are the biggest and best around." She brightened. 'However, he is writing a history of the fort—he has a university degree you know. I'd have to say he's a rather book-ish farmer, a *rara avis*, these days…Not what you'd expect of a lands-man among the Cumbrian fells, eh?" Her voice trailed off and she sipped her tea. "But it was rather jolly, wasn't it—finding all those glittery old coins? That boulder certainly scoured them clean." She shifted in her chair and changed the subject. "I look at all the rocks left over from the last ice age and think: wouldn't it be fascinating if they could talk? This land has been inhabited for so long and so little has been found to give us any idea how the people lived, where they came from, where they went…I find the Druids fascinating but so very little is known about them either. And were there early men here—like the ones in France who painted all those haunting im-ages of long-ago beasts in the caves?"

She eyed Hawkeye and Bhu Fan curled up on the settle by the fireplace. "I'll bet they'd have a few tales to tell, too." Wisteria blushed. "Don't laugh; somehow, I have this idea that cats have a race memory that goes back further than ours—"

Bhu Fan raised her head and peered slit-eyed at Wisteria. Hawk-eye gave her a grin. *Sometimes humankind isn't so dumb as we'd like to believe, are they?*

Cottia laughed. *One has to remember it's like Wisty says; this land has been inhabited for a very long time by all sorts of creatures long gone and still here. No doubt some of our perceptions are bound to have rubbed off on the present day mantoms.*

Bhu Fan looked at her companions with that superior smile Hawkeye knew so well and turning, gave her paw close scrutiny as she extended her claws.

Right. Only they're too self-absorbed to get it…

CHAPTER NINE

BETH LOOKED AT THE three cats perched around Wisteria's snug kitchen. *You'd think,* she muttered to herself, *they'd all had a big bowl of this jersey cream themselves. What I'd give to know what they're thinking!* She nodded absentmindedly, arose, took her plate and mug to the drainboard beside the sink and looked at her hostess. "I think I'd better go check on our juvenile delinquents, Star and Angel. In all the excitement of the afternoon, I forgot all about them."

"And if there's a way to trouble," Chad added, putting his cup aside and rising from his chair, "those two will surely find it." With that, all three headed for the cattery, Bhu Fan and Hawkeye on their heels. The little Korat was shaking her head. *They're not there,* she said softly to Hawkeye.

The big tabby stopped suddenly and looked at her in alarm. *What!?*

Star and Angel. They're not here. Bhu Fan started up again as they all entered Wisteria's cattery at the side of her thatched cottage. *They have floated away.* Hawkeye, who was staring openmouthed at his friendly neighborhood seeress, followed her into the cattery, his heart sinking. That rascal Star couldn't stay out of trouble to save his soul. What had he gotten into this time?? He didn't doubt for a moment Boo knew what she was talking about. She'd proven that time and again.

Blast! uttered the little Korat angrily. *I should have picked up on it sooner. That'll teach me to ignore fuzzy head!*

Beth stood in the middle of the common room looking all about her, her arms folded across her chest. No sound. All was quiet. The queens gazed sleepily at the group when Wisteria turned on the lights. Nowhere, though, did Beth see her two youngsters. Their baskets were empty. Wisteria walked around the edge of the room, peering closely into each and every enclosure. She knew they wouldn't be in there, they *couldn't* be in there, but she had to do something. She opened the door to the supply closet. Nope.

"Star! Angel?" She called, her voice rising, quavery with fear. "What have those little beggars done with themselves?"

No response.

"Would they be in the garden?" asked Chad, frowning.

"I shouldn't think so at this time of night but we can certainly look." Wisteria gritted her teeth and sucked in her lower lip, trying to dampen down her alarm as she pushed open the door to the garden. She checked the cat flap. It had not been secured. "Oh, dear," she muttered to herself. *Am I getting* that *absentminded??*

Again Beth called to her missing pair. More grown than kits they might be—but to her they were still kittens. Particularly when they were so clueless. Well, maybe curious was a better word but that didn't help. They were *not* where they were supposed to be.

All was silent in the tall shadowy enclosed cattery garden. Light lingers longer in the northern latitudes. And it never gets truly dark in high summer. "If the kittens are here they'd surely come to us—" Beth muttered softly. She had a sinking feeling she didn't like at all, her heart beginning to pound; disappearances like this really sucked, as Cheryl's teenagers would say. Oh, for the day when microchips were also GPS locators!

"Look!" said Chad sharply, pointing his finger at the back fence and taking his wife by the hand. He strode swiftly to a spot along the fence between two rose bushes. Wisteria quickly joined them and peered down at the black hole. There was a large gap in the fence where the lattice work had been pushed apart, a hole certainly big enough for a pair of young cats to squeeze through. They stood mute while the creatures of the night around them whispered among themselves.

Before anyone could stop her, Bhu went slithering through the gap and sprinted down the incline to the lake, a silvery wraith skimming over the ground. *Wait for me, Boo,* cried Hawkeye, taking off at a gallop behind her as Wisteria unlatched the garden gate. Three anxious people went quickly down the slope after them, stumbling a bit in the dark, thankful that ambient light from the north kept it from being a stygian blackness under the fells.

Soon they came up behind the little Korat, standing poised at water's edge, one paw lifted tentatively. All any of them could see was an impression in the damp gravel where a small rowboat's keel had been pulled up. Where its owner had disappeared to was anybody's guess. Gone to her neighbor's maybe? A couple of boot prints were barely visible further along and a few small paw prints filled with water still reflected the starlight. They gazed across the mile or so of gentle waves at the lights of habitation winking fitfully against the backdrop of the fells across the lake.

Wisteria let out a little cry. "Could it be? Is this what happened to Freddie?"

"What?"

"Paul came to call with his fishing companion, Maid Marion," Wisteria smiled briefly, "Maid Marion being one of his lovely Coons. Early last spring it was—and they brought me a bucket of fish. We had a nice visit. Maid Marion made herself right at home and after tea, we played Scrabble for awhile. Paul loves word games." Wisteria concentrated on the memory. "He came again a couple of weeks later as he'd seen I needed a door re-hinged and this time, when he walked back down to the lake for his boat, which he'd just pulled up out of the gravel as the lake is placid most of the time—" The woman gazed again at the twinkling lights at water's edge beneath the fells on the far side of the lake. "—It was gone." She looked at her companions in the pale moonless night, their faces mere shadowed outlines. "We thought it had just drifted away. The lake's quite wide here, you see. But Paul can come by boat quicker than car, as you've no doubt noticed from our trip to Hardknott…the far side of Windermere might as well be on the moon. If a wandering cat or a lost one—

"I drove him home and the next day, I realized Freddie was gone. I couldn't find that cat anywhere." She turned her back toward the water; a breeze was blowing softly from the land out across the lake. She started slowly back up the Slope toward her cottage with her visitors, Bhu Fan and Hawkeye trailing slowly behind.

"Now I wonder if Freddie got curious and hopped into Paul's fishing boat and ended up heaven knows where; I mean a motorboat of some sort may have gone skimming down the lake and its wake caught Paul's boat and rocked it loose—do you suppose," she ventured, "someone else might have left his boat here for some reason and it got accidentally hijacked by another curious pair of small stowaways?"

Chad put his arms across the shoulders of both women. "If they floated away, they'll come to no harm, Wisteria—not as long as the weather holds. We'll set out bright and early in the morning to look for them. That boat has got to land somewhere; it won't just bob about out in the middle of the lake."

Wisteria said nothing. Lake Windermere being the longest lake in England, it would be like trying to find those poor little scraps in another country. Somehow, this didn't seem the time to explain that to Beth and Chad. One could only hope that someone kind took them in.

Thump! went the loud report as the little rowboat banged up against the pilings next to a pier on the far northwestern edge of Lake Windermere. Star and Angel were instantly awake. Dawn was slowly creeping down the fells that loomed over them. The two young cats jumped up on the prow and looked all about. No strange creatures were around to threaten them. A few birds twittered from the trees overhead, looking down at the two young creatures curiously. Distant sheep up on the fells still lounged close to their drystone walls out of the swirling wind. The planked walkway jutting out into the lake appeared to lead up to a path toward some sort of habitation. Someone had planted all sorts of shrubs, herbs and flowers along the walkway. If any nearby mantoms were up and about, however, they were keeping very quiet.

"Where are we, Starry?" Angel asked as she hopped up on the rough wood of the pier and crouched down, peering all around them.

"How should I know, twitbrain?" complained Star as he landed softly beside the little silver torbie. "I didn't bring my maps with me." He, too, looked around to make sure there was no danger lurking nearby.

"Well, there's no need to be sarcastic," riposted Angel as she made her way slowly to the moss-covered steps which led up the hill to a dwelling of some sort. Only the roof line showed above blazing scarlet rhododendrons and clouds of pink clematis blossoms tumbling over a tall latticed wall along one side of the path.

Warily, the two young cats moved in that direction. Other blooming bushes guarded the pathway, wearing flowers that neither of them could put a name to. Aside from the bird song, a few indistinct sounds were muted. No human voices called, no noisy vehicles started up. Aside from the roof tops, there was nothing to see that might tell Star and Angel what they were approaching. At least no dogs barked and growled. No raptors wheeled menacingly overhead.

"Do you think mantoms up there will take us back to Wisteria's?"

"Huh! How they gonna know that's where we came from?" Star gave Angel a   stern look and shook his head as they progressed up the hillside slowly and with great stealth. *Queens! I ask you!* The young tom muttered under his breath. Suddenly he stopped in his tracks.

"Listen!" he commanded.

Angel gazed at him curiously, but did as he said, one paw frozen in mid-step.

"Is that a *feline* I hear up above?"

"Sing a song of sixpence, uh pocket full of ryyyeeeee,
Four and twenty blackbirds baked in uh piiiiie…
When the pie was oh-pend, the birds began to sinnnnnggg
Now wasn't that uh dainty dish to set before a kiiinnnggg—"

A huge black and white tom was leisurely strolling down the path toward them, contentedly amusing himself with song, his tail to the perpendicular, waving back and forth in time to the music. And wonder of wonders, he was a Maine Coon! In his black mask and huge splotches of the same color on his shoulders and flanks, he looked like a clown who'd escaped from a circus. The two youngsters blinked. For all his comical dress, however, there was something rather grand about him. Star and Angel held their ground.

"Hullo!" he said, almost to himself, pulling up short as he spied the two. "What have we here? I don't believe I've seen you lot before."

He gazed at the two young cats fearfully crouched in front of him, poised for flight. That wouldn't do. He sat down, smiled and brought his bushy tail around in front of him, picked it up and gave it a quick wash. He gazed at Angel and Star with a bright twinkle in his eye. "I'm Freddie," the big tom declared between licks, "who might you be—and where have you come from?"

Star stood up boldly. His interrogator had a bit of Shere Khan's grace about him. And no aggressiveness at all. "I'm Star," he stated, "and this is Angel. We got floated away in that little boat down there from across the lake and," Star took a deep breath, "we're lost."

"And very hungry," spoke up Angel, coming to stand close to Star's flank. "Do you know where we might find something to eat?" She sat down and wrapped her silky tail around her paws. "I'm really *very* hungry," she repeated, in case the big tom hadn't heard her the first time. Angel was not accustomed to missing out on breakfast. Or any other meal, for that matter.

The big tom looked down at the young maiden queen with a benign expression on his face. *Kitlings!* He bowed respectfully. "Well, come along with me, Mistress Angel, and I'll see if there's breakfast at the house. My guv is usually very generous to guests with visiting felines. There's no reason he wouldn't be to felines who come without guests." As he started back up the path, he looked back over his shoulder, while Star and Angel puzzled over guests with and without felines. Hunger was warring with trust. Slowly the two youngsters got up and trailed along in the wake of the big black and white tom.

"You lot aren't from around here, I know. You talk funny. Are you from America? My former mistress, Wisty, was always playing hostess to people from America—"

Star suddenly perked up. "Wisty? You mean Catemom at CumbriaCoons?'

"The very same."

Star sucked in his breath. He suddenly remembered that he had come from MerryMaines to replace a big tom named Freddie who had disappeared under mysterious circumstances. Did he dare tell this big tom he, Star, was supposed to be his *replacement*? Me replace *him*?? How would he react? And if he took offense, how were they ever to find their way back across the lake to CumbriaCoons? He stopped suddenly. What if Freddie didn't *know* how to get them back to their new home? After all, he'd not gone himself—and he knew Catemom must grieve for him….what a pickle!

Star clamped his mouth shut, sighed and followed Freddie and Angel up the fragrant path, carpeted as it was with the tiny leaves of lemon thyme, to the Bed and Breakfast Freddie spoke of. When they came to the small patio under spreading copper beeches on the back side of a tall, stately old house, they stopped. Seated at a table there was a man of middle years with greying hair and a square jaw which seemed to be perpetually on the verge of a grin. He was very relaxed, reading a newspaper while he drank his tea.

"Tom," he remarked, looking over at the small trio, "who've you got there?" He put down his paper and gazed benignly at the newcomers.

Star and Angel paused to flee back down the way they'd come. While this mantom didn't look like he would do them any harm, the kits had gotten very wary in the past few hours.

It's okay, Freddie cried quickly in a soothing voice. *That's my guv'nor. He doesn't know my real name. How would he*? Freddie sat down and licked a whisker. *He and the missus took me in when I almost drowned.* Without further explanation, he added, *He has no guests at the moment so he's taking it easy.* Seeing the skeptical look on Angel's face, he added, *he'll fetch us something to eat.*

"Wherever did you find them, Tom? That's certainly a handsome pair of moggies." The mantom picked up his tea cup and rose from his seat. "I'll bet they're hungry, eh?"

While Freddie, Star and Angel stood watching him, the younger cats still apprehensive, the mantom walked into the kitchen and returned shortly with a stack of bowls and a plate of table scraps. Angel, who'd never seen table scraps in her whole life, nevertheless fairly danced up and down. The offerings might not *look* familiar but they sure smelled familiar.

Star, however, had other things on his mind. How were they going to get this thoughtful mantom to understand and help them get back to CumbriaCoons? He knew they'd never make it on foot. Freddie certainly hadn't. And what about Freddie? What did he mean: he'd nearly drowned? Star shook his head as he stuck his nose tentatively into his bowl. He had a lot of things to sort out. But nothing was gained by doing his thinking on an empty stomach.

✿ ✿ ✿

"I've put the word out on the internet, Beth. But I'm the only Maine Coon breeder in this part of Northern England except for Nepetacoons and she's a bit distant up at Shap. Not many of the cat lovers hereabouts would have any idea about Coons; long-haired cats certainly—but Coons? However, since both Star and Angel are 'chipped', it should be easier to identify them if someone finds them." She didn't add: *and tries to claim them.* No use in making Beth and Chad feel any worse than they already did. She didn't want to admit that she'd certainly had no luck finding a "chipped" Freddie either.

Beth nodded, although she looked very glum. She'd been through this sort of distress before when Beowulf was kidnapped, an incident that Wisteria certainly knew about. Beth had lucked out then, thanks to Hawkeye and Bhu Fan, but Wisteria wasn't so sure she'd be so rewarded this time around. Star and Angel were, after all, in alien territory and would have no "homing" instinct for CumbriaCoons.

Chad had departed, if reluctantly, for Scotland, where he was to meet up with the contingent of wildlife coordinators on the matter of beavers. Nobody had yet assured themselves that the newcomers were going to settle in and take hold in their new habitat. There was much to-ing and fro-ing among the experts. Chad felt himself hardly an expert on the *castoridae* family of large rodents but all the same, he had a great deal of practical experience with beavers. The game warden still wasn't sure how he'd drawn the short straw on this adventure but he wasn't going to knock it, having been provided with such a great place for a honeymoon. He paused in his ruminations as he carefully drove along. Or it *would* have been if that reckless pair of curious youngling cats hadn't wandered off.

Hawkeye and Bhu Fan, sequestered in Wisteria's cattery just in case they had a notion to go walkabout, were chatting up the queens, hopeful of getting information about the lay of the land and where their small charges might have gotten to. But the CumbriaCoon queens, alas, were no help. None of them had ever gotten any further than the garden. Except for Cottia and briefly: Volet, who'd seen a bit more of the world. And somehow, they didn't think that Star and Angel could have been swept all the way up the lake to Fellshadow Farm. Well, maybe, but again maybe not. "Hawkeye, my peasant," began Bhu Fan, looking up from behind one elevated slender leg getting a wash, "We've got to get back to Tatty Bumpkin."

"Huh?" queried Hawkeye, as he cleaned his whiskers of broiled fish. "What's Tatty Bumpkin got to do with our missing kits?"

"I'm not sure—but Tatty knows this territory and his farm is also home to Sir Francis."

The big brown tabby looked momentarily confused. "Sir Who—?"

"Sir Francis, the old shaman of Tatty Bumpkin's family. He *knows* things."

Hawkeye looked thoughtful and pierced his small seeress with a sharp eye, "—as in the way your Royal Highness *knows* things?"

"Exactly."

✡ ✡ ✡

CHAPTER TEN

T HE OFTEN FICKLE ENGLISH summer—which some years didn't deign to come at all—held for the next few days: dry and clear and warm. Chad was at work in Scotland, Beth and Wisteria explored the environs of Lake Windermere on the lookout for their missing cats. It was disheartening work and their return of an evening to Rose Cottage saw them too exhausted to eat. They'd get up in the morning, rush through a meager breakfast and head out again. On this particular morning some days after Star and Angel disappeared, however, they were momentarily diverted by a phone call.

"Eh, that you, Wisteria?" a resonant baritone came over the line. "Paul here." There was hesitation on the other end of the line. "Can you stop by the farm soon? I've got something to show you."

Wisteria grew excited. "Is this about the coins, Paul? Do you get credit for the find?" She looked around, wide-eyed, at where Beth was sitting with her coffee mug in mid air as they puttered about in the old kitchen, her two cats alert and interested, listening as they were doing from the middle of the new sheepskin basket Beth had bought for them to take home. At Wisteria's glance, Beth put down her mug and she, too, listened.

"Oh, it's my land all right. But no, this isn't about that...it's a litter of kittens I've got, you see." Again the well spoken farmer hesitated.

His mates at the pub would howl if they thought he was courting his lady friend with a litter of kittens. "Come for tea, can you, maybe this afternoon?"

"Um, um, yes, Paul, that would be lovely...And we need to tell you about our bad luck here—but I'll not ruin your morning with that. We'll see you shortly."

Paul Mellish's family had worked Fellshadow Farm and herded sheep among the crags of Cumbria since time out of mind. Over the centuries, it had prospered—insofar as such a hard way of life could be said to prosper. However, thanks in part to some ancestor who had invented some newfangled piece of machinery for carding wool, it did better than most. Paul himself had been to university. And on to teaching history in an exclusive so-called "public" school (which wasn't public at all but very private) outside York. But that life had not suited him at all. He loved his books but it didn't take him long to realize that teaching was not for him. His upbringing had been so vastly different from his students that he was really hard-pressed to reach them. And being shut up inside all the time was just not rewarding enough for a son of the fells. When his parents died, he gathered up books and came home, married Marion, settled on the farm and raised three sons (now out on their own). It was a hard life, riskier than most, given the vagaries of the weather, but a satisfying one, helped by that stipend from the woolen mills. At least until Marion died of cancer and he found himself saddled with his very opinionated old maid sister who, herself, had retired from teaching in the local comprehensive. Since then he'd done his farm chores— which kept him away from Lavinia's harangues—and puttered about writing a history of the Roman occupation, another project his pub mates would no doubt josh him about. At least he could count Wisteria Cate a close, non-judgmental friend who shared his love of books and cats. And at his age, he told himself, he expected little more. Sister Lavinia had seen to that.

Wisteria herself wasn't exactly sure what Paul was up to in the matter of kittens but she was certainly curious. All the cattery chores were done, thanks to lots of help from her visitor and they could continue their search on the way to Fellshadow Farm. She grabbed up a book she'd borrowed from him, one by their favorite mystery writer, Stuart Pawson, and headed north, Beth asking tentatively as they headed out the door, "Is there another way to Paul's farm besides the road over Hardknott Pass?" At this, Chad, who had just returned from Scotland, guffawed softly. When his wife gave him a stern look, he subsided and gave her a playful hug.

Her hostess gave Beth a kind look and laughed. "Of course there is, love. The Hardknott Pass roadway is mostly traveled by tourists. It's not the sort for tractors and herded sheep." As they crossed the garden to her vehicle, she added, "There's a proper road, a bit north of the fell passes, that we'll take today." Her eyes twinkled. "—But not nearly so exciting. And we can look for those two wretched kittens as we go."

Beth blushed a bit as they approached the Taurus and stammered, looking at where Bhu Fan and Hawkeye stood waiting beside the car. *How do they always know?* She shook her head in exasperation at the perception of her cats. "Is it all right if we take my cats? I don't want *them* disappearing on us."

"Of course. I'm sure they'll find Paul's cats quite friendly. After all, they've already met one of them."

"Tatty Bumpkin." Beth exclaimed, as she hooked her seat belt. "I love that name. It's so nicely eccentric."

Wisteria smiled as they drove along the winding road beside the lake. "I'll have to ask Paul about that. Odd, isn't it? All his other cats have rather aristocratic names: all knights and ladies…Sir Francis is the oldest. He's been there as long as I can remember. Big silver mackerel tabby Maine Coon. Most of Paul's are moggies—a bit of this and that. But Sir Francis was a gift from a professor who used to spend his summers on the place in the old shepherd's hut, digging here and there, writing some sort of history of the Roman times." Wisteria paused for breath, turning upwards through what Beth had come to think of as Sherwood Forest, all carpeted with a swath of bluebells. "I think that's who stirred Paul's interest in writing a history of the Roman occupation and Mediobogdum.

"He's a Maine Coon, Sir Francis, that is. But Paul has no idea if he came from a proper cattery or if—" Here she paused to glance at her seatmate as she negotiated a tight curve, "—or if he's like your foundation cats." She chuckled softly. "He's certainly a law unto himself. A bit like your Hawk."

"Not Shere Khan?" Beth queried. "You remember The Great One?"

"Of course, I remember that big handsome tom. No, Sir Francis has been neutered for years. But still, he has lots of lady friends. And like Hawk he's infinitely curious. For all his no longer being intact, he's still king of the castle." She added, "Most of Paul's girls are spays, except for Lady Lucy and Maid Marion. He's very responsible about his cats."

Encapsulated in their big carrier on the back seat, Bhu Fan and Hawkeye were listening closely to this conversation. *Do you think this Sir Francis can help us find Star and Angel, Boo?* Hawk paused and shot a piercing look at the little Korat. *And how did you manage this little invitation to tea?* The big shaggy neuter, knowing her as he did, had no doubt that Bhu Fan had worked her subliminal magic on *somebody.*

But Her Highness wasn't talking. At least not to her favorite peasant. She was straining to see the tall intimidating fells out the car windows as they went zipping by, squinting from the glare of a bright cobalt blue sky reflecting off the now-distant lake.

Not too far from here, I think, she muttered cryptically, *not too far.*

Seeing his cratemate's unfocused gaze, Hawk didn't ask any more questions. He knew she probably couldn't hear him anyway.

Shortly after their misadventure, however, Freddie and his new charges sat about on the deck at the Bed and Breakfast having a postprandial wash, the two young reluctant immigrants still keeping a wary eye on their human host. They had never met any mantom who was less than he seemed, but a lot had happened in the past few days that made them slow to trust their luck. While Star's wariness was simply feline caution, Angel herself had not forgotten that it was an English shopkeeper in Manhattan who had spirited them away from the big cat show when the so-called Animal Rights Militia showed up.

"I say, Dex, what have we got here?" A smiling short, plump and pink-clad woman came through the kitchen door, escaping strands of grey hair flowing behind her as she set about straightening chairs and sorting tables, the bun at her neck loosening dangerously. She, too, had taken advantage of no visitors at their establishment to spend a few days with a sister in Cartmel.

At the sound of her voice, Starry and Angel cowered and poised to run.

It's okay, Freddie assured them, *that's my guv's consort. She's a good sort. A bit free with hugs and kisses but then I don't suppose we really ought to complain about that…there's some out there who're just as quick with a kick and a shout.*

The two young cats gave Freddie a long look. Star had a feeling that Freddie knew about this from experience. That thought made him sad. Having never been mistreated in his whole young life, Star blanched at the images it conjured up in his mind. Then he remembered Smudge's accounts of what his life had been like in the dark city before he met up with Shere Khan and the gang escaping from the pet store thieves. Forewarned is fore-armed, Smudge had cautioned him on occasion—and one always needed to have a bolt hole.

"Tom found them somewhere, Bev, and they certainly don't look like strays. Can't say I have any idea how or why some blokes would turn them out."

"Well, no matter, Dex. They're lovely, aren't they? Particularly that little silvery one. They're welcome here until I can find good homes for them."

The woman squatted down, wiped her hand on her apron, pushed the errant gray strands behind her ears and held out fingers toward Angel. The silver torbie was still digesting what the ladyqueen had just said and found it a bit off-putting. *Find us homes, Freddie? What's she talking about?* Angel's eyes grew large with alarm and she slowly backed up.

My guv's consort is a big help in this neighborhood. When she finds any of us homeless, she takes us in until she can find other homes for us… I got to stay cus' I welcomed all her guests and they liked me (actually I was looking for Wisty—but they didn't know that). Freddie walked over to where Angel crouched down. He could see she was still skeptical. *Look at me, you lot, when I jumped in the lake—trying to swim home, don't you see? She pulled me out, brought me up here and dried me out, fed me—and I've been here ever since.* Freddie sighed sadly. *That water was just too long and cold. Try as I might, I couldn't make it home again.* He sat down close to Angel's shoulder and waved his tail over her back. *Don't be afraid.*

Angel submitted herself to being stroked while Star stared at Freddie, frowning. *You tried to* swim *home, Freddie?* The young black tom queried, finding such a notion quite scary.

Freddie sighed again and licked one errant whisker. *Aye. My own fault I'm afraid. I'd been adrift for some little time when the boat landed me a bit north of here.* The big tom looked abashed. *I was looking for Maid Marion, you see, she'd been to visit Wisty with old Woolly Socks.* Freddie brightened. *I found her all right—at the big farm up among the fells north of here.* The big cat smiled slyly. *We had a nice visit but the old neuter up there, Sir Francis, said I couldn't stay. Too many mouths to feed already there, he said, although he was nice about it. So I started home. But there was no way except to swim and I learned the hard way that was not a good idea...* Again the big black and white tom looked sad. *So this is where I ended up*

Star's heart sank. If this was as far as Freddie had gotten in his trek toward home, what chance did he and Angel have?

Seen from this angle, Bath Merryman thought, Fellshadow Farm was quite imposing. It had looked so tiny from far above on the precipice behind the ancient breastworks of the Roman fort. The house was rather plain greenish plaster of some sort and utilitarian with the usual complement of tall chimney pots. But at the same time, fragrant carmine climbing roses angled all about the front of it, relieving the sharpness of corners and small square porch. Hollyhocks bloomed at the corners and the windows were all clean and shiny bright. Squat blue petunias spilled over low brick borders across the front of the house, faintly aromatic.

Paul Mellish met them at the door. "Let's have tea first, shall we? Then I'll take you out to the barn and show you Lady Lucy's kittens."

As his guests murmured assent and preceded the farmer into his house, Bhu Fan and Hawkeye looked at each other and detoured to a barn set at some little distance from the old farmhouse. Beth watched them go and, satisfied as to their destination, followed Wisteria and Paul inside. She knew her cats would not go far. Then she grimaced. She wouldn't have thought Star and Angel would have gone far either. But there was no point in dwelling on that right now.

The interior of the venerable old stone barn was dark and smelled of leather, hay and cattle feed; a few chickens pecked and scratched here and there, carefully avoiding the cats. Cobwebs swung from the beams and cross braces. For all that, the place was tidy and well cared for, the hard packed dirt floor free of debris. Tatty Bumpkin met them just inside the door.

"Hullo again," he said cheerfully, "Come to see Lady Lucy's kitlings, have you?"

"Well, actually," admitted Hawkeye," we were looking for your senior shaman, Sir Francis—but we wouldn't be adverse to having a gander at new kitlings." The big brown neuter smiled benevolently as he watched Bhu Fan stroll down the breezeway and into a stall at the far end where five wee heads were poking out in curiosity. Seeing Bhu Fan coming their way, they quickly disappeared back inside, giggling.

When he and Tatty Bumpkin stepped through the same opening, there was Her Highness sitting just outside a large box filled with soft sheepskins.

"Good afternoon, my lady," Hawk said, bowing his head as he approached the box. (He, too, had watched a few old episodes of Miss Marple on Simon's TV). The little Korat and the new momcat turned their gaze on Tatty Bumpkin and her favorite peasant. "Good afternoon to you, sir," returned Lady Lucy, a soft blue smoke tabby with white Maine Coon, her pristine paws crossed in front of her. "Hawkeye, look here," commanded Bhu Fan as she gently poked one slender paw toward the tangle of kittens lying belly up, watching beside their dam. She touched a small male. "Does this kitling not remind you of Riddle—and Shere Khan?" Hawkeye peered closer and then looked at his cohort, a bit confused. "I'm not being negative, Boo Lady Lucy— but this wee one is a blue smoke—like his, er, handsome dam—Why should he be reminding me of our brown and red toms back home?"

Bhu Fan smiled that superior smile of hers that always made Hawkeye feel like a, well: a dumb barn cat. Carefully, she rolled the little tom over on his paws. "What do you see now?"

"Bast's balls!" exclaimed Hawkeye and ducked to avoid Bhu's swipe at his head.

"No blasphemy, Hawkeye!" she retorted as Tatty and Lady Lucy looked a bit startled. "You do see it, don't you?"

"The *Mark of Minai*," Hawkeye admitted, "but how—?"

"The mark of who?" asked Tatty Bumpkin, "You mean that little white spot in the middle of his forehead? Is that supposed to mean something?"

"Oh, I'd say offhand," mused Hawkeye, gazing at his new acquaintances with delight, "it means we're all cousins." He shook his head in wonder. "How 'bout that?" He laughed delightedly as Bhu Fan sat beside him looking smug while the little tom in question, rubbed one paw across the top of his head, not at all certain that spot would rub off or not and if it didn't, what did *that* mean?

The new momcat cocked her head in uncertainty.

"We will come back to see you, Lady Lucy, and explain about that teardrop in wee one's forehead." Bhu Fan added, backing out of the stall. "Right now we need to find Sir Francis. Before Bethmom and others come looking for us. I don't know how much time we have." Seeing the uncertainty on the faces of Lady Lucy and her offspring, she hastened to reassure them. "It's okay. Little teardrop marks a lot of Coons in Maine and means most have come from same place along inland sea."

Looking at the little blue tom, she added, "Hawkeye's sire wears that same mark, little one, and he's a very famous tom!"

The small kitten sat up straighter and turning, giggled at his mum, while his siblings looked on with barely disguised envy.

✧ ✧ ✧

CHAPTER ELEVEN

THEY FOUND SIR FRANCIS in the tack room, all hung about as it was with harnesses, antique horse collars and assorted gear, along with barrels of grain and sacks of other feed. As it appeared to be the custom, the old neuter was stretched out on a woolly brownish array of sheepskins. He smiled at his visitors and invited them to share his bed.

"You've come about the old fort, haven't you? And I believe—" he eyed the little Korat, "—that you are the discoverer of the coins... I've been waiting for that to happen." He gazed about at Tatty Bumpkin and Hawkeye, nodding his head happily. Sir Francis did love a fresh audience.

Hawkeye looked at the old silver shaman with reverence, imagining all his ancient tales of derring-do the big brown neuter could tell his sire and grandsire, Minstrel, when they got together when he was once again home. "From what I hear, sir, those coins go back to an era so shrouded in the mists of time, as my venerable old grandsire would say, as to be lost in memory." The big Maine Coon settled himself and crossed his front paws. "Does your family history go back *that* far as well?"

Sir Francis looked at Hawkeye with amusement. "Our ancestors here are, I think what you'd call: *a mixed bag*, He laughed at the peculiarly American phrase. "They only acquired the name 'Maine

Coon' when they became so revered in your country. Actually, 'Highland Forest Cats' would be more *accurate* here. Some of our forebears came from the mountains and deserts by the inland sea, certainly, then more from the great northern forests… Every wave of invaders, it seems, brought our felinekind with them and while the conquering mantoms might not have prospered—they certainly weren't always a pleasant lot—their cats managed to melt into the landscape and form their own clans." He gazed out the big window that looked toward the Irish Sea. "Actually, though, our kind was here long before the mantoms." Sir Francis, stroked his chin with one paw and added, "*felis silvestris grampia*, if one is to be correct; actually the rarest wild cat in the world."

His audience waited, eyes large and disbelieving. Were there *cats* here *before* mantoms?? How could that be? Even Bhu Fan was staring in wonder:

"A wild feline was here *before* mantoms existed?"

"There was this wild cat here before there *were* mantoms, yes, at least as we know them in the present day!"

Raising his paw to quiet the skeptical murmurs; "There was," he began, "a wild cat here since the time when that channel of water between us and that huge land of many languages to the east of here did not exist. They *walked* from those parts as the ice retreated northward, having evolved long before modern humankind." Sir Francis smiled wickedly. "This was *before* mantoms—those latecomers—even knew then this land of fells and forests was here," he added with emphasis.

Seeing the disbelief on the faces of his visitors, the old shaman grinned like Alice's Cheshire cat. This lot hadn't heard his tales of prehistoric felines and Roman times like Maid Marion, Tatty Bumpkin and Lady Lucy had. His tail gently waved up and down in delight. Oh, how he did enjoy a receptive audience!

"Oh, yes. He was, if I may say so, a contemporary of the huge woolly beasts with long tusks—and it's just as well they didn't compete for food." Sir Francis looked wry. "Or doubtless, he would not have prevailed." Laughing he added, "The woolly mammoth certainly did not." Their narrator lifted a paw and brushed it across his face. "But that's another story and I'll save it for another time.

"Suffice it to say, there are very few of his handsome kind left and most—though not all—are hiding in the Scottish Highlands. Thus he has acquired the name of that place." The old neuter's eyes half-closed slyly. "Although I number one or two of the more adventurous ones among my acquaintances, those big fellows…"

"What?"

Sir Francis ignored the question. "He is now called the *Scottish* wildcat—and I'm quite sure that he is among your forebears, as well, in your home country, some having mated with the more agreeable cats from the northern forests on the other side of that channel of water which makes this an island now. No doubt his offspring joined the explorers and were taken west by the Viking raiders who arrived here before they sailed across the icy sea." Looking thoughtful, he added, "No doubt his thick heavy coat helped his descendants to survive those frigid treacherous waters. And of course, our coats grew longer and more silky with that infusion from our Southern ancestors—" He peered closely at Hawkeye—"And became what they are now, young sir, for you and me."

Sir Francis shifted on his sheepskins and took a moment out to clean his whiskers, putting his thoughts in order. A diversion was in order. He would not betray his wild cousins' home range among the fells and forests hereabouts. Nor divulge the fact that one of their kind was an ancestor of Lady Lucy.

He thought for some moments and his eyes, like Bhu Fan's often did, grew unfocused. Might as well get to it.

"Here in this bit of valley before the so-called Dark Ages uncounted moons ago, were the huts of a horse trader. To us, primitive; to the Celtic Britons, the farm of a well respected tribesman. No one remembers his name—we were never concerned with the names mantoms gave themselves. What we do know is that he supplied ponies to the other native tribesmen who sold their wares to the spear-carriers up above where the invaders had their—forum? It was little better than the wattle-and-daub huts here belonging to the horse trader, but they dominated and also, on occasion, bought horses from down here." The old cat smiled briefly. "And the Britons, whatever their livelihood, be they horsemen, traders of other goods and services, hawkers or hunters, were all too happy to take the invaders' money: coins, denarii, obols—the matter of exchange had many names. But no matter. It was ever thus. Mantoms enjoyed accumulating wealth of one sort or another; whatever bought them pleasure...

"The cats that were here had to shift for themselves but they were tolerated by the mantoms because they were useful in controlling the rats and mice." Again Sir Francis smiled on his audience. "Although certain clever ones managed to insinuate themselves into the households and huts of the women who also seemed to have to shift for themselves; for the most part, treated little more thoughtfully than their mantoms' beasts of burden. There were no ladyqueens at the fort—that stockade was what they called a 'garrison'. The Romans' womenfolk , however, did inhabit dwellings around the lake down at Ambleside." Sir Francis burst into laughter. "Thank Bastet for the ladyqueens! They were much more attuned to our felinekind and more inclined to keep them as—wonder of wonders—pets!"

Sir Francis' audience chuckled appreciatively and made themselves more comfortable, enjoying the warm sheepskins spread about for them. Even those in his audience who had heard this tale many times, in spite of what the old neuter might think, enjoyed it once again. Except for food, nothing was more pleasant than a good story.

"Now the horse trader took as great care with his cats as he did his horses and ponies. Not only did they keep his grain stores free of varmints but the inhabitants up on the fellside acquired them, too, paying out good money when disease and misfortune overtook the feline population up there." The old cat paused again and licked a paw, getting his story in its proper sequence.

"As I said, the commanders up there and the higher ranks did on occasion also buy cats from him to take down to lakeside for their ladyqueens as they spent a large part of the time separated from their consorts—women who were inclined to get into mischief if left all alone too long." Here a knowing look and a snicker passed among all the cats stretched out around the old silver tiger.

"And," he added, "the ladyqueens were inclined to pick out the prettiest kittens. How not?" And again that knowing look passed among his audience.

"Certainly a man who knew how to breed better horses and ponies would know how to improve his felinekind—would he not?"

Bhu Fan, Hawkeye and Tatty Bumpkin returned their storytellers' knowing smile and vigorously nodded their heads. How not indeed!

"On the occasion of the particular happening that's come down to me, the horse trader and his daughter were about to make the difficult journey around the tall escarpment—I think it's called—up to the fort with a pair of ponies for the soldiers up there. And in her saddlebags, Drusilla-the-daughter, had a pair of Drusilla-the-dam's kittens for a buyer there as well (we know the horse trader's daughter's name only because she gave it to one of her cats: Drusilla-the-queen). The kittens, by name Cottia and Casandra, I must add, were the ones who passed the tale down to *their* kittens and thus to us." Sir Francis cleared his throat, got up from his bed and padded over to his water bowl for a few laps.

"Our informants said that for some reason, their mistress was uneasy on this particular day. Someone it seems, had warned her sire the day before that there might be trouble soon between the invaders and the tribesmen…It appeared there'd been a so-called 'holy' mantom in the vicinity who was urging the natives to rise up against the solders in order to serve the Britons' Druid gods and wrest their land from the foreign pagans."

A look of disgust crossed the old neuter's countenance. "Utter nonsense, if you ask me. What's it to the gods how mantoms carry on?"

"However, the horse trader decided to go up on the fells anyway. The Romans had asked for two of his best ponies to fill their horse troop and the denarii he'd earn would help him pay all his debts. Drusilla's kittens, which he'd thought his most handsome to date, would allow his daughter to purchase some trifles she'd craved from the vendors outside the fort. And he knew she'd painted a pottery jug—as she was well known for her artistry—for a visiting scribe who'd requested it to take back to—Rome?—with him when he went.

"And so they arrived at the forum. The centurion of the horse troop paid the horse trader, who furtively passed off the coins to his daughter. She secreted the coins in the jug, thinking they would be safer there should some craven soldier or tribesman accost her and her sire before she could find the craftsman she sought and the scribe in the forum. She stuffed the jug into her saddle bag and set the kittens on top.

"But as her father looked around, there seemed to be very few tribesmen, vendors, craftsmen or otherwise, present." Francis rolled over on his side, shaking his head. "What could the man have been *thinking*—after all, he'd been warned!" An unhappy look crossed Sir Francis' face. He did, were he to admit it, have sympathy for all those creatures, two-legged or four, who were put upon and suffered through no fault of their own just by being in the wrong place at the wrong time.

"It was midday when the aroused tribesmen rallied on the other side of the pass and attacked the fort. The horse trader and his daughter had sat themselves down beside the burn up there for a meal of cheese and hard bread. The kittens, not yet delivered to their new owners, were romping in the grass beside them.

"When the marauders came screaming down from the summit, the daughter, Drusilla, grabbed her saddle bag and stuck it into the soft under-bank of the burn and jammed it with rocks. The two kittens, terrified of the noise and the clash of arms, went skittering across the grass, leaped over the edge of the precipice at the back side of the fort and, being small and nimble-pawed, they managed to hop from one outcrop to the next like wild goat-kids until they made their way to the valley below and escaped into their own hut to hide."

Francis sighed deeply.

"What happened, Sir?" asked Hawkeye, "to the horse trader and his daughter?"

"We don't know. I imagine like so many innocents caught in the crossfire between combatants, they perished. And there was no one skilled enough, or thought it was important enough to record their side of this conflict. Either by mouth or written hand. The scribe, if he survived, might have written about the skirmish when he returned to his home, but of course, we'd never know about that." Sir Francis sighed again.

"Cottia and Casandra said the horse-mantom and his daughter were never seen at the horse traders huts again."

"Did, did, the wild ones win battle and drive away the fort's foreign soldiers, sir?" Bhu asked, not at all sure she wanted the answer. While the acts of humankind she often found wanting, she liked to cross all the "T's" and dot all the "I's".

"No. the soldiers drove them off—or so it's come down to us. The horse trader's consort was allowed to stay where she was. She continued to raise the horses for whoever needed them and cats for the grain stores." The old neuter paused and brought one paw across an ear. "But after that, she never sold Cottia and Casandra. She kept them all their lives on her own hearth." A rueful look crossed his face. "And she knew better than to ask for payment for the two horses her consort had taken to the fort that day." The old shaman looked wise. "The original payment for the horses, I'm sure you know, are the coins you found, Bhu Fan, such a short time ago—"

"Bhu! Hawkeye! Where are you?"

At the sound of Bethmom's voice, her cats thanked Sir Francis hastily and trotted out of the barn.

Well, at least we know where those coins came from and how they got to be in that rivulet, Hawkeye sighed, *but we still don't know where Star and Angel are.*

No, we don't, responded the little Korat, *but I have an idea we will before the day is out.* Bhu Fan gave her friend a thoughtful look. And *when that search is resolved, we must come back here, Hawkeye-my-peasant, and learn more about Lady Lucy's ancestor. The wild one.*

Huh?

You want to now more about your ancestors, don't you? Bhu Fan looked sly.

Hawkeye was purely confused. But not worried. He'd been on the teasing end of Bhu Fan's machinations more times than he could count. He'd do as his sire counseled and *wait.* Sooner or later, the haughty princess would enlighten him.

CHAPTER TWELVE

AS THE TWO CATS walked out of the barn with Tatty Bumpkin, who was determined to be a good host, they met up with Bethmom, Wisteria and Old Woolly Socks, Chad having asked permission to take a close-up look at Paul's drystone walls. He was intrigued; if it was one thing Siberia Farm had in abundance, it was rocks... Not sure exactly what was on the minds of their humans as they saw three coming toward them and one going off in another direction, the cats sat down and waited. Obviously they weren't leaving yet as it appeared the three humans were headed for the barn. Divining what was on their minds, Bhu Fan jumped up and trotted back into its dark, aromatic interior and turned into the stall where Lady Lucy was curled up around her 5 multi-colored kittens.

The three adults knelt down in front of the blue smoke queen's box and smiled. Kittens always brought such a reaction; it was the way of things with humankind who had been enslaved by felines. Paul reached into the box and carefully extracted a small male and held him out to Wisteria.

"Paul!" she exclaimed. "This baby is a carbon copy of Freddie! I can't believe it." She turned wide eyes to the grinning farmer. "Do you know who she mated with?" Wisteria held her breath and hoped.

Paul Mellish shook his head, "Not whom you'd like, Wisteria." He grinned roguishly. "But close." The man patted her shoulder and turned to gaze pointedly at Tatty Bumpkin.

"Tatty? Wisteria marveled. "But I thought he was neutered."

"He is—now." Again their host laughed. "I suppose you could say it was a Last Hurrah." Paul turned back to his guests and explained. "I prefer not to keep a tom as they always go walkabout and that's worrisome out here." He paused and furrows appeared in his still nicely chiseled countenance.

"I wanted you to see this little chap because you're more up on feline genetics than I...Tatty's out of Maid Marion and I never figured out what 'travelin' man'—" the man looked at Beth and smiled, "I do love your American slang—came calling as all her kittens were either red like her or blue." He pointed upward to where the red queen lounged on the divider between stalls. "Her kittens—Tatty's litter—were born early autumn last year. And because he was red like all the others, I didn't think much about it."

As Wisteria fondled the little male in her hands, the farmer, brown muscled arms showing below rolled up sleeves, gazed fondly once more at the nursing queen, who exchanged a look with her former consort and smiled.

What, what!? exclaimed Hawkeye as he playfully bumped the red neuter's shoulder and chortled as only one rascal can to another.

Hush! Bhu Fan admonished. *I want to hear this.*

Paul looked again to where Tatty Bumpkin had set about grooming himself with gusto while the two visiting felines looked on.

"But! If you look at that big scalawag, you see that he may be all red and white but his markings are identical to Freddie's! And I'm thinking, love, that he just has to be a Freddie son—ergo, this fat little sausage is a Freddie grandson!"

Wisteria, her silvery hair twining around her still pretty face like tendrils of ivy, held up the kitten and scowled. It certainly seemed within the realm of possibility. And if that was the case, where had Freddie gotten to? From what she and her visitors had surmised with the disappearance of Star and Angel, she already had a pretty good idea how he might have gotten *here*. And to Wisteria's dismay, that was about to be confirmed. Or as much as one could confirm anything where their cats might be concerned.

The man paused and sat back on his heels, turning his attention to his friend. "Remember when I lost my boat from your shoreline last spring and you drove me home? A few days later it turned up at the dock next to the Pack Pony—there's deep water on that side of the lake below the pub." He hung his head. "I never thought to tell you, although at the time I wasn't aware that Freddie had gone missing."

Paul looked intent. "But see here, Wisteria, suppose Freddie was aboard when my rowboat slipped away and landed close by that place. Which is no distance from here." The man again had an abashed, if sly, grin on his weathered face. "Suppose Freddie came calling on Maid Marion, er, did the deed and then got run off by Sir Francis? That bugger might be an old neuter but he's still king of the castle around here."

"—And Freddie couldn't get home!" ventured Wisteria Cate. "He might have gone back to the pub. He was always a gregarious soul." The woman, bright blue eyes shining, got to her feet. "We need to go look, Beth."

Beth Merryman, who had been very thoughtful during this exchange, all the while nodding her head, was examining the rest of Maid Marion's kittens. "By all means. And I hope, where we find Freddie, we find Star and Angel as—"

She stopped in midsentence and picked up a fuzzy little blue male. She held him up closely to examine him. The kitten stared back at her owlishly. A look of total wonder crossed Beth's heart-shaped face.

"Great balls of fire, as my nanny used to say." Beth turned to her friend and held out the wee tom. "This baby wears the Mark of Musket! Can you believe this, people???"

✿ ✿ ✿

Star gazed at the newly arrived bed and breakfast guests speculatively as they sat at their leisure on the patio under a bright blue, cloud-dotted sky, eating a proper full English breakfast. It was obvious to the young tom they were Americans. But he wasn't at all sure that was any advantage to him and Angel. Something about them was off-putting and he thought with longing of Bhu Fan, who could certainly define his wariness for him. The little blue Korat could read mantoms like he could read a mouse trail.

The ladyqueen was loud-spoken, rather obese, a bit overdressed. Yet for all that, she appeared to be friendly, taking great interest in things going on around her and addressing their hosts with respect. Star picked at a bit of leaf stem caught between his toes as his gaze shifted to the lady's consort. He, thought Star, catching Angel's eye where she crouched under a nearby chair, her head cocked, was another kettle of fish altogether.

This mantom was entirely outside Star's experience. He was very short, dressed in a loud check sport coat and black trousers, which he constantly brushed off as if the cats had personally targeted him with their long wispy hair. He had a voice sharp as a sword and he never looked directly at whomever he was speaking to. If he pierced anyone with his small flat, close-set, slate-colored eyes, it was with a look of contempt for that individual's lesser intelligence. Star was just as glad he and Angel had not attracted this man's interest. Just what would The Great One think of him, Khan's very homesick offspring wondered.

The couple had been discussing the day's prospects. Should they wander over to Hawkshead to see Beatrix Potter's home or go to Dove Cottage where the poet, Wordsworth, had once resided? The fancy glassworks at Ambleside? The Castle Rigg stone circle at Keswick? Or the ancient Roman fort remains at Hardknott Pass?

"Well," said their host cheerfully, "all those places are certainly within a couple of hour's reach and worth seeing." He hesitated and laughed, "though I have to say, Mr. Pullet, I'd not have taken you for a man interested in the likes of Peter Rabbit."

The man's wife and their hosts laughed at this remark but Pullet himself remained stone-faced. Mrs. Pullet, knowing his volatile temper, sought a distraction. She looked about for something to direct their attention elsewhere and spotted Angel watching them from her spot under a nearby chair.

"Do you think, Beverly," she said, "that I could take that pretty little silver and orange cat with us when we go back to London? You did say she had just shown up, didn't you?" Mrs. Pullet paused and clicked her tongue against her teeth as she reached for another scone. "She'd look lovely in our Berkley Square flat against my new maroon leather sofa and chairs…after she'd been declawed, of course." The scone quickly disappeared and she reached for another without taking her eyes off their hostess. She'd intimidated more than one store clerk with that look.

The B and B hostess hesitated as she cast around for the little silver torbie who had suddenly disappeared into the shrubbery. Beverly Bishop was consistent in her attempts to place cats that had wandered into her vicinity. But she was also rather picky about her placements. This couple, who had not visited them before, certainly appeared to be well-off. But the word "declaw" put her off. She knew very well that some Americans practiced this form of cruelty on their felines and she found it offensive. She was sure they didn't cut the toes off their dogs when they scratched at their leather couches and dug up their gardens, all the while thinking nothing of mutilating their cats and kittens that way.

"Mrs. Pullet," she declared, thinking fast, "I don't know… that little one bites. I really don't think she'd make a good *house*cat—"

"Oh, that's no problem. I think Jerry could quickly break her of that habit."

Her husband responded to this declaration with a wolfish grin as he finished off a slice of bacon in one bite and picked up his newspaper again.

Inwardly shuddering, Beverly paused. She had not taken to Mr. Pullet either.

"—She does well enough here in the garden but I daresay she's litter-trained."

At this, Mrs. Pullet's mouth turned down. "Too bad," she sighed. "She looks just like a breed of cat we have in the States called the Maine Coon. I was thinking after Jerry's stint in London, I'd take her home and show her off as a Limey Coon." The woman reached for yet another scone and laughed at her own joke, not realizing that "Limey" might be a pejorative and thereby offensive to her hostess. After a moment or two, chewing diligently, she added, "it really shouldn't be any great difficulty to box train her…And I'm perfectly willing to pay you for her." Mrs. Pullet had already decided that her hostess' reluctance in the matter was merely a ploy to get good money for the pretty young cat, which she knew had to be a purebred Maine Coon, no matter how she had turned up here. She sighed. It was the same the world over. Money was the bottom line. Even in cats. She gazed at Beverly as if the matter was settled and sipped her tea.

I say, ventured Freddie, himself not impressed with his guv'nor's guests, *let's go down to lakeside, shall we, for a spot of fishing? I know where there's a little pool of tasty hatchlings."*

Yeah, agreed Star. *An' I think we ought to stay there until these mantoms leave and go home.* He wasn't exactly sure how he was going to keep the pushy Americans from laying their hands on Angel but he'd think of something. At the same time, he didn't want to alarm her beyond her present fearfulness. Best to get themselves out of sight and off the visitors' radar.

Sitting on a flat stone near Freddie's pool of silvery fish fry, the three cats were thoughtful. Freddie had become protective of his two fugitives and concerned that the pair of guests at the B and B had designs on Angel. He knew that if she were taken away from Star, he would be disconsolate. The two weren't siblings, he knew. But they might as well be. How to prevent it? He was going to have to talk to Star. The big tom took a long look at the young queen, suddenly aware of his own keen interest in the pretty silvery torbie with her snowy Elizabethan ruff. She'd make quite a handsome queen soon. Too young for him, but…His stomach rumbled. Hatchlings didn't make much of a meal.

"Come, kitlings, it's time to go eat something more filling. The loud mantom and his consort will have gone for the day. Mistress Bev will have something—"

"—No, we can't," interrupted a shrewd young black tom. "If we go up to the dining place, I'm afraid your mistress might snatch Angel up and take her off somewhere until the ladyqueen comes back and wants to take her away. She offered your guv's consort money for Angel—remember?" The look on Star's face disheartened Freddie. *Would Mistress Beverly do that?*

"I'm not so sure, Star." Freddie pondered, stretching himself out on the rough planks of the pier. "I saw that look on her face when that guestlady said she'd have Angel's claws cut off." All three cats shuddered at this prospect. "Bevlady is a good heart. I don't think she'd stand for that. More like, she'd *hide* Angel 'til they've gone away."

Star looked skeptical. Angel had said nothing. She merely looked stricken and picked up a dainty white paw to gaze at it.

"I'd rather die," she declared vehemently.

Freddie nodded his head and chewed on his lip. "Okay, we'll go along the road a bit and hide under the hedge that rings the pub's patio until the Yanks have gone. Blokes there come outside to eat and drink their beer. They get careless and drop crisps 'n chips 'n sausages."

"Pub?" Star asked confused. "Chips? Crisps?" Sausages he knew, but the other words?

"Food," declared Freddie and smiled. "We don't quibble; we just eat."

As all three shared a chuckle, Angel asked, "what's a pub?"

"It's a 'public house' called the Pack Pony and it's very old. Most every village has one; mantoms have been coming there for moons beyond measure to drink ale and stout an'—well, no matter. It's a gathering place and they've always been good about handing out tidbits…I check it out ever so often." Freddie frowned. "I'm still hoping, if truth be told, that I might see Old Woolly Socks there and maybe Wisty." The big black and white tom sighed. "But we have to stay outside. If we went in, we'd likely lose a tail. The buggers can be a rowdy bunch and they don't always watch where they put their big feet."

"Heavens to Betsy, Khan, I think you and Smudge are going to grow to that spot…" Beth's house sitter stood there with her hands on her hips and looked at the two lounging cats, a gentle smile on her face. "But with Magic and Madame visiting at Cheryl's, I don't guess there's all that much around here to keep you guys entertained."

Martha went back out to her car for the rest of her groceries, chatting cheerfully at the two cats stretched out in the bright morning sunshine. As she walked into the kitchen and put her sacks down on the old porcelain topped table, Khan opened one eye and stretched. Life was good, if lazier than usual. Smudge merely rolled over and licked a paw. Martha exited the house and went back to her car for Sweeper, Chad's other cat who had been injured in the City after getting loose with Shere Khan and the others from the pet store thieves. He had been to the vet for his check-up.

Once free of his carrier, he sat quietly with Smudge and Shere Khan indulging in a bit of gossip under the porch swing.

"Where's Beowulf? " asked Sweeper, looking around for his sire.

"He was upstairs last I looked—watching that confounded blue jay. Why?"

Shere Khan skewered him with an eye. Something in Sweeper's demeanor boded ill. The Great One hadn't attained his healthy old age without being very sensitive to things going on around him. Sweeper had had more than his share of troubles. Khan went over, gave him a lick on his ear and merely said, "So what's up?"

"Isn't Angel one of Beowulf's grandkits?

"Yep...is there something he should know?"

Sweeper sighed, ducked his head and explained. "Martha stopped by the Post office—she doesn't like the computer, y'know."

Khan was quick. "There's bad news from Bethmom and Chad?"

"Yeah." The muscular smoky neuter gave the old tom a sympathetic look. "Star and Angel have...disappeared."

A look of consternation crossed Shere Khan's face. "Abducted?"

"No. It seems they just got curious...you know how Star is, Khan; he'd chat up uh, uh, stray...*dog*. Or check out the open door on somebody's truck just to see what was inside." Sweeper slumped onto his belly. "Fool kitling. He and Angel went exploring and just...disappeared. At least that's what Bethmom's card said." He looked toward the back door. "I think Martha is that upset but she's trying not to think about it."

Shere Khan nodded his head sagely. "If Star and Angel went off on their own, Bhu Fan will find them. No need to upset Wulf." He smiled tentatively, his own heart thumping for his errant offspring. "Her Royal Highness could find an ice cube in an avalanche."

The sound of a distant vehicle coming up their farm road arrested their attention. Martha heard it, too, and stepped out onto the porch. A large official looking white van and its satellite pickup truck slowed and stopped at the gate opposite the back door. Beth Merryman's cat sitter paused warily. There'd been more excitement in this little center of Maine than she'd cared for lately. The last white van that showed up had almost ruined their plans for the Moosery. And so far as she knew, Beth hadn't been expecting anyone from the state health department, as the logo on the van's sides declared. Certainly not the county humane bunch as well.

The drivers of the two vehicles hopped down from their vehicles and approached the waiting farm wife as she stood, her hand gripping the cell phone in her apron pocket. She didn't know what this was all about but Gaston was working at the Dickens' place over the hill if she needed him.

"You Miz Merriman?" the tall, skinny beanpole of a health department official asked, officious looking clipboard in one skeletal hand.

As Martha shook her head, she looked at the county humane officer hiding behind his leader. Harry Armstrong knew very well she wasn't Beth Merriman. What was going on here? As she gazed sternly at him, the humane shelter boss had the grace to look sheepish. He shrugged his shoulders helplessly. Evidently he'd been no match for the arrogant bureaucrat from down state confronting Martha Michaud.

"No, Mrs. Merryman is away right now—and you knew that, Harry!" She directed this statement to the official she knew and then turned back to the state's man. "What do *you* want?"

"We got a complaint from somebody who bought a couple of kittens here; said conditions were overcrowded—" the man looked unsympathetically at Martha,—"and nasty."

Martha's mouth dropped open. Who? What? Then she remembered. Could this be that couple from Lincoln who'd given Beth such a hard time?

She had delivered a pair of Gracie's kittens to a couple when she had business down that way, thinking to do them a favor, only to find that, for once, she'd misjudged her buyers (or at least felt less than comfortable with them). They were a pair of scam artists who owned a kitten mill—well, that was Cheryl's term for them. But that came later. At the time, Beth had no real excuse to back out. The kittens had contracted ringworm a month or so after they left. The buyers, obviously without thinking through the consequences, got very irate and claimed she'd sold them "diseased breeding stock". Beth, however, knew they were not "diseased"; ringworm being no more than a minor malady kin to athlete's foot that neither killed, maimed nor was incurable, which they'd more than likely picked up in their new home—such as it was. They certainly weren't *breeding* stock either. Beth never sold breeding stock to strangers. It had been a real mess before she got the kittens back and left the would-be buyers to the mercy of their own county sanitation officials.

This, Martha decided grimly as she watched her interrogators start removing pet carriers from the van, was those people's revenge. Her back was up.

"Overcrowded and nasty," she harrumphed. "Stuff-and-things: those people have never even *been* here to see what the cattery looks like!"

"We're going to have to confiscate all Miz Merriman's cats," the health department stated, ignoring this, while Harry Armstrong looked on with bowed head. "The healthy ones will be returned most likely...the sick ones will be destroyed."

Martha came down the steps with blood in her eye. "There are no sick cats here, mister, and you—"

The official moved closer to Martha while Harry hung back. Obviously, Martha realized, he wasn't going to be any help. And jobs being as scarce here as everywhere else right now, he wasn't about to jeopardize his by coming to her defense.

"Lady, we're doing our job. If you interfere, I'll have to call the sheriff. And you'll find yourself in court—and the varmints will most likely have been all gassed by then!"

Martha exploded, "Well, you just call Jim Proudfoot; you *do* that, you, you goat-head!" She got right up in the tall hook-nosed bureaucrat's face. "His daughter has one of Beth's cats. And he'll most likely arrest *you* for threatening me!"

Before the state health department could react to this challenge, a loud roar arrested the two men in their tracks and the thunderous running hooves of a very large, clearly disturbed bull moose froze them in their tracks. The huge ungulate, obviously alerted by all the loud angry voices and knowing he was not where he had any business being, lowered his head and came straight at the two officials as Martha, quicker on her feet, retreated to the kitchen door. Carriers went flying in all directions as the two men dived for cover.

The moose, having made his escape from Beth's shed where he'd been feasting on a tasty bushel of apples, barreled on down the road, shaking his huge head as he quickly distanced himself, trailing a cloud of dust. Martha scanned the porch and driveway for Shere Khan, Sweeper and Smudge. They were nowhere to be seen.

After some little time spent picking up their equipment and slowing his heart rate, the van's driver ripped open the kitchen door and glared at Martha.

"Let's get on with it, lady. We got to get back to town before dinnertime. We've wasted enough time here." He loomed over Martha, his fists tight. That she'd witnessed his embarrassing and undignified dive for safety did nothing for his state of mind, let alone his ego. And Martha Michaud was smart enough to know it. Taking a deep breath, she drew herself up. Slowly, she came out of the house. As she stepped off the porch, she could hear another vehicle tearing up the road in the distance. She smiled to herself and led the health department and Harry, if more slowly, to the old barn of a cattery.

Gaston got out of his truck just as she was reaching for the barn door, which to her surprise was gaping wide. But she didn't have time to think about that now. She gave her husband a grateful look as he approached, a large and angry bull of a man himself. As she stepped inside, she stopped dead. And stared.

The cattery was empty.

Martha blinked. The two officials looked around at the very spotless, well organized cattery and then stared at her. Gaston came up behind his wife and he too peered into the cavernous room, running his hand nervously across his luxurious moustache. Moving more softly than one would expect of a man his size, he inspected all the enclosures, walked inside each of them and glanced through the window at the outdoor runs behind them. All the doors were unlatched and open.

Nothing.

There was not a single cat or kitten to be found anywhere at MerryMaines.

The state health department official glared, speechless, uncertain now that he saw the condition of Mrs. Merrimans' cattery, empty or not. Harry Armstrong ducked his head and grinned to himself. *Serves you right, you toad*. Martha and Gaston looked at each other. Their innocence in the matter of absent critters was all too obvious. And genuine.

Not sure exactly how he'd been thwarted and not wanting his witnesses to relate to boss, judge, sheriff or whomever, his undignified scramble from the angry moose, the state health department's enforcer retreated to his vehicle grumbling to himself but resigned and roared down the driveway. Sometimes you win and sometimes you lose. With any luck, nobody'd ever hear about this little moose attack. Or missing cats.

Harry Armstrong, who knew all the parties involved in this little incident—in particular, the big volatile carpenter— waved his hand and smiling weakly, retreated to his pickup, departing without a word. Let Gaston cool down and then the two of them would no doubt hash over the matter tomorrow at the All-Nite Diner in Gilby over coffee with the rest of the regulars. He needed to talk to Gaston anyway. He'd heard some disturbing rumors about other missing cats.

Gaston and Martha walked back inside the cattery and stood in stunned silence. "Where on earth have they all disappeared to, chéri? This is totally weird." She wrung her hands helplessly.

Gaston, not saying a word, all the while shaking his head, lips tight, chewing on his moustache,inspected the cattery enclosure doors once more. His wife certainly wouldn't have turned all the cats loose; she'd had no idea they were in jeopardy. He was as confused as she was.

Suddenly, something caught his eye. He squatted down and inspected the latch on the door to Simon's quarters. A large white tuft of cat fur was caught in the device. He carefully removed it and stood up, smiling broadly at his wife, who had come across the floor to quickly inspect what he held in his hand. He didn't know whether to laugh, cry or cuss.

"I don't know where they've gone, that's for sure—but I sure know who engineered their escape!"

The two of them stood there and grinned at each other uncertainly. Gaston hugged his wife.

"We'll find them, Marthy, I daresay that wily old rascal Shere Khan has herded them off somewhere. The Moosery probably." He shook his head in wonder. "But how did he *know* to do that?"

CHAPTER THIRTEEN

A T BETH'S EXCLAMATION ABOUT the "Mark of Musket" on Lady Lucy's little tom, as she and her friends stood over the fat little kittens in Paul Mellish's barn, Wisteria hesitated. Freddie had been gone for months. What were a few more hours? She curbed her inclination to rush out and start another search for him as she held up the little blue male with white feet, belly and muzzle that Beth had handed her, her mind now shifting into line-chasing mode, a habit of breeders who wanted to mentally sort through their cats' pedigrees.

That white dot *was* disconcerting. But according to what Beth said, it had "surfaced," for lack of a better word, on Maine Coons going back to Colonial Times and one of the earliest chroniclers of the breed had said it was first observed in Musket, a tom sired by Jig, who had come from the Middle East on a ship belonging to Capt. James Merryman. And the little white teardrop in the middle of a cat's forehead was known thereafter as the Mark of Musket. (Wisteria wasn't to know, of course, that the cats, whose oral traditions were much more detailed and older, called it the Mark of *Minai*, after pretty ancient enamelwork developed by the Medes.) Wisteria shook her head and smiled at the kitten whose tiny claws were hooked over her finger. If she hadn't known better, she'd have sworn he cocked his head and grinned at her, taking in their whole conversation.

I yam the leader of the queen's nave-eeee, I yam, gaily sang the little blue tom as the feline visitors looked to Sir Francis for explanation.

We've a radio out here in the barn, you see, the old shaman explained, chuckling. *Old Woolly Socks likes to listen to Gilbert and Sullivan as he sweeps and sifts. The kittens are great mimics...*

Bhu and company weren't exactly sure who Gilbert and Sullivan were but they laughed out loud at the kitten's *chutzpah.*

Beth, Wisteria and Paul looked at each other and Beth felt exasperated. Alas, there was just no way they would understand the joke, although she didn't doubt for a minute that some joke had passed among their cats. She turned to Wisteria.

"What are you thinking, Wisteria?"

"Oh, just that from what you've told me about Jig and Musket, other longhaired cats could have been claimed off that quay and sailed on ships to England as well as America." She looked thoughtful, "No telling *how* many cats carry it...but it does make a good tracer, doesn't it?" Wisteria glowed with self-satisfaction. "And I am that pleased that we Brits just might have a piece of the Maine Coon pie."

Smiling with delight at this observation, Beth and Paul stood over Lady Lucy's nest box, Beth with hands in her pockets, Paul with a wisp of straw in his teeth. The farmer/scholar hadn't seen his old friend this animated in a very long time. What a lovely lady she was! He blushed and turned away lest they catch him as embarrassed as a schoolboy.

Wisteria put the infant down and gently picked up his dam. While Lucy was not accustomed to being held, she did not struggle in the lady's arms. As the woman hugged her close to her chest and ran sensitive fingers through her thick coat, the blue smoke queen found she rather liked it.

But why is she holding me, Tatty? She asked her erstwhile consort, as he spent more time with humankind than she did and was more likely to be familiar with their habits.

Bhu Fan, who had leaped gracefully to the top of the stall's partition to keep a better eye on things, answered for Tatty Bumpkin.

She's checking your coat.

Whatever for?

All our pelts feel different. Some are coarse—Bhu Fan made a face —*some are fine, some of us have undercoat*—Bhu Fan giggled, —*and some of us have no coat at all.*

At this, Hawkeye joined in the Korat's merriment. The others, all of whom had never been far from home (and had certainly never seen a Sphynx), merely looked quizzical.

Paul Mellish's eyebrows lifted and he looked to Beth before breaking into a smile. "Your cats carry on regular conversations, don't they?"

"Oh, yes," Beth responded, "right now, they're probably discussing Lady Lucy's antecedents." The game warden's wife, whom Chad had often called his sweet southern Yankee, looked to Wisteria, batted her eyes and mimicked, sniffing theatrically, "Well. You know, her grandmother was probably no better than she ought to be. But her father was a prosperous shopkeeper in Soho and her other grandparents did come from Yorkshire gentry and wouldn't you know? This girl we've had such high hopes for—why, she's fallen for a, a *ne'er-do-well* from Cheapside who hasn't a ha'penny to his name!"

At this age old scenario which parents had defined and classified since their ancestors carried spears and provided dowries, the three people in the barn all laughed at the accuracy of it with great good humor.

Wisteria, still a bit distracted, handed Lady Lucy gently to her American visitor. "Run your hands through her coat, Beth, and tell me what you think."

Beth did as she was bid, all the while looking off in the distance, tongue in the corner of her mouth as she concentrated.

"It's like thick plush velvet, Wisteria," she uttered, her eyes growing large. "Our Coons have long hair certainly, falling from shoulders, belly and britches, but they have no undercoat. Not like this—and I'm not really sure this is, technically speaking, an undercoat." Beth frowned, her face still animated, and then she shook her head and laughed. "It's heavenly to feel, very different; almost as if she was the result of a cross between a Maine Coon and one of our Canadian lynx."

"Or," Wisteria Cate wondered, looking more closely at Tatty Bumpkin and Maid Marion, "if she has our own native cat in her background."

Beth looked a question when their host, who had quickly caught Wisteria's drift, chortled to himself and shook his head in derision.

"The Scottish wildcat," Wisteria explained, her head cocked at the amused farmer, daring him to contradict her.

No longer able to contain himself, Paul Mellish laughed out loud. "Now, Wisteria, I don't think we've got any of those around here. You'd be hard pressed to even find them in the wilds of the Scottish Highlands!"

Before he could explain to an interested visitor about the elusive Scottish wildcat, he touched his old friend's shoulder with affection. "But come, let's go find Chad and see if we can't pick up the trail of Freddie. If he and your kittens escaped the same way, they might well have crossed paths. And if I know Maine Coons, they like to stick together." He added, "The Pack Pony is the logical place to start. If there's food to be found for hungry critters, that's where it'll be."

Once again, however, the fickle weather asserted itself with cold rain and icy fog, leaving the trees high on the fells coated thickly as flocked Christmas trees. Beth and Wisteria confined their quest to the computer, asking various online friends of Wisteria's for help. But no one had seen the elusive pair. Chad made another trip to Scotland, coming back as coated with rime as the highland trees and the ladies contented themselves with clipping claws and brushing coats to a fine sheen while the game warden wrote up his notes for his own bosses.

Finally, the weather gods took pity and the skies cleared again. Beth and Wisteria could only hope as they made the trip once more to Fellshadow Farm that the lost cats had found shelter *somewhere*.

The picture-book pub with its thatched roof and Tudor exterior looked as if it had been plunked down like a Shakespearean stage set in its entirety, just waiting for the playwright to appear and exclaim, "the play's the thing!" The dark interior was chopped up into a number of low-ceilinged small rooms, all smoky plaster and black beams which made Beth Merryman feel, if enchanted, almost claustrophobic. A fireplace, decorated with the ubiquitous horse brasses hung about the wall sat in the "public bar", where most of a crowd was gathered. The "saloon bar", through another door next to a dining room, was all but empty. There was much laughter and discussion all about and an occasional "thump" reverberated from the dart board beside the fireplace as another missile hit the bullseye, while its various contestants cheered or moaned goodnaturedly.

Paul Mellish was greeted warmly by a good number of the Pack Pony's clientele as he herded Chad, Beth and Wisteria up to the long polished bar, its dispenser of good cheer standing behind his taps with a shiny empty glass in his hand.

"Evenin', Paul," the barman said as he passed an order to his barmaid. "What's your pleasure?"

As Paul ordered them each a glass of the local brew, Beth Merryman looked around the room again. One door led to the saloon bar and dining area while another led to the gents' and ladies'. Past the loos, she could see a door to outside tables and chairs clustered around a flagged patio. For the most part, the regulars seemed to ignore their little party and she was just as glad. Beth could take center stage when she had to but for the most part here, she preferred to stand in the wings, watching, listening—and learning. Not a pushy Yank, she!

Beth looked closer at the patrons both inside and outdoors. They appeared to be a mix of local farmers and tradesmen, families and tourists. Not American tourists, she decided; these were obviously Brits. And a realization popped into her mind. She grimaced at her own silly mistake. Somehow in her provincialism, she'd always thought of "tourists" as boorish Americans, the two descriptions being interchangeable. Judging from the very English group at a table in the middle of the room, however, whose accent with its weird inflections she could barely understand, Beth's countrymen had no corner on *that* behavior. Their accents unintelligible maybe, but their derision for their fellow Brits, local and otherwise, was all too clear. She chuckled to herself—and missed Cheryl, who would no doubt be just as amused by the raucous ones, who were obviously here to lord it over the local gentry.

Paul put a cold glass in her hand and led them all out to a patio aglitter with fairy lights and lanterns at the back of the pub. The night was cool and clear and a number of merrymakers had the same idea, clustered as they were about the various tables and chairs. The area was not large, bounded as it was by a low wall covered with some sort of flowering vines. The view beyond was of the lake, a mirror of glass reflecting starshine back at them, a glow of pale orange hovering over the fells to the north.

As the four of them sat down, Paul spoke up. "Brian, the barman, says he's seen several cats around but this isn't anything unusual. There usually are and he's not noticed any particular strange cat among the regulars." He took a long swallow of his ale and licked his upper lip of froth. "But then he says, he's personally a dog man himself—"

Before Mellish could finish his sentence, there was an ear-splitting howl from the top of the wall. Two dark shapes erupted into the crowd, leaping from table to table. Drinkers suddenly jerked back, some almost upending drinks and chairs as a pair of woolly cats bounded across the small tabletop islands, each of them coming to rest excitedly in the laps of the two women who had just sat down. And to their audience's amazement and much laughter, the two ladies, instead of being annoyed by this assault, were quite obviously jubilant as each of them folded a large cat in a delighted hug, tears rolling down gleeful faces.

Paul grinned happily as Wisteria exclaimed over Freddie and Beth gave Star what-for over going off like he had but Chad looked alarmed. His wife suddenly realized what brought such consternation to her husband's handsome face.

Where's Angel?" he exclaimed, hurriedly standing up from his chair, and looking all around the patio.

✧ ✧ ✧

"Dammit, Karen. We're lost! You and your big ideas." Jerry Pullet was red-faced with anger, gripping the steering wheel as if it were a weapon he was going to tear out and use to teach his wife a lesson. "If this is a short cut to A595, I'm a footballer for Manchester United!"

Karen Pullet merely gripped her door handle on the unfamiliar left passenger seat, her lips compressed grimly. The road was only wide enough for one vehicle and it was snaking up and down and over hills and fells with blind curves and stomach-lurching humpbacks.

"That damned Dex. I'll bet he knew you were sneaking off with that stupid cat you had me trap." He raised one hand to display the scratches and punctures across the hairy back of it. "It's a shortcut, all right; a shortcut to Hell." In annoyance, he stabbed the accelerator with his foot. He, too, was not comfortable in the unfamiliar right-side driver's seat.

It was the wrong move to make. The car leaped forward toward the crest of a rise just as another vehicle came over it straight at them. Instinctively, Pullet jerked the car down onto the narrow, almost nonexistent shoulder where they bounced out of a ditch and came to rest with a loud thump, sending both of them skyward, seat belts painfully trying to restrain them.

The box on the back seat, which had not been belted in, bounced and bumped to the floor, the one string holding the lid shut flying loose. The box's prisoner squeezed out, looked around, shook her head and hunched down among strewn suitcases and packages behind the driver's seat and waited. The occupants of the front seat didn't give their reluctant passenger a thought. Dazed, with hearts racing, they slowly unbuckled and got out to survey the damage. The other vehicle had already disappeared around a curve behind them and vanished, either unaware of their predicament or not caring.

The front bumper of the rental car was a bit dented but there seemed to be no major damage. Well, maybe, maybe not. One tire, the right rear, was flat. The angle at which their vehicle had come to rest was a bit precarious but Pullet thought he should be able to get it jacked up. His wife stood in front of the hatchback VW trying to calm herself and figure out where they were. It was a vain hope. She'd never been here before.

While bracken covered the rising fell on the right side of the cut, on her side of the narrow tarmac, a forest rose up the side of a gentle hill, thick with old trees, a carpet of blue wildflowers underneath their spreading leafy branches. Hardly in the mood to admire scenery, she turned back to her husband.

Pullet, having decided on a course of action, released the latch on the rear hatch and raised it to look for the spare tire tools. At that moment, a small silver streak shot past him and disappeared into the woods, galloping at full tilt.

"Stop her!"

Pullet turned and gazed at his wife from beneath his black bushy eyebrows, a look she had learned to read and fear long ago. Karen Pullet shut her mouth, turned her back on him, her hands jammed in her coat pockets and walked up the road without a word, disappointment, anger and fear all mixed together in the set of her shoulders.

✡ ✡ ✡

"Why, yes," Dexter Bishop said as he stood with his wife in the front hall of their B and B the following afternoon. "Old Tom there did find a pair of young'uns and bring them here, over a week ago, it was." He looked fondly at the black and white cat so firmly attached to Wisteria's shoulder. "That young black tom you've got there and a pretty little silvery-orange girl."

"—And that wretched American stole the little tortie," his wife, Beverly, declared vehemently. "I tried to discourage her. The wife, that is. She wanted that cat, pretty little thing that she was, but when she said she intended to declaw her, I tried to discourage her. That should never be done to any poor animal."

Beth, Chad, Wisteria and Paul stood there in dejection, their two remaining cats clinging to the two women. The barman at the Pack Pony, knowing his neighbors' love of cats, had directed them to LakesEdge Cottage B and B in hopes of finding the missing member of their feline trio.

"Come along," Bev encouraged, "we'll go out on the patio and have a cup of tea. I'll miss old Tom; he's a good cat but I'm glad his rightful owner has found him." Their hostess chattered away, bustling down the hallway, through the sitting room and kitchen and out onto the patio. While she busied herself making tea, her husband pulled out chairs for Paul Mellish, with whom he'd thrown a few darts in local competitions, and his friends.

"The wife was okay—or so I thought," he began, "but I can't say I cared for the husband. Bloody know-it-all." He looked at Chad and Beth with apology. "Beggin' your pardon, Mrs. Merryman, but some of your countrymen just don't know how to be good chaps in another country."

Beth nodded ruefully while Chad echoed her sentiments. "How long have they been gone—and do you have an address for them in London?" Chad asked, thinking of the daunting task before them.

"Oh," Dex laughed. "They never got to London." Seeing the confusion on their faces, he hastened to explain.

"Mr. Pullet asked me for a shortcut to the main motorway south. But his wife wanted the 'scenic route' by way of Morecambe Bay." The man ducked his chin and grimaced. "Pullet himself had been such a plod, telling us how they did things so much better in America: better roads, better cars, better food—you know?—I was that sick of him, wasn't I? Pushy git. So I sent him along the way over Hardknott Pass toward Ravenglass. I figured that would make a believer of him."

Beth was squirming in her seat. "But, but, you said they didn't get to London—"

Their host laughed. "No, they had a bit of disputed right-of-way with a Range Rover and ended up with a deflated tire and a bent wing pushed into a tire which immobilized their front end."

"So where are they now?" Beth and Wisteria were ready to launch themselves in search of Angel's abductors.

"They're in Ambleside at a garage—or were—I know because they called here." Dex Bishop favored his visitors with a wicked smile. "Mrs. Pullet was in such a rush to be off she forgot her handbag—with all their credit cards in it."

"Served her right, it did," declared Beverly, stepping onto the patio with her best tea tray. "That's what she gets for stealing that pretty little silver moggie."

Their hostess sat down and went about the ritual of pouring tea, giving them her version of a wicked grin. "Dex told her husband we'd be glad to swap his wife's handbag for our cat they'd taken away—"

"Such language!" Bishop sputtered. "Good thing he wasn't talking to Beverly. She'd have set him straight, she would."

Beth found herself holding her breath. "So what happened? Did they bring Angel back?"

Dex turned grim. "The cat got away from them when they had their accident. Near the forest where the road forks and goes around the fells to the north." He shook his head in apology. "I gave the lady her handbag. Don't suppose we'll have any return business there— not that I'd say we had a vacancy if they did come this way again. But I wish I could be more helpful about that little lost puss."

Beth Merryman felt like she'd just been jabbed with a sharp pin and all her air had spewed out. Wisteria, she could see, was just as deflated.

"Not to sound like some comic book character, honey," Chad Merryman said, patting his wife's knee, "but this sounds like a job for Supercats."

Beth perked up. "Hawkeye and Bhu Fan, you mean?"

"The very same."

CHAPTER FOURTEEN

O UT OF BREATH WITH sore pads and a pounding heart, Angel looked back over her shoulder. She could no longer see the road or the hated humans. She crawled into the tangle of fallen branches which seemed to have been a lair fashioned by some creature much her own size. There she collapsed in a heap, curled up in a tight ball, closed her eyes and tried to shut out the world. Too tired to think at this point, Angel finally slept. At least she had escaped: no declawing in her future now!

Her growling stomach awakened her. The young queen had never hunted for her dinner in her whole life. Nor had she had any chance to learn from her dam. One hardly had to stalk a bowl of kibble. What was she to do? Without Freddie and Star to give her protection and company—and direction, if she would admit to it— Angel was badly frightened. She'd never been on her own before. How was she to cope? Cautiously, she rose up and peered out of her tiny cave. She jerked her head around, ears swiveling. What had she heard? A rustling in the forest duff? There was movement in the dead leaves. Slowly she put one paw out of her hiding place. Instinct was all. Feeling sorry for herself just wasn't going to cut it. Nor fill her empty stomach. Moving stealthily and silently on her belly, she approached the gray squirrel scrabbling in the undergrowth. A twig snapped under her paw. The squirrel's head came up and he flew just as she pounced.

Before she could right herself to chase the scrambling rodent, a loud deep voice cried in triumph as its owner materialized a few feet in front of her, snagging the fleeing squirrel out of the air as he landed, scattering dead leaves in all directions.

Taken by surprise, Angel stood up tall and looked in the direction the creature had taken. Her eyes widened. A large very muscular cat was dismembering the dead squirrel. She moved closer, angry now. That was to have been her meal. Without thinking, she carelessly pounced on her usurper.

"That was my prey!" she declared, claws extended. "You stole my breakfast, you wretched creature!"

The two cats rolled over in a noisy, fur-flying melee and Angel quickly realized she'd bitten off more than she could chew, if that wasn't putting too fine a point on it. Her adversary had the advantage of weight and skill. There was nothing for it but to capitulate. Panting hard, her mouth open to suck in more air, she glared at the big tiger striped cat who had now turned his back on her and returned to his kill. Having wiggled out of his grasp, she backed off and stared at him with hostility, all the while assessing the feline in front of her.

Angel blinked. She'd never seen a *wild* cat before. And make no mistake about it, all her instincts told her this tom was certainly wild in the true definition of the word. His coat was thick and heavy, if not long—wispy long hair would have been to no advantage in these dense woods and gullies. Yet, in another life, he might have been a Coon. He was of a proper size and had that look of majesty about him. His pelt was the mackerel tabby pattern, all browns, golds and blacks with its striping running vertically down his flanks. It was a pelt that certainly had been to his evolutionary success as it would have made him invisible in his native Scottish Highlands, which were not all that far from these very fells. His eyes were a vivid green-gold, with a look in them both piercing and fearless.

He stood over his kill, now looking easily at Angel. "You put up a good fight—for a quine."

"What's a 'quine'?" she ventured, looking hungrily at the squirrel and licking her sore scratched shoulder.

"A girl," he responded. "But this is my territory," he continued as if she hadn't spoken, "and all the prey in it are mine." He gave her a sly smile. "But I must say, you did distract this critter long enough for me to get him." The big cat put a large paw on the squirrel and tore off a piece of hide. "Not bad for an amateur. These blighters are wily prey, not easily brought down." The tiger tom chewed thoughtfully.

Angel stood her ground. "Compliments are all very well, ruffian, but I was hungry and that was *my* squirrel." The silver torbie glared at her adversary. "But then I guess, having grown up with no manners, you could hardly be expected to honor any code of sportsmanship." Angel's eyes half closed. She sat down, licked a paw and brought it carefully across her face. "What do they call alley cats in your country? *Moggies*?"

The big tom arrested his efforts to de-fur his kill. Wordlessly, he glared at the young queen in front of him. It dawned on him that this silky feline was not native to these parts. Not that it mattered in his scheme of things.

"I am *not* a moggie! I am not an *alley* cat—whatever *that* is, nor have I ever begged at any mantom's hovel. My ancestors came here before any of humankind ever arrived; my kind were contemporaries of cave bears and woolly mammoths. I am known among mantoms as the Scottish Wildcat."

Angel's body language clearly indicated that she was not impressed. "Well, ruffian, did your dam ever bother giving you a name? Or do I just call you 'Thief'?"

"I am Derryth," he answered peevishly and then sat back on his haunches, annoyed at this young queen's indifference to his exalted status. Normally a solitary creature, the big cat was really a bit disconcerted by this, this *house*cat who was obviously not going to go away and leave him to himself, mouthy little thing that she was. How to get rid of her?

"I have taken the hide from this squirrel and if you will just go away and leave me to my endeavors, I will share a bit of it with you." He added, "But only if you will then go on your way."

Angel didn't commit herself. Right now, what she wanted most in the world was to fill her empty stomach. She came up to the de-furred feast and daintily helped herself to a haunch. The taste was a bit gamey, she thought, not what she'd care for as a steady diet but at the moment, since it was all that was offered, she'd take it. As for going away, how could she possibly know where to go? As she helped herself, she thought: what would Bhu Fan do if she were in my place?

✡ ✡ ✡

Dawn in high summer over the Cumbrian fells was magical. All the colors of the spectrum shimmered against their grassy heights. The drystone walls that slashed this way and that across the pinks, golds, rich browns and vivid greens gave the landscape surrounding Lake Windermere the look of a painting by Mondrian. Add a few sheep, soften it a bit and it became a Monet.

Bhu Fan, however, was not exhilarated by her surroundings, enchanting though they might be. She sat unmoving in Wisteria's cattery looking coldly at Star. It might not be visible, but her throne was certainly there. Hawkeye lay at her feet, spread out across the floor like his sire, Shere Khan at his most relaxed, deceptively so. He knew what was coming. And though he had not met the fabled Freddie before, he was quite pleased to find that he'd become young Star's advocate.

For his part, CumbriaCoon's prodigal son, was quite awed by Wisteria's visiting royalty. Like Violet and Cottia, he was automatically programmed to revere blue blooded aristocrats no matter what the breed. Bhu Fan might be a small slender, shorthaired blue grey Korat from the other side of the world with enormous (and judgmental) green eyes but that she was also descended from ancient kings and chieftains, he didn't doubt for a moment. And one did *not* gainsay royalty. With any luck, though, Freddie would have a word or two in defense of his young friend.

"Well, Star, what have you to say for yourself?" Bhu Fan was obviously going to show no mercy. It was one thing to go haring off and get oneself lost. It was quite another to lose one's co-conspirator in the process. And as far as Miss Uncongeniality was concerned, one was guilty until proven otherwise.

The young black tom, who all this time had been sequestered in a corner, a self-imposed exile, now came forth to face the music. Although he knew that while he might not have been the instigator of his and Angel's escapade, it would not do for him to shift the blame where it properly belonged. Add to that, the guilt he felt over his inability to rescue Angel from the clutches of her kidnappers, knot-head though she might be, was squarely weighing him down. He drew a deep breath and shook himself, knowing he could only throw himself on the mercy of the court.

"I wasn't quick enough," he admitted, wrapping his bushy tail around his paws. "I didn't see it coming."

"Didn't see what coming?"

"That ugly little mantom whose consort wanted Angel."

"Explain please,"

"Freddie 'n Angel 'n I were all sitting in the garden next to the outdoor eating— patio? behind the lodging place. We'd found a sunny spot in a corner next to the stone wall…Freddie excused himself to, ah, go take care of business. Angel hopped up on the wall and was giving her face a wash. We'd all just had breakfast, you see…I suddenly felt thirsty so I got up to go to the water bowl by the back door on the other side of the patio." Star became agitated and started going in circles. "At that precise moment, that vicious mantom suddenly stood up on the other side of the wall and dropped a blanket over Angel." The young tom's countenance grew bleak. "She fought, she really did…and I know," he added with satisfaction, "she drew blood." Star sunk down on his paws. "But by the time Freddie and I got across the patio and the garden and up on the wall, they'd stuffed Angel in a box, thrown her in a car and taken off." Star looked at Bhu Fan, his large gold eyes unutterably sad. "I was too little and too late."

"Now, Star," encouraged Freddie, "don't blame yourself. You couldn't have known what that pair of uglies was going to do. We'd all heard Mistress Beverly tell that guestqueen she couldn't have Angel. It's not your fault they weren't honorable."

Bhu Fan sat quietly for a moment. While Star was here and Angel wasn't, she had a pretty good idea which of the headstrong ones was at fault for this whole misadventure. Not that it mattered whose fault it was. Laying blame was not going to solve anything. She turned her eyes on Star and said gently. "Well, we'll just have to go find her then, won't we?—But not you, young sir, you will stay here with Freddie."

Star looked at his inquisitor and his shoulders slumped. Hawk-eye walked over and gave his young sibling a lick on the ear. "It's okay, squirt—Boo just doesn't want to put you at risk again. It's bad enough Angel is lost; you get lost again and Catemom is a two-time loser."

Wisteria pulled her car into a lay-by off the narrow twisting road to Hardknott Pass. Beth, Chad and a pair of quasi-bloodhounds followed her out of the car and walked back down the road to where Dex had said he thought the Pullets had gone off the pavement.

Bhu Fan and Hawkeye paused by the muddy tire tracks burrowed into the ditch and started trolling back and forth at forest's edge to see if there were any signs of Angel. Chad, an experienced wildlife tracker, leaped over the ditch behind the two cats and helped the two women across. Beth and Wisteria stood there for a moment. Beth sighed, smiling nostalgically. Looking into the blue-bell carpeted deep woods with its ancient trees, she'd have expected to see Little John or Robin Hood pop out from behind a large oak and greet them—or pull a bowstring.

Mentally shoving her fantasy aside, she looked at her cats, who were now carefully plotting a course between the ancient trees, Chad close behind. "I saw a couple of small paw prints at the edge of the forest and the distance between them would indicate she was moving fast," he declared, "and our two catly bloodhounds here have found a little path. Step carefully."

In single file behind the cats, Beth, Chad and Wisteria plodded into the forest, Chad marking their way with a piece of chalk in his hand. He didn't want somebody to have to come looking for *them*. He had no doubt the forest opened up as it climbed the hills toward the fells but it was unfamiliar territory to them. It was also an old growth forest thick with game and prey. Or so it seemed to an American game warden. He wasn't sure if this was good or bad insofar as their lost cat was concerned so he said nothing to that effect.

Bhu Fan! Called Hawkeye, coming into a small clearing, *see here!*

The little Korat abandoned her course and hopped over to the spot where her old friend had his head stuck in a small tangle of branches. It was obviously some creature's lair. He stuck his head inside.

Empty, he said, disappointed.

Without speaking, Bhu Fan crouched down and entered. *But Angel was here*, she cried, backing out, a tuft of silver hair in her mouth.

Chad, Beth and Wisteria quickly came to stand over them. "Yep," said Chad, almost as if he'd understood what the little Korat had said, "Angel sure hid in there—at least for a time."

He began ranging the perimeter of the small clearing, Hawkeye with him. The cat suddenly started digging among the leaves of the forest duff.

Chad squatted beside him. Shortly the remains of a gray squirrel were revealed, with the obvious indications of having been some creature's partial meal. Bhu Fan sniffed in disgust. *Ugh*, she complained to Hawkeye, *Not what I'd want for breakfast*.

The big Maine Coon neuter gave her a teasing smile. *Not so good as bangers and mash, huh?* he ventured, referring to that typical English fare offered by their hostess. He did love some of the British slang.

Bhu Fan ignored his dig and sat back on her haunches. *Somehow*, she said, looking up at Chad, certain he'd get her meaning, if not her words, *I don't think Angel suddenly turned into Xena-warrior-princess and brought down this smelly beast.*

"What do you think, Chad?" Beth ventured, coming up behind him. The game warden was looking up into the trees where he heard squirrels scrambling and chattering about over their heads.

"A wild creature brought down that squirrel. Burying a carcass for later dining is your typical wild animal behavior." He smiled at his wife. "And somehow, I can't see our pampered Angel going feral."

Wisteria was squatting down on the upper edge of the clearing where a tiny spring was seeping up to the surface. She eyed its muddy path toward lower ground. Nodding to herself, she stood.

"Well, um, look here, Chad, Beth—" she called, "I don't think our Angel was alone."

"What?!" the two Americans cried in unison, coming to stand by Wisteria, who was pointing downwards.

Immediately, Bhu Fan was there. Gently Chad barred her way as he squatted down. He didn't want her messing up what he was seeing. "Easy, Bhu, don't trample the paw-prints we see—I think you're right, Wisteria." The game warden closely examined the pug marks in soft earth. One set was certainly larger than the other and not so smudged with hair on the bottom of the paws.

"Wow!" he whistled. " I don't know who our girl has met up with—" his eyes scanned the clearing as only a naturalist can, "—but whoever has led her away, is a much bigger feline. I don't think, though, he/she has been aggressive toward Angel...I see no blood anywhere—or pieces of hide."

"Reeoow!" cried Hawk, looking back over his shoulder. He was in a thicket of undergrowth further up the hill among large boulders with young saplings and dense yews snaking over them. *They went this way!*

Chad looked grim. "C'mon back, Hawk!" he commanded. "There's no way we can follow you in there. Nothing bigger than another cat could." He shook his head at the two women.

"I hate to say it, Wisteria, but I think you can kiss Angel goodbye. We'll never find her up here. She could be anywhere, particularly if she's joined up with another cat—and it's a tom if I'm guessing right."

"Well," Beth murmured, putting her arm across her friend's shoulder in a friendly hug. "At least she isn't alone and maybe her new companion will keep her safe...or she'll find a homestead somewhere like they did at the B and B and become a pet." Beth sighed deeply. "One can only hope."

Bhu Fan, who had been listening to the exchange, looked up at her human family thoughtfully. As Hawkeye came up beside her looking disappointed, the little Korat shot him a look.

Not to worry, she said confidently as she turned and started back the way they had come, *Angel is okay. She's a survivor.*

Hawkeye looked long at his cohort, respect for her intuition, if one could call it that, and concern for Angel warring with it. He did not like the idea, any more than Chad, Bethmom and Catemom did, of going off and abandoning the search for Angel. That she might have chanced upon a consort made him a smidgeon easier but he didn't like their going off all the same. If it had been up to him—

The little Korat smiled, perceptive as always. *It's time for tea,* she murmured and stared back to the road.

Reluctantly, Hawkeye followed. If Angel's disappearance was really cause for worry, Bhu Fan wouldn't be so sanguine about it. He could only trust Bastet—and her unappointed seeress.

CHAPTER FIFTEEN

MARTHA MICHAUD LOOKED UP from the pile of mail she was sorting as she came out of the Stacyville Post Office, hoping for a letter from Beth telling her they'd found Star and Angel. At least *she'd* been able to get Dr. Watts wife, Vickie, to email the cattery in Cumbria that Gaston and Cheryl had found the MerryMaines gang at Chad's camp out in T-3 township…that had been a hoot! Gaston had unlocked the door to find Shere Khan spread out on Chad's bearskin rug with all the cats here and there around him, just like he'd been giving a stern lecture on celibacy. Martha chuckled to herself. At least they were all safe and sound. She'd worry about any "Oops-litters" later…She reckoned they'd go round up everybody soon and bring them home. No hurry now. If they'd played musical romances, what's done was done by now. Gaston had seen to it that they had plenty of kibble and water and left them to their leader, Khan. But who would keep *him* in hand? Martha giggled to herself. Maybe she ought to have Cheryl bring Madame du Maine home and take her out there. She'd certainly see that things went as they should. And that included Shere Khan.

"Wait up, Martha! I need to talk to you."

She looked up to see Harry Armstrong hurrying toward her from his county dogcatcher's truck parked just up the street. Martha waited, frowning. She'd not forgotten his bringing the state health Department know-it-all down on Beth's cattery.

"Harry, you miserable—I don't even want to talk to you. All of Beth's cats have disappeared (she wasn't about to tell him otherwise, not until she knew that specter of the state people was gone) and it's all *your* fault."

"I thought Gaston hid 'em in the old Hartman barn, Martha, I really did. And that guy from State, he's left. I think he had second thoughts about that idiot of a complainer when he saw how clean that place of Beth's was—Well, it don't matter…" The humane shelter boss waved his hands in apology. "I can't help *that* but Gaston says he knows where they are 'n the State's SOB is gone but—" Harry ran out of breath and shrugged his shoulders, "—that's not what I wanted to tell you. And Gaston left the diner this mornin' before I could tell him."

Harry Armstrong looked so serious, Martha felt a bit sorry for him. He was not all that articulate or well educated but the man really did try to find homes for all the unfortunate dogs and cats that, one way or another, ended up in his shelter. Talked Doc Watts into spaying and neutering those he caught before giving 'em back to folks who couldn't afford to do it themselves. And she knew Beth helped out with a monthly donation. Martha dropped her mail in a basket on the front seat of her little Chevy pickup and turned to face Harry, arms folded across her chest.

"There's talk," he began, "among some of the low-lifes around here about a long-time poacher and overgrown juvenile delinquent whose name it ain't worth my life to mention, who's trappin' cats… not just our Coon cats, just any well fed critters he can lay hands on… he likes housecats because they're easier to catch, not bein' so wary 'n all." Harry's face turned purple with anger and frustration and he jammed his hands in his pockets to keep from maybe stabbing Martha in the eye as he ranted.

"He told his buddies he takes 'em out to that shack he lives in close to the timber company road—and uses 'em for target practice." Harry took a deep breath and tried to get himself under control. "You don't want to know the details …says it sharpens up his co-ordination for pickin' off bigger game. An' sometimes, he doesn't even trap 'em, he just shoots 'em on the fly from his van." The man took a few minutes to gather himself and look Gaston's wife in the eye.

"You'd know who I'm referrin' to, Martha, but you didn't hear it from me. That sorry scumbag purely hates cats. Says they're evil; creatures of the devil." Harry ground his teeth and his jaw twitched. "If anybody's evil around here, it's him." The man turned and headed toward his truck. "Seems it all started when his wife threw him out. He's worse now—and she's taken her little Annie and left the country—gone to kin up in New Brunswick."

Martha looked after her informant as he hustled away back to his vehicle before anyone saw him, her brow wrinkled. For some minutes after he drove away, she didn't move. Just stood there leaning against her truck. She knew very well who Harry had been talking about. Gary Styles. For sure-- and some wild creature had left some telling claw marks on his face and head! Martha ruminated for long moments. He'd had one go at Chad that she knew of—and after what happened on his and Beth's wedding day, she wouldn't be surprised if he hadn't had *two* shots at the game warden. She also knew couldn't anybody touch him unless he got caught in the act. And so far, Gary Styles had either been slippery as owl's grease—or so intimidating that nobody dared speak out against him for fear he'd come after *them.*

Making up her mind, she walked around to the driver's door, got into her truck and headed out to Siberia Farm. She needed to call Cheryl and Gaston. They needed to get Beth's cats home and locked up in the cattery—Shere Khan, too. And she'd move a cot out there for her husband to sleep on if need be.

"Lord love us—I'll be so glad when Beth and Chad get home," she said out loud, shaking herself. "Target practice, Dear God!"

"Come along, quine, you're going to have to keep up. When we're in the open like this, the eagles can spot us." The wild tom paused and looked back over his shoulder. "And I have no wish to get snatched aloft." Derryth laughed. "Don't like heights; they make me dizzy."

Angel ignored her guide's good humor. She'd learned from him that there were heights—and there were *heights*. She'd perched so high up in trees with him it made *her* dizzy. At the same time, she didn't doubt that caught up in the talons of a flying eagle was not a situation either of them wanted to be in. "The ground here is stickery," she griped, changing the subject. "And the nettles are tearing at my coat." But she looked up at the sky nevertheless. She'd heard the tale of Madame and Bhu Fan's escaping the clutches of that great barred owl and she didn't have any desire to be snatched up either.

They were out in the open, making for a copse of trees nestled in a hanging valley. The sky was an intense cloudless blue, the color of those eyes she'd admired on a Siamese at the cat show in New York City. She'd wished she had eyes that beautiful shade of sapphire but her dam had admonished her to be satisfied with the pretty green-gold eyes she had, telling her that most blue-eyed Maine Coons, pretty as they were, were also usually deaf. Pushing aside such thoughts, she hastened to catch up with Derryth.

He wasn't a bad sort really. He'd shared his prey with her and showed her how to avoid fur sticking in her teeth. He'd also showed her how to drink off her paw. She'd seen Coons drink that way; she'd just never tried it. She didn't like any part of herself being cold and wet. He wasn't the most entertaining conversationalist. But then, why should he be? Spending so much time so solitary just surviving. He'd hardly know about how things went at cat shows, what the newest cat toys were, which new kibble was good and which wasn't fit for cockroaches and who was courting whom. But he had shared his fur-lined lairs with her and one evening when they'd hunkered down in a hollow log to get out of a cold, foggy rain when she'd been so miserably (and vocally) damp, he'd told her tales of his sire, a chieftain among the clans who avoided mantoms assiduously and his dam and how she'd shown him how to hunt and how each of his siblings had gone off to carve out a territory of their own. He'd missed them all, if he were to admit to it. But soon he'd learned to live on his own and reign in *his* own territory. Otherwise, he'd have surely gone very hungry. Angel found it hard to imagine living such a lonesome and chancy life by choice.

"Quine! Quick!" The wild cat commanded out of the blue, his ears swiveling; "Dogs!"

Without looking back, Angel exploded into a gallop, trying her best to keep up with her leader as he raced through the tall grass. Hearing the insistent howls and yips behind them, adrenaline pumping, she ran faster than Derryth thought a pampered young housecat could manage. The two of them made for a cluster of tall boulders at forest's edge. The wild tom leaped to the top of one and as Angel scrabbled up behind him, trying to get purchase, he reached down, caught the nape of her neck and pulled her up, turning only long enough to see how close the yapping hounds were behind them.

Too close, he judged and leaped for a low branch on a nearby oak. Angel watching, made the leap behind him. She almost missed but managed to grasp the branch until she could get her hind claws into the bark. Righting herself, all out of breath, she followed him along the stout horizontal branch. The big tom then leaped to another branch, this one on a bushy ancient yew. Further up into the tree by way of its main trunk the wily cat scrambled. It made for difficult climbing so thick were its branches. But at the same time, it was much more concealing and even a neophyte like Angel could grasp the importance of that. At last Derryth settled in a wide crotch, the young queen close up beside him. They looked down at the hounds, now sniffing around, trying to pick up their scent trail. But the cats, having leaped to their refuge from bare rock, had left no scent along the ground for the dogs to follow.

"I thought," Angel whispered, swallowing great gulps of air, "the only dogs around here chased after those woolly goat-like creatures—what do you call them? Sheep?"

"Normally, yes," the big cat answered. "But there are a couple of mantoms who bring their hounds up here in summer to train them."

"Train them? What for?"

Her companion looked down at Angel, his big green-gold eyes going cold. "They think we make good substitutes for the foxes they like to run to earth further south, poor wretches." Seeing Angel's consternation, he gave her a lick across one ear. "There's nobody up this way to see them and complain about 'em using them an' us for what I've heard called 'blood sport'."

Angel stiffened fearfully.

He hastened to reassure her. "But today, their mantoms are evidently too far behind them to give us any grief."

The two cats looked down at their pursuers who still didn't appear to know where the two felines were. Fortunately, the branches of their stout elderly yew were so thick as to give both pursued and pursuers a very sketchy view of anything really distinct, either up or down. The hounds were coursing back and forth, noses to the forest detritus beneath them. Angel shuddered. They were so tall and brawny and there were so many of them. She didn't want to even imagine what would have happened had they fallen into the midst of the excited hounds' melee. She closed her eyes and turned her head into her companion's shoulder. Presently, hearing a distant whistle, the dogs retreated hastily in the direction from which they'd come.

The big tom relaxed. Angel stuck to his side, finding comfort in his close muscular company. Some sort of strange feelings suffused her. She shook herself, trying to throw them off. She was depleted; the adrenaline rush had drained her dry. She didn't want to move and her eyes had grown heavy.

The big tom, a veteran of many chases, let her sleep for awhile. He found that he didn't want to move either. She felt sort of warm and comforting; friendly.

"We'll go now," Derryth said softly after awhile, nudging her. "I know where there's a little cave high in the rocks with a spring and small fish in a burn."

Without a word of complaint this time, Angel trailed behind her guide as he descended to the forest floor and then scrambled upward into another oak, whose branches, being much more open, made the going easier. In this manner, they made their way along one stout oak branch to another reaching toward them. Imitating the squirrels, which were giving them wide berth, they traveled across the forest, tree to tree, the questing hounds left far behind.

Presently, Derryth leaped down to the soft spongy forest floor and made his way along a path only he could make out, Angel close behind. The wild tom stopped at a pool below the spring he'd spoken of for a drink. As Angel came up behind him and caught sight of her reflection, she groaned out loud.

"My pretty pelt! What has happened to it? I look so raggety-taggy." She whimpered and dropped dispiritedly on her paws.

Derryth looked around at her and backing away from pool's edge, chuckled playfully and lifted a comforting tail over her shoulder.

"You're alive, aren't you?"

CHAPTER SIXTEEN

F REDDIE, OVERJOYED AT BEING home again, was holding court from his elevated perch in CumbriaCoons' premier wire-enclosed stud suite (Wisteria had told him as she lovingly inserted him into his suite that she didn't want him "making up for lost time with the girls.") With Star stretched out on the carpet just outside as his prompter, he was regaling all the queens of CumbriaCoons with his wild—to hear him tell it—adventures on Lake Windermere, his harrowing trek through the fells, the ghosts of Mediobogdum and his coming at last to Fellshadow Farm where resided the beauteous Maid Marion. Geoffrey Chaucer couldn't have told it any better: "The Wandering Tom's Tale", perhaps. He talked of his retreat to the LakesEdge Cottage Bed and Breakfast and his rescue of Star and Angel. Only he was hard-pressed to put any kind of positive spin on the ending of *that* tale. Somehow he and Star should have been more alert to Angel's possible abduction— and prevented it.

Violet and her little blue troop were loose in the cattery's common room, bright-eyed with excitement. She did love storytelling time. Foxglove, her littlest tom was stalking Bhu Fan's lazily moving tail. Gentian was playing slap-paw with Hawkeye, while Lobelia, Violet's one little female, was trying to entice a very glum Star into a wrestling match. Star was resisting, growling in mock ferocity.

"I might as well be wrestling a butterfly." At this, Lobelia squeaked in protest, leaped at the black tom and grabbed him around the neck. He rolled over in seeming submission, a small smile crossing his face. The kittens, as one might expect, were unaffected by the grownups mixed emotions over recent events. They lived for the moment.

That Angel was no longer among them caused little distress among Wisteria's queens beyond dismay at her being lost. They'd hardly known her. Freddie's return, on the other hand, was cause for celebration. He had been a great favorite of the ladies—and his fostering of Star was also making the queens sit up and take notice. More than one, to include the calculating Violet, was taking the black tom's measure. He was a mite young but growing quickly and turning into a very handsome Coon. And his remoteness only seemed to make him that much more attractive to the lassies. The Crown Prince of CumbriaCoons perhaps?

Star, however, was not feeling all that entertaining at the moment, quite content as he was to leave the field to Freddie. It wasn't that he harbored any romantic feelings for Angel. She was much too familiar, too full of herself and too bossy for that. At the same time, she had been, he felt, his responsibility. The two of them had been thrown together eons ago (or so it seemed) on the other side of a long sea and were expected to come to this, a fine cattery in the Lake District of Northern England and excel. And now she was lost in the fells and he had no way of finding her. Star put his head down between his paws and gazed sadly into the distance, seeing nothing. It was the *not knowing* her fate that was weighing so heavily on him. If he could only believe that whoever had discovered her out there in that dark forest would take good care of her, it wouldn't be so worrisome to him. Bhu Fan and Hawkeye seemed to think she'd crossed paths with a tom who was wise to living free. But given Angel's bossiness, that would have to be *some kinda cat*. He shook his head and sighed.

Violet, who had made friends with Bhu Fan, insofar as one can become friends with royalty, sauntered over to where the little Korat was having a wash in a sunny patch beneath a window, while still playing happy tails with wee Foxglove, who giggled gleefully as he chased her whippy tail.

"Where has Wisty gone with your friend, Your Highness? And her consort: Chadtom? They left awful early this morning." Somehow, Violet expected Princess Bhu to know everything. Wasn't that what royalty was for?

Bhu Fan looked up from her toilette and thought for a moment.

"Chad has gone back to Scotland"—*now why does Scot-something ring a bell*? She shook her head; it was trying to go all fuzzy again. "Chad's gone back to Scotland," she repeated, "to see to the beavers. Catemom and Bethmom have gone somewhere to visit other catteries. I not know where…"

"Manchester and Yorkshire, I think," put in Hawkeye, who had ambled up to the pair. "I think they wanted to take their minds off of Angel's disappearance." Hawk spread out on the floor and waited. He wanted a private word with Boo. No sense in spilling the beans to everybody. He'd overheard an interesting conversation between their two moms.

"What?" asked the Korat a bit querulously, when Violet had left them to go feed her brood. She was still smarting over her inability to conjure up Angel for the searchers, even though she was sure the silver torbie had come to no harm, wherever she was at the moment.

"I heard Bethmom and Catemom talking at breakfast about some pretty little van-patterned queen at a cattery called Musicoons. D'ya think they'll bring back a consort for Starry?" Hawkeye paused, his eyes alight. "They took a carrier with them…"

Bhu Fan skewered her favorite peasant with a stern eye. "Starry, I think, is still a bit young to take a consort but I do notice he is showing signs of imminent tomhood." She pursed her lips in concentration. "But a young queen might just take his mind off Angel." The haughty Korat thought for a few moments. "I rather think it was Angel who wanted to go adventuring that night and Star went along to keep her out of trouble…He never had any acquisitive feelings for her; it's just that he felt, big-brother-like, she was his responsibility. Besides," she added with a sly secretive grin across her face, a thought having just occurred to her. "Angel just may surprise us all:.*A Fine Romance*, as old song goes…"

Hawkeye returned Boo's imperious gaze. "Well, Your Highness, that's all very well and good for giggly kitling queens—but winter is

coming one of these days and somehow, knowing how Angel likes
her creature comforts, I very much doubt her 'fine romance' is going
to keep her warm—and safe—up there among those big old cold
rocks."

Bhu Fan looked up at Hawkeye and to his amazement, faltered.
"I can't see *that far* ahead," she admitted and bent nervously to her
composure grooming.

"Okay, everybody, play time is over! Time to hit the road for
home."

Gaston, Martha, Cheryl and a stranger swept a glance at all the
cats scattered about in Chad's cabin, as they came softly into the
room and started stacking carriers along one wall. Everybody appeared to be in good shape and relaxed in their temporary quarters.

Shere Khan gazed up at them and along with Beowulf, Smudge
and Sweeper, set about reassuring the rest of the gang that it was indeed time to go home and therefore, they should all co-operate and
allow themselves to be crated. The cabin was, after all, not nearly
so roomy as their cattery and the cats did, ever so often, like a little
privacy. Especially the queens. They were quite unaccustomed to
the toms mixing and mingling, even toms so laid back as Rio and
Simon. The kittens had been a special trial to Khan, always pester-
ing him for stories. But he'd gotten his own back there, as Smudge
learned to his cost when he had been indiscreet enough to snicker
at his old friend, thereby finding himself on that same hot seat. Well,
at least he had a few war stories of his own to entertain the wee ones,
for which harassed momcats had been very grateful.

The Great One eyed the stranger now and only Cheryl's added presence reassured Himself that Harry Armstrong was friend
instead of foe—after his bringing the state's mantom down on
MerryMaines. But as he watched his humans going about the business of loading everybody into their crates, he noticed the humane
shelter boss handling various queens and kittens gently and with
confidence. Suddenly Khan also recalled that when the moose

scattered the two mantoms who had come to confiscate Beth's cats that day, this one had been very slow about getting to his feet and gathering up various crates and carriers. His apparent sloth had given Khan and his three cohorts enough time to get everybody out and gone. Had that been deliberate? Had the man seen Khan's little exodus sneaking away from the cattery?

Like Martha and Gaston, he'd known who the man was and what he did for a living. Not much that went on in Penobscot County passed him by unnoticed. He also knew from his acquaintances in Patten and Gilby that some of those same friends had gotten a second chance in the scheme of things because of Harry. There'd been no euthanasia in *his* shelter. Shere Khan chewed on a whisker. Perhaps the mantom was here to make up for his subservience to that officious health department enforcer.

At last, all the cats, save Shere Khan, Smudge and Sweeper were loaded in Gaston's and Cheryl's vehicles. Well, Beowulf would ride shotgun with Gaston and Riddle was sent along home to Singletary's farm. That he had showed up to visit with Kazandra just about the time Khan had led them all out to the camp hadn't been a surprise. The big red tom had a sixth sense where his consort was concerned. And he knew as well as Shere Khan how to get into the cabin through the woodbox, which opened both from outside and in.

"C'mon, Khan, you, too, Sweeper, Smudge, we haven't got all day," admonished Cheryl, bringing The Great One out of his musings. "Let's herd 'em up and head 'em out."

Obediently, the three cats followed her out, watched as she locked the cabin door and hopped into the van beside her. Khan put his paws up on the dashboard and looked over at the driver. She laughed out loud. "Are you going to backseat-drive on me, Khan? Give me directions?"

He withdrew from the dash and settled contentedly beside Smudge and Sweeper, a grin on his face.

Will Chad and Bethmom be there when we get home? They'll be glad we scarpered out to the camp on our own, won't they?

I sure hope so, Smudge, Shere Khan answered, thinking hard. Riding herd—to use Cheryl's analogy—on this bunch of felines has certainly taxed his powers of persuasion. *I surely do,* he repeated, hoping as well Madame would think so when next he saw his own consort. Or he'd have an awful lot of explaining to do.

Very wary after their near encounter with the fox hounds, Angel crept along behind Derryth as they moved toward some destination only the big cat had in mind. It seemed an awful long way, however, and her paws, not yet forest-toughened were terribly sore. But she knew him well enough now to ascertain this crafty tomcat did nothing and went nowhere without purpose.

Again they were out in the open with only the rocky remains of the last glacier anchored in the ground around here and there with the yellow blooming gorse butted up against them as if for protection from the hated wind. Angel disliked the stickery, weedy bushes. They were almost as bad as the nettles that attacked her every chance they got. She didn't care much for the bracken either. Nowhere in her homeland were there growing any scourges such as these. Not that she'd know if they did, cattery bred as she was. But she pushed mere facts out of mind and concentrated on their course.

Her companion paused at the base of a particularly tall sandy-colored tetrahedron close to the edge of an escarpment that loomed over a lush green valley below. Without explanation, Derryth scrabbled to the top of it, gazed around and then lifted his head to howl. Only, Angel realized, her escort wasn't howling in the excited tones like those of the hounds they'd escaped. He was—singing. She almost laughed to herself, remembering her first encounter with Freddie singing his song about sixpence and blackbirds. Derryth's song was no nursery rhyme; more like it was a call or a signal to someone down below. She didn't understand the words but their music echoed across the valley and back again.

Suddenly and instinctively she glanced over her shoulder and glimpsed, to her very great alarm, a fast moving shadow behind her. She shouted a warning.

"Derryth! Eagle!"

In less time than it takes to tell it, the big tomcat had launched himself off his perch and disappeared, his song abruptly cut off. All Angel heard as she flattened herself to the hard ground, closing her eyes tightly, was a rush of wind and the cry of a very angry raptor as he winged off in the distance over the valley, screaming defiance.

"Derryth!" she called, her heart in her mouth. "Derryth! Where are you?" Thoroughly distraught now, she got to her paws, circling around, calling again. Had the eagle carried him off?

Oh, please, Bastet, not Derryth!

At that moment, there was movement among the thick branches of the gorse on the lower side of the rocks. Her companion came crawling out from under and sat down on his haunches, blinking a bit, as if to recover his balance.

"It's okay, quine, I'm okay." He grinned derisively. "Avoided flying once again." He shook his head, clearing it of cobwebs.

Angel rushed to him, checking him over very closely. There was a long scratch along his back but thankfully it wasn't all that deep. Had the eagle grazed him? He had a few tufts of fur missing here and there, lost no doubt by his dive through the thick gorse. The big cat limped a bit but seemed to be none the worse for it. Angel started to exclaim as she attempted to lick his wounds.

He pushed her aside gently. "I'm all right," he repeated. "Just landed wrong. Twisted my paw. No need for concern. That worthless bag of moldy feathers and I are old enemies." He looked up at an empty sky. "I'll outlive him yet!"

Derryth brought his gaze back to Angel. "Come, quine," he said, something like sadness in his voice. "We don't have much time. It grows late." The big cat got to his feet and started down the escarpment, picking his way from one grassy outcrop to another, keeping one eye skyward. Angel followed him wordlessly. She had been terribly afraid the huge bird had carried him off. And the thought of being all alone up here without him was almost more than she could bear. Where did such intense feelings come from?

They'd reached another level where the land dropped away behind them. To her surprise, Angel spied a big silver neuter, his mackerel tabby tiger-like stripes glowing in the late afternoon light,

sitting on a ledge as if waiting for them. And to her even greater surprise, he looked like a Maine Coon. She glanced at her escort. The
other cat's appearance seemed to surprise him not at all.

"Sir Francis."

"Lord Derryth."

Angel blinked. It seemed to her that this stranger all but bowed
to her companion with great deference. She looked hard at Derryth.
Wild or not, he did seem to have an aura of lordliness about him.

"I heard your call," Sir Francis chuckled with a broad grin. "It
would seem that nosy eagle heard it as well."

Derryth shook his head in embarrassment. "What I get for not
paying attention." He paused. "I trust all is well with you and your
clan at the big mantom's barn?"

"Tolerable, tolerable," the older cat replied. "And I trust, my lord,
all in your fiefdom is as it should be?"

Derryth shot a glance at Angel, who was thinking the title certainly suited him. "—Excepting eagles," he admitted," who recog-
nize no sovereignty but their own, marauding dogs—and wandering quines."

For the first time, Sir Francis turned his attention to Angel who
stood uncertain, not sure whether she should be insulted or flat-
tered by Derryth's last comment. She stayed close to his shoulder
and waited, a bit uneasy. She wasn't real sure just what this meeting
was about but that her escort had called it was now quite obvious.

"You'd be the missing queen Angel from Wisty's establishment,
would you not?"

Angel's jaw dropped open. "You know me?"

The old neuter laughed. "By now I imagine every cat in Cumbria
knows about you and your escape from the ugly ones. Quick thinking, that."

Angel digested this, suddenly feeling terribly torn between two
worlds.

Derryth turned to her. "I brought you to Sir Francis, quine, because I was sure he could see that you got to your home down by the
lake."

Angel turned on him quickly, her jaw again slack, her brow
furrowed. "You don't want me to stay with you, Derryth?" she

murmured in a small voice. Expressing herself was suddenly very difficult.

The lord of the forests looked long at her, regret in his eyes. "It's not that I don't want you with me, quine." He gazed at his acolyte with affection. "'Tis that I want you safe. You weren't born to the uncertain wild life of the forests and fells. Your chances here would be, well, slim. And," he added with humor, "I don't think the menu is really to your liking." He grew serious once more. "This is no life for you."

Angel gazed at Derryth for a long moment without speaking. Truth to tell, it *wasn't* the life for her and she had become pragmatic enough to realize it. Still…would she ever meet another one such as this?

"I will miss you, Derryth. And I would wish for you many fat squirrels—and no heights to make you dizzy—" Angel's voice broke and she dropped her eyes to the ground, faltering.

"Memories of you, Mistress Angel, will keep me warm amidst the winter snows." So saying, Lord Derryth dropped his head and rubbed along her side, running his tail over her back. "Go with Sir Francis now. Before I change my mind—and condemn you to a diet of furry teeth and rodents."

Angel gave him a very private look, smiled at his attempt to lightness, sucked in a deep breath, turned and followed Sir Francis down a narrow path toward Fellshadow Farm.

✡ ✡ ✡

CHAPTER SEVENTEEN

T HE LANDSCAPE UNDULATING ACROSS the Yorkshire countryside, punctuated by the ever present drystone walls cheek-by-jowl with row upon row of terraced houses, their chimney pots piercing the sky like a scene out of Dickens, made Beth Merryman shake her head in wonder. It was like seeing tall apartment buildings lined up out in the middle of nowhere; city dwellings transported to a place they just didn't seem to belong. Like in the middle of a cornfield. Then Wisteria's route would, by chance it seemed, bring them past a cluster of buildings butted right up to the edge of their roadway as if there was no room for them at the back amidst hills and dale; villages dotted with pubs (almost always with one named "The George and Dragon"), garages, news agents, a church or two and car parks, all manner of private residences, where stepping out the front door always put you at risk of being run over by horse, motorbike, or heaven forbid: a rollicking lorry. Or worse: a tour bus. Beth had never seen so many mammoth tour busses on roads hardly adequate for a motor scooter. And while so many places in Yorkshire bore delightfully odd names like Alderman's Head, Birdsedge, Meanwood and Hades, she wasn't real sure why those tour busses would be exploring such places. Still, she could just visualize one of the passengers coming back into her cottage after her tour, telling her husband, "Well, we've been to Hell—and it's not nearly so hot as the vicar would have you believe." She snickered to herself. Perhaps it was all the very lovely multi-colored gardens that attracted the busses. Even in window boxes. (Well, with one's doorway opening right onto the road, where else could they put them?) Nowhere in all her travels had Beth Merryman seen such beautiful gardens…Nor such inventive ones.

And suddenly, they had reached their destination. Wisteria parked the car in front of a row of semi-detached houses(which Beth would have called "duplexes"), tall and narrow with tiny garden walls marking off each pair, set down along a narrow road where the only other inhabitants in sight were sheep gazing at them over the ubiquitous drystone, moss-covered walls on the far side of the roadway. "Musicoons" proclaimed a small plaque beside the fire-engine red door of the house right in front of them. Wisteria took the carrier from the back seat and the two of them made their way up the walk. Beth laughed out loud. The large sitting room window before them was lined with cats: standing tall, stretched out, some fast asleep and crowded everywhere with rambunctious, curious kittens. The two of them were certainly being closely vetted by the furry occupants.

Spying a lovely silver torbie queen in the middle of this row of feline inspectors, Beth felt a terrible pang of regret. Was there any chance that such an array of lonesome houses might be somewhere up there amid fells and forests in Cumbria, a place where Angel might find refuge?? She had to think so. All else was unbearable.

Violet gave each of her kitlings a proper bath and retreated to her outdoor run for a nap in the sunshine. It wasn't that she didn't love the three little mites; it was just that like all overworked momcats, she needed a little time to herself. Wisty and her visitors had gone off somewhere and so, with things very quiet in the cattery, she'd indulge herself in a snooze where there was a gentle breeze to massage her fur. Bhu Fan and Hawkeye, stretched out in the common room appeared to be doing the same. Violet had checked on her wee ones as she went through her cat flap and they were all tucked away in their nest box sound asleep.

Well. Not really. Little Foxglove, already called Foxy by his siblings, was restive. The little blue and white tom might be the smallest of the litter but he was also the most inquisitive. And when he lifted his head from the tangle of kitlings and saw this multi-legged fuzzy creature moving across the floor of their enclosure, he quietly lifted a paw, stealthily left the fleece-lined box and with his belly to the floor, approached the slow moving arachnid.

It ignored him and kept to its trajectory. Where was it going? What was it going to do when it got there? What had it been doing in *his* quarters? Why hadn't mum told him about such weird critters with so many legs?

Foxy nosed the spider. It reared up on its hind legs, looking very fearsome for such a small creature. The kitten jerked back. Felines, even the smallest, have quick reflexes. The spider proceeded along its chosen path, Foxy following along, head and tail low to the floor. Moving objects are impossible for kittens—or cats, for that matter—to ignore.

The spider went under a warped trim board near the cat flap at the back end of their enclosure. Foxy inserted a paw in an attempt to fish it out. Surely something even smaller than himself couldn't hurt him. Energetically, he kept scrabbling after his quarry, one paw then the other under the base board. Suddenly there was a soft crack and the board came away from the wall. A small dark hole loomed up ahead of him. A mouse hole? Maybe. Big enough for a kitten at any rate. As his eyes adjusted to the darkness, Foxy could just make out a dim glow at some little distance down the tunnel to—what? Another enclosure? And where had the spider disappeared to?

"I'll get you, you bugger!" declared the tiny kitten with determination. So saying, he wiggled into the small hollow tunnel.

"Well, my dear, what did you think of the Musicoon cats? Laura and Jane? I thought that big red boy of theirs, Midnight Sun, was quite handsome." She chuckled softly, still concentrating on her driving. "He all but glows in the dark." Seeing her friends' Maine Coons always brought a bit of cheer, no matter how down she might have been beforehand.

Wisteria kept her eyes on the roadway. There were very few straight ones in Yorkshire. This one was winding one way and another. Like a snake on uppers, Beth thought, and often it appeared to be tunneling through a narrow defile between towering vine-covered cliffs on both sides of them. She had been wondering how many eons it had taken some sort of river or wash to carve out this gorge in the earth. She turned her attention to her driver's comments.

"That big red classic *was* quite handsome—lovely muzzle, intense deep red," Beth mused into breederspeak, "but I was also taken with the cream and white mac, Flagship, from our American cattery Boundingmaines. I do enjoy seeing how our exports have turned out...And the brown classic from Katmea...

"Odd, that." Beth thought for a moment. "That there should be only two tabby patterns in Maine Coons: classic and mackerel... Somewhere along the line, you'd have thought more diversity would have shown up—unless you count the 'van' which is a pattern only now being recognized in the Coons." She laughed. "I guess you could call that a gift from the Turkish Van breeders, all of whose cats have just the head markings and the same color tail... No matter: the place was—as I expected—spotless. Lovely cats, Jane and Laura very friendly..." She grinned with fond remembrance. "But if I consume any more tea and scrumptious scones before we go home, I'm going to look like Colonel Blimp—and what would Chad think about *that?*"."

"Chad is no doubt thinking the same thing about himself up there in Scotland—after all that's the Land of the Scone—but I can't imagine him *fat* either...you're very lucky, Beth, that your husband is fond of cats, too. Game manager or not." As Wisteria spoke, the two woman laughed. Their visit having been quite pleasant and productive; it provoked much conversation as their journey meandered back to Cumbria. To cat breeders, their felines were a topic they never tired of. No matter what the country.

"Meorrrow!" came a comment from the back seat. *How come I didn't get any scones? Lar and Jane always share. What and where are we going anyway? There are more than enough bumps and swings along this tarmac. Making me dizzy, it is: I just-don't-need-all-this-aggravation!!*

Wisteria gave Beth a meaningful glance. "She sounds just like your Bhu Fan. I'd have thought cats didn't gripe so. But I certainly know complaints when I hear them."

"Yep," agreed Beth, smiling. "That little girl is *not* a happy camper." She turned in her seat to face the Pet Taxi secured on the seat behind her. A pristine white face with neon amber eyes peered back at her, her lynx tips making exclamation points above her head, as if to give emphasis to her displeasure.

Well? The cat said, plain as day. *How long am I going to be shut up here like some thievin' hamster?*

Beth reached out and poked her fingers through the metal latticed door of the carrier. The cat, unable to contain her curiosity, sniffed at them. *Catnip? Surely not!* Why did this ladyqueen's fingers smell of catnip? *Of course!* She licked her muzzle and sighed. *She brought some to the cattery. Lovely stuff, 'nip. I'd go anywhere for catnip...*

At this series of chirps and muttered trills, Beth giggled and turned back to Wisteria. She grew solemn then. "I feel so badly about Angel." She sighed, changed the subject and gazed again at the white queen on the back seat whose few markings were quite vivid. "One doesn't see many Maine Coon queens with that van pattern. But what a perfect red rosette she has on top of her head—and that fluffy red tail looks like it belongs to a fan dancer. You think this pretty little queen will perk up Star? She is totally unlike Angel."

"We can but hope," replied her seatmate. "I hadn't intended to mate Angel with Star but I did want different bloodlines from each of them to cross down the road." Wisteria paused. "I'm like you, love. I want no inbred cats. Linebred Maine Coons have suffered enough from that. Not so badly as purebred dogs but bad enough." She kept her eyes on the winding road as they turned northward onto the M6 motorway.

"Look at our poor English bulldogs. They've inbred them to such a huge grotesque shape that they not only can't mate naturally but all puppies have to be delivered by c-section. It's all very well for some people to like *ugly* or extreme—but not at the expense of an animal's health and well being."

She shook her head, silvery curls spinning around her face. "Well, anyway, this little girl's dam came from Amsterdam: Patchwork Cattery. And her sire is from Moonshine Cattery in Germany—"

"*Moonshine*—??" Beth interrupted, laughing. "Does she know—??"

"Oh, yes—she does *now* but she takes the unexpected American connection to your potent whiskey with good grace. And her lines, well, both cattery's lines, are not anywhere close to mine. So we should get lots of nice healthy kittens." Wisteria paused, "—that is, if she takes a shine to Star."

The driver giggled at what she had just said as she glanced in her rear view mirror at her new acquisition, who appeared to be listening closely to this conversation

. The young queen sniffed. *My family tree is quite internationally famous; you should know that. And just who is this Star tom? Is he famous in America? And just why should a world famous champion like me care anything about him anyway? Pfft! I was just enticing Middie and he certainly did glow like a Midnight Sun—*

"Let's hope she makes Star sit up and take notice," remarked Wisteria, unaware she was interrupting the van's tirade. "With their co-operation, we should get some quite lovely high white torties."

Beth nodded her head vigorously. "For me, birthing kittens is like Christmas morning. You just never know what feline genetics is going to give you: reds, blacks, browns, blues, silvers, cameos, whites—and any number of combinations thereof. Solids and tabbies. And of course, high white babies with orange, black and white are always the flashiest of all." Beth chewed on her lip thoughtfully. "You're so right, Wisteria, Star being solid black and this little girl red and white, well: that's the classic combination for high white tortoiseshells!"

Beth turned her attention once more to the lovely little queen on the back seat, her luxurious snowy white coat punctuated with the carmine rosette on her head and the same vivid red on her bushy tail. Starry would have to be hopelessly brain dead not to be enchanted by this awesome queen. Now what she'd think about *him* was another matter entirely—

"What are you going to name her?"

"Chrysanthemum," Wisteria said happily, "Chrysie for short."

CHAPTER EIGHTEEN

THE SMALL BLUE KITTEN, Foxy, oblivious to danger for the simple reason he'd never been exposed to any, came merrily out of the hole which was a very small drain through a storage closet on the back side of the cattery. Old farm houses such as Wisteria's had always had sheds and box rooms and such attached to them willy-nilly, in addition to a barn set close by. And the older they were, the more pockmarked such add-ons were with drains and holes and tunnels for small rodents, insects and simple erosion, even thorough Rose Cottage had been upgraded and remodeled to some extent as a cattery, with a lot of those small buildings torn down. Some of their hidey-holes, however, had survived unnoticed by human tenants busy with other things.

Foxy blinked in the bright light. All around him were roots and stems of the roses and other perennials which Wisteria cultivated next to the wilder enclosed cattery garden. Wisteria Cate took her name to heart as well; her namesake's vine, which was slowly encompassing the netted cat garden, sprang from a trunk thick as a young oak. It had been the first thing she had planted when she inherited her cottage and set up her cattery. The farmland around it had long since been sold off but her husband's parents had kept a large acreage of it surrounding the old farmstead. She was widowed by then, her one child having immigrated to New Zealand with her new husband; Donald's parents gone, too, and she needed something to focus on besides getting the cottage modernized and its thatch replaced. Having seen Maine Coons at a local cat show and fallen in love, she shortly set about the arduous task of learning to become a cat breeder. Wisteria did not, however, neglect her gardening. She set about designing one with rocks, terraces, raised herb beds and seeing its soil enriched and planted. It was this endeavor that had taken her to Fellshadow Farm for a load of fertilizing cattle manure.

If Paul Mellish hadn't loved cats, too, it's doubtful their friendship would have, well: blossomed. But that was the icebreaker, so to speak. From that beginning, it didn't take long for the two of them to discover similar tastes in books, music and, of course, gardens. That it might have become a more romantic relationship was thwarted by a crafty if infirm sister to Paul, who had been a disruptive influence in their family since she'd learned at the age of eight how to manipulate all manner of situations to keep her family at loggerheads. Power. Lavinia Mellish knew how to wield it to her own purpose—until she came up against Wisteria Cate, who neutralized her adversary's machinations by the simple expedient of ignoring her. This state of affairs might well have irritated and annoyed the spinsterish sister but at the same time, it did serve her purpose. Wisteria adroitly avoided letting the charming scholar/farmer get too close. She was not about to find herself locked up in a relationship that included the conniving Lavinia. But their friendship endured. By the time of the old girl's death (she was Paul's senior by 12 years) Wisteria felt herself a bit long in the tooth for anything that smacked of "dating", candy and flowers or, come to that: sleepovers. So there the matter rested. At least it did for her. How Paul might have felt about it, she had no idea.

The tiny four-footed explorer would have had no idea either about such matters of the heart. Or care. On this particular morning, all he knew was that the spider had led him into a whole new and enchanting world, wherever *he* might have gotten to. Foxy wandered the pebbled walkways between elevated beds of basil, thyme, rosemary and other assorted culinary enhancements, taking in everything around him. He played tag with a huge (to him) dragonfly. He batted at flower petals liberated from their bordering anchorage by an errant breeze. And like Peter Rabbit, when he came to a fence of willow wands, his curiosity about what might be on the other side lured him under and into another interesting and lively realm.

Whatever were those quick, grey, furry long-nosed varmints even smaller than he, with the skinny tails and rounded ears, creatures who scurried about, gathering up seed heads among the tall grasses bending almost to the ground, heavy with even more seed pods? Leaping forward, the curious kitten intended to find out.

Paul Mellish stood beside the drystone wall behind his barn. He'd been replacing a few flat rocks that a willful heifer had kicked loose. When he'd seen a large silhouette riding the thermals over the escarpment to the south, he galloped to the house and grabbed up his field glasses. He'd seen that shadow once before and he was debating with himself. Was it or was it not a sea eagle? Or a golden? Neither huge, rare raptor had been seen in these parts in more years than he could count. But it was too big, he surmised, to be a merlin or its like or anything else native to the fells. Mellish thought of himself as a "birdwatcher"—as opposed to being a "birder". The former title indicated an interest; the latter a dedication. Whatever his mates at the pub might call him, he wanted to identify that huge raptor all the same.

The shadow had disappeared over the fells by the time he got back to his station beside the wall. Paul's shoulders slumped in disappointment. Sighing, he lifted his binoculars one more time and scanned the cliff to that point where it stepped down toward his paddocks. Just in case he'd missed a nest up there amidst the outcroppings.

"*What*?" he mumbled out loud as he sharpened the focus on his field glasses, frowning as he did so.

Outlined against a sky gray with gathering dark pregnant clouds, he saw his old cat, Francis, sitting patiently on an outcropping about halfway down from the escarpment's highest point. "What is that old bugger doing up there? Francis rarely leaves the barn."

The man panned the escarpment again and caught sight of two other cats approaching his old silver tiger. Even more curious now, he steadied his glasses by bracing an elbow against a clothes line pole and shifting his weight. One of the cats, the leader, was a large, healthy looking—oh surely not—"It can't be: a *Scottish wildcat*?? I don't believe this!" He took down his glasses, scowled in bafflement and put them to his eyes again.

He studied the cat as closely as he could, intent on getting all the details firmly in his mind so he could tell his mate at the pub, Charlie Priest, who was an amateur naturalist, exactly what he'd seen. They had debated the possibilities once or twice of the wildcat venturing this far south as he felt the pressures of habitat destruction. Both men knew he was definitely an endangered species, with maybe only 400 left in the wild.

He frowned again as the second cat came into focus. A *Maine Coon*? What? What? Of course! He chortled in triumph. "It has to be! Wisteria's missing silver queen!"

Now smiling broadly to himself, Paul Mellish watched as the three cats appeared to be holding some kind of conference. Then the wild tom appeared to be saying farewell to the other two and trotted away from cliff's edge, quickly disappearing from sight. Francis got up, turned and headed down the narrow path toward home, the little silver queen dejectedly plodding along behind, head and tail low.

Paul lowered his glasses. Was it his imagination or did the two cats seem to part with regret? "I'm a hopeless romantic," he admonished himself. "Cats don't feel like that—do they?" He sighed, realizing he'd never really know. He shook off the fantasy.

"At least," he remarked to his audience, a pair of curious heifers peering at him over the wall, "I'll have good news for Wisteria and Beth when they come home from cruising the dales of Yorkshire."

Paul put away his binoculars, strode into his kitchen and, keeping watch out the back window that opened onto his garden, waited for Sir Francis to bring his ward home—which he knew the old boy would surely do. As he watched and waited he minced some leftover chicken, added a dollop of cream and upon seeing the cats enter the barn, scooped some of his offerings into a bowl and went out to greet them.

Francis, seeing Old Woolly Socks, called a greeting and ambled forward down the barn breezeway. Angel, whose mind had been distracted all the way down that path she felt fit only for goats, looked up at the brawny farmer and stopped in her tracks, poised for flight.

"It's all right, Angel, I mean you no harm." Paul spoke softly and stood quite still, slowly lowering himself to his knees, certain he'd look less threatening that way, no matter his creaking joints.

He knows my name? Queried the silver torbie, looking in Sir Francis' direction, the tip of her tail twitching.

Oh, yes, Mistress. Old Woolly Socks is a great friend of Wisty's and your Bethmom. He is very kind. No need to be afraid of him.

Paul, still squatting, extended his fingers, his face giving nothing away. Within himself, though, he was appalled at the young queen's condition. Her coat was clumpy and bound up with burrs and sticks. Her tail, well, her tail probably added a stone to her weight; ah, "pounds" they call it in America...Whatever the extra weight, it was a very over-used feather duster burdened with all kinds of seed pods and forest detritus.

Slowly gathering confidence, Angel moved toward the mantom and sniffed his extended fingers. She gazed up at his face and cocked her head. He did have a kindly look to him. This mantom was certainly not like that scrawny scut who had smothered her in that blanket. She rubbed herself against his bent knees. She was, after all, a Maine Coon; conditioned to laid-back friendliness. And Sir Francis *had* vouched for him. Carefully, he picked her up and headed for his kitchen.

"Angel, poppet, we can't let Wisteria and Beth see you like this. You need a proper bath before I invite them to tea."

Angel gazed up at Paul Mellish and slowly relaxed. She had almost forgotten how pleasant it was to be cosseted and unafraid. Her rumbling purrs alerted everybody behind them as they left the barnyard, bringing forth big smiles among Fellshadow's felines.

Sir Francis smiled after the departing pair and winked at Lady Lucy, who had stuck her head out of her stall, her curiosity aroused. Satisfied that he'd done right by his lord of the forest, the old silver shaman stuck his nose into the bowl of creamed chicken Old Woolly Socks had put down for him and sighed. Virtue does have its rewards. And, tom howdy, as Hawkeye would have said, he had a good (if cautionary) tale to tell Lady Lucy's kitlings.

Paul filled the ancient stone sink in the kitchen with warm water and got out the tools he used to clean his sheep fleece and, occasionally, his cats. He put her bowl of creamed chicken in front of the little silver torbie and while she nibbled ravenously, he untangled her knots and combed out the sticks and nettles. It was slow going; he didn't want her to back off should he hurt her, tugging at her coat. The man, sensitive as he was to the animals he lived with, had no doubt she'd been through a traumatic ordeal and greatly in need of a bit of tasty nourishment, readjustment—and much TLC.

The young queen looked up at her hairdresser and licked the cream from her whiskers, gratitude plain in her eyes—or so Paul liked to think. As he watched her, he continued to get all his bathing equipment assembled, talking nonsense in a soft voice as he did so.

Having accomplished this, he checked the temperature of the water in the sink and gently inserted Angel, not at all sure how she'd react. But this cat was a veteran of the show halls where pre-show bathing was *de rigueur*. For a fastidious feline who'd spent many days with few opportunities to sit and perform her toilette, the warm sudsy water was cat heaven. Never mind the old wives tale about cats hating water. What Angel *didn't* like was the *cold* wet, like frigid rain and icy streams with all kinds of unknown snares on their rocky and often sharp, slick bottoms. At this moment, she luxuriated in the warm suds and relaxed to Paul Mellish's gentle fingers massaging her torn coat. She'd think about Lord Derryth when she retired for the night, hopefully curled up on a warm and fleecy sheepskin like the ones she'd seen in the barn.

After a series of warm rinses and all kinds of questions from her groomer that she of course couldn't answer (although she did like the sound of his deep voice), Angel went happily limp as Paul wrapped her in a towel and rubbed her dry, her eyes shut, a smile on her face.

"There. Now, M'lady, you look like a proper queen ready for your court."

Mellish stepped back to admire his handiwork. She really did look more like a Maine Coon now. A few snagged patches left her coat a bit uneven but on the whole, it had fluffed out very nicely. Getting some meat on her bones would take a little longer. Running a comb through her fluffy tail, he gave her a bit more chicken, after which he deposited her on a fleecy cushion in the sitting room. Seeing her settle down, he smiled to himself and went out to tend to his farm chores. It was growing late. Certain that Wisteria and Beth would not have returned yet from Barnsley in South Yorkshire, he'd call Wisteria in the morning. There was no hurry now. Angel was safe. He thought it would be a nice surprise for them.

As he leaned his manure fork against one wall of the barn and started back toward the house through the breezeway, he paused to check on Lady Lucy and her kittens. Sticking his head into the old stall where her nest box sat, he saw to his surprise, the whole tribe gathered there. He almost laughed out loud. Sir Francis was sitting in the middle of a circle of cats and kittens, all of whom he'd swear had been listening to the old boy tell them about his trek to the top of the escarpment and back. Shaking his head in delight, he headed on toward the house in the gathering dusk. "Now I *know* I'm a hopeless romantic." But he was grinning to himself all the same.

Having returned to Rose Cottage where they deposited Chrysie into her new quarters, the women, retreating to the house, had fallen, tired and happy, into the two comfortable easy chairs in Wisteria's sitting room. They sat in companionable silence for awhile. Beth gazed at the mesmerizing landscape over the fireplace, trying to imagine how the Castle Rigg stone circle would look transplanted to the crest of the hill on Siberia Farm where the littlest Viking had been laid to rest. Somehow, she felt strongly, the two would have gone together... Her hostess, her lips pursed, appeared to be in deep thought as well.

"You know, Beth," she ventured," I'll wager that Paul would give you one of Lady Lucy's little blue males—I'm thinking of the blue boy with that very thick and plush coat—to take home with you. The litter is old enough to leave now...Both Lady Lucy and Tatty Bumpkin are registered Coons and I think the little chap might give you more genetic diversity—and if he passes that lovely coat on to his offspring, I think it would be a real plus for showable kittens. What do you think?"

Beth Merryman, coming out of her fantasy, cocked her head and was silent for a few minutes. "It is a lovely litter—and that one little guy is so fuzzy, he looks like a child's teddy bear. I'd love to have him." She frowned. "But I'd rather buy him than accept a gift from Paul. I don't like to take advantage."

"Oh, he wouldn't think that. He's a lovely man, Paul is. Look on it as a wedding present." Wisteria beamed widely.

Beth nodded her head in agreement. "I really liked him—and he's single, isn't he?" She sent a sly look in Wisteria's direction.

Her hostess rolled her eyes heavenward, fidgeted and ignored the question.

"I daresay the cattery chores can wait until tomorrow. All seemed to be well when we took Chrysie out there. Let's have a quick bite and go to bed, shall we? I'm a bit tired after that long drive and I know you must be as well... Chad home in the morning?"

"Supposedly," Beth smiled, "if the beavers don't decide to 'move house.'"

CHAPTER NINETEEN

OXY WASN'T SURE WHY the mice didn't want to play with him. Whenever he approached them, they scurried away. No matter. There were butterflies and waving wands of tall grasses to amuse him. Birds tumbled through the air and sang from distant perches. Things were *so interesting* out here! The kitten jumped and scampered among thickets of wild herbs and heather.

But then his stomach began to rumble. A bit tired by now, he wanted to curl up and take a nap. Only there was no fleecy place to sleep—all he saw besides grass and weeds were a few piled up rocks. And there was no mum to feed him. Foxy began to doubt the wisdom of leaving the cattery. *I think*, he said to himself, watching a very large flyer overhead, *I better go home*.

He turned around. And turned once again. Which way was home? He looked up. For some reason, deep in his bones, he knew that bird hovering overhead meant him no good. He looked around again. All the mice had gone to ground. Foxy checked on the bird again. It was large, very black with sharp beady eyes and a terrible beak. Time to hide! But where? Nothing in the kitten's cosseted experience had prepared him for this sort of scary situation. Now he began to be very afraid. The raven had him pinpointed. That pile of rocks beside the path. Could he squeeze in there? Just as the big bird swooped, Foxy scuttled into a small aperture in the stone pile. There was just enough room for him to turn around and back away from the opening. Just out of reach of that probing beak. He listened to the raucous cries of frustration as the raven tried to get at him. The small kitten knew enough not to move. Finally, the big corvid gave up and, still muttering to himself, flapped away.

The awful rapid beating of his heart slowed. Foxy waited. Something instinctive told him to wait, to stay where he was. He realized the day was drawing to a close. Hungry as he was, he slept. Tomorrow, he was sure, he'd find his way home.

Bhu Fan and Hawkeye were having a leisurely wash when the little Korat realized that Violet was pacing up and down at the front of her enclosure in a very agitated manner on the far side of the room, muttering to herself. She strolled over to the blue queen. "Is something troubling you, mistress?"

"Foxy is gone!" she cried. "I can't find him anywhere!"

"When was this, Mistress Violet?"

"This morning. I left the kitlings to nap in the sun outside and when I came back in to tend them, he was gone. I can't find him anywhere...I'm so afraid!" Hawkeye peered upward at the latch on Violet's door as Bhu Fan climbed the screen to get a better look into Violet's boudoir, as she called it. "I see something, Hawk. Open door."

The big brown tabby did as he was bid, frowning wryly to himself as it seemed he was always Bhu Fan's lackey. Well, not really. He knew who the brain in the family was. Pulling down the latch wasn't even a real stretch for a Coon some four feet tall with extra toes. On his hind legs, that is.

The two cats tumbled into the room, Bhu making a bee-line for the back corner. She put her head down to where the end of the baseboard had come away from the wall. The anomaly wasn't visible from any distance but when approached obliquely, its hidey-hole was evident. The three cats gathered there and peered into the dark little tunnel. Violet called out frantically to her missing kit. Silence. Bhu Fan, who was the smallest of the three, stretched out flat on her stomach, peering intently into the hole. There was no shadow against the distant glow of light. She stood up and looked at Hawk and Violet.

"We must get outside, Hawkeye, where hole is at other end." She looked at Violet. "You stay here, Mistress, and tend Gentian and Lobelia. We'll find Foxglove." She sighed and shook her head. "Little toms. They just will let their curiosity get the better of them."

Bhu Fan looked at Hawkeye. "Well, what are you waiting for, peasant? Get us out of here."

The big brown neuter blinked, turned and headed back into the common room, the little blue Korat on his heels. He knew there was a cat flap into the cattery garden. But judging where the garden was in relation to Violet's outdoor run and the mouse hole, Hawkeye knew that wasn't the way he needed to go. He prowled the common room. Nobody paid him any mind. They were all intent on watching dust motes as late afternoon sunlight streamed through the windows.

There was the door to the front of the cattery through which most visitors and kitten buyers came. There was a door to a storage closet where supplies were kept. There was a door on the far side of the building that led to Wisteria's cottage. Parsing all this out, with Boo poised beside him, it was this door to which he trotted. Reaching up, a paw on each side of the knob, he turned it easily. The door slowly swung open and the two cats found themselves on the flagstone path to Rose Cottage and, to their right, a way through Wisteria's garden along the outside wall of the cattery.

It was this direction Bhu Fan took, her head raised, turning back and forth, peering in all directions. Hawkeye pushed the door closed and followed his leader.

"Blast!" cried Bhu. Where the small tunnel exited, there was no sign of an errant kitten.

Hawk, momentarily amused at the expression she'd already picked up from Freddie, gazed about. The empty garden was bordered on the far end with a fence of willow wands. "Well, there's no help for it," Bhu grumbled and with Hawkeye beside her, the two trotted to the back of the flower beds and leaped over the latticed fencing.

"Bast Bespoke, Boo," exclaimed Hawkeye as they landed on the other side. "That kitten could be anywhere!" His heart sank as he looked around him. Before the two of them, the open meadow seemed to stretch for miles. To Hawk's left, the land appeared to slowly rise upward like a bread loaf with too much yeast, the fell's shoulders striped with tall trees in its declivities. To his right, past where Bhu stood silently with just the tip of her tail moving, the meadowlands sloped down to a roadway beyond which the lake placidly waited. The landscape appeared as empty as the mountains of the moon.

"I say, Wisteria, can you and your visitors possibly come for lunch? I've a largish pork pie in the oven and it's much too much for me to eat alone...Chad has retuned from Scotland, has he? That's good. There's certainly a feast here...besides, I've something here I'd like to show you." He paused a moment, listening. "—Oh, certainly. I think that little boy blue of Lady Lucy's is old enough to leave the nest...It would be my pleasure." He paused, "I thought I'd name him Fellshadow Centurion...Yes, yes—I got the idea from your misadventure up on the pass at that old Roman pile." The man chuckled as he added, "I could hardly call him after some crusty old coins, could I? I mean, a kitten named *Denarii*?? But the fellows from whom they might have been taken, I thought, would serve very well. After all that was 2000 years ago—I can hardly bear them any malice now." He paused and laughed quite merrily. "I'd be quite chuffed to have one of my Coon cats in America."

He put down the phone and looking around, realized he'd better get busy and do a bit of housecleaning if he was going to have company. It wouldn't do for Wisteria to find him a sloppy housekeeper. He grinned at his feline visitor who was curled up asleep on the fleecy window seat and set to it.

Having put off their cattery chores until they should return home to Rose Cottage from Fellshadow Farm, Wisteria and her company set off for the Hawkshead ferry and the North. Now more at ease with Cumbrian fells and curious roadways, Beth relaxed, ignoring the twists and turns and frequent pauses to let other vehicles pass. Chad brought them up to date on the suspenseful reintroduction of beavers into new habitat in the highlands, which passed the time pleasantly enough until they arrived at Paul's plain-Jane of a farmhouse. The game warden's work was done now; he and Beth could spend their remaining time wandering about the Lake District, enjoying pub nights with Paul and Wisteria and getting their feline cadre ready to return home.

As they got out of the car in front of Fellshadow Farm, Chad rubbed his wife's shoulder, "Would you like to go back by way of Hardknott Pass—and look for some more coins?" He looked slyly at Wisteria—"if we've enough gas?"

The three of them were laughing as their host came out the door to greet them, Tatty Bumpkin in the lead, bounding down the flagstones. When Paul looked a question, Chad repeated his conversation to the ladies about Hardknott Pass.

Paul grinned ruefully, his hands deep in his pockets. "Officialdom is giving me a real headache about the coins you lot dug up. Now they're talking about moving me off my farm and doing a dig up there." He waved his hands, "but no matter. It'll be years before they make a move. Come, no need for those blighters to ruin our lunch."

Wisteria scooped up Tatty Bumpkin as they strolled along and gave his head a kiss as Paul ushered his three visitors into a sitting room replete with bookcases from floor to ceiling, an oil painting over the fireplace mantle of some eerie Scottish castle—and their host grinning like the Cheshire cat. As they set about sorting themselves out and getting seated, Beth did a double take and sucked in her breath. Her eyes wide, she lit up like a moon rocket, her hands moving quickly to her face in disbelief.

"Oh, my sainted Aunt Agatha! *Angel!*"

As Wisteria spun around, the silver torbie stood up and stretched on the window seat where she'd been napping after a bit more chicken with cream.

"Rhiow!" she called in turn, as she hopped down and trotted up to the visitors. Holding back and grinning broadly, Beth was all but bouncing on her toes. A thunderstruck Wisteria released Tatty Bumpkin and scooped up Angel. Holding her close under her chin, Wisteria's smile as she faced her old friend, would have dazzled the sun. She spoke to Mellish as Chad clapped him on the shoulder.

"Wherever did you find her, Paul?" The woman was running her fingers through Angel's now silky pelt. "I know she didn't look like this when you found her! Not coming off the fells…" prattling away; anything to damp down her emotions, Wisteria fairly glowed with happiness as did Beth Merryman behind her. Paul Mellish was thoroughly gratified. Like Sir Francis, he felt virtue really did have its own rewards. He wanted to grab up Wisteria and hug her, cat and all.

"Miracles really do happen, don't they?" she added, tears running down her cheeks. She brushed them away with her free hand and beamed again at Paul, waiting for an explanation.

"Well," he admitted, seeing the fond look on Wisteria's happy face beamed at him. He couldn't help himself. He blushed and thrust his hands deep in his pockets.

"it's a long story, love."

Bhu Fan and Hawkeye returned to the cattery from their hunt to find, to their surprise, a newcomer sitting relaxed in the middle of the common room holding court. However, they ignored her for the moment. They needed to speak to Violet. And that didn't go well. Poor Violet was beside herself with concern for her missing offspring.

"We'll find him," Bhu Fan assured her." I think he's out there in meadow somewhere. And now it's dark, I have an idea he's curled up in a rock cave sound asleep. It would be natural," she added as

Hawkeye shot her a look, "for him to do so." It didn't take a seer, her response to Hawkeye indicated, to figure *that* out. "Hawk and I will go out again at daybreak and hunt for him." Bhu Fan looked a question at the agitated queen. "Do you know anything about mantoms who live in that house on far side of meadow?"

Violet paused in her pacing. "No, I can't say I do. Wisteria meets with them sometimes but from what Freddie has said in the past, they're more fond of dogs than felines."

"Dogs?" Bhu Fan exclaimed, trying to keep fearfulness out of her voice. "Do you know what kinds of dogs? I mean are they little yappy dogs or big hunting dogs?"

"Oh, they're big dogs. Their mantoms have brought them along the meadows sometimes. I've seen them out there, walking along through the tall grass." Violet didn't need Bhu's questions to alarm her; she'd already cottoned onto what she was inferring. Her eyes grew round and large. "They're great big shaggy yellow dogs with long bushy tails…but, but, I've never seen them that they weren't on a string with their mantoms on the other end." Violet almost cried. "You don't think—"

Hawkeye hastened to calm the blue mantled queen. "Don't go there!" he admonished. "Don't think the worst, Violet. If the dogs are always leashed, they're not likely to harm Foxy—and if," he added, hoping it would ease the momcat, "their mantoms walk them, they may find the little guy and bring him home." A sudden thought struck him. "And as soon as Catemom realizes in the morning that the little guy is missing, I'm sure she'll call her neighbors and set them about looking for him, too." The big brown tabby sucked in his breath as Bhu Fan echoed his sentiments.

Violet nodded her head and tearfully returned to her nest box, Gentian and Lobelia peering out of its opening. It wouldn't do to alarm them as well. She curled up around her two kitlings and tried to force herself to relax. Tomorrow couldn't come too soon.

Hawkeye and Bhu Fan exchanged a glance and without speaking, turned and strolled over to the group in front of Freddie's enclosure where he, Star and a couple of Wisteria's half grown kits were clustered around the newcomer. And what a newcomer she was! Hawkeye thought to himself. He sneaked a furtive look at Star. The young black tom, it would seem, was speechless with enchantment. Hawk grinned and glanced at Bhu Fan. "Well, at least, *there's* one thing to the good," he whispered. Bhu Fan smiled slowly at this and stretched out close to Freddie. She'd interrogate the big black and white tom when this snowy white and red van had taken herself off somewhere else. And Star she'd speak to as well—when he could find his voice again.

In the meantime, she would find out what the young queen had to say for herself. "And you are—?" she asked, trying to keep her natural hauteur out of her voice. Bhu was, after all, not on her own ground. And for some reason, this queen appeared to be, well, formidable.

The newcomer turned her limpid gaze on the sleek blue Korat. 'My name is Chrysanthemum. I came from Musicoons in Yorkshire. Your Wistymom brought me here today." She lowered her eyes. "They've been telling me about you." She looked up at Bhu Fan and gave her a catly curtsy. "You're Princess Bhu Fan, aren't you? Visiting here from America?

"I'd love to hear all about what it's like to be a royal princess; feline, that is. Our human royals certainly seem to make a good thing of it." She lowered her eyes again. "That is…if you don't mind my asking."

Bhu Fan swelled up with pride, momentarily brushing little Foxy's plight from her mind. Hawkeye and Freddie exchanged a glance and hid their own smiles. Star came out of his trance long enough to shake his head. Maybe staying at CumbriaCoons wasn't going to be so bad after all. Any cat who could put Bhu Fan on her mettle was his kind of girl.

CHAPTER TWENTY

I T WAS A CHEERFUL trio who brought Angel into the cattery that afternoon and set her down among the cats gathered there. The silver torbie queen herself seemed to be glad at long last to be home. Freddie paced his doorway screen, calling out his greetings. Beth smiled at this homecoming as Chad left to go finish writing up his final notes and begin their packing for their homeward journey. Wisteria puttered about doing her long overdue cattery chores, crooning to her cats as she did so.

Beth stood in the middle of the common room, her smile slowly turning into a frown. Something was out of sync. She looked around, her uneasiness growing. Where were Hawkeye and Bhu Fan? She stood there and circled in place. Her two cats were just not there and had they been, she was sure, they would be nose to nose with Angel. Further, the blue and white queen, Violet, was also pacing up and down, very vocal, her two kittens in a clump behind her. Beth bit her lip. Violet's *two* kittens?

She walked over to Violet's enclosure as the nervous queen looked up at her in a pleading sort of way. The door, while closed, was not latched. She stepped inside.

"Wisteria—"

Her friend looked up immediately from where she was scooping Freddie's litter tray. Something in Beth's voice brought her quickly into Violet's quarters.

"What's wrong, love?"

"Doesn't Violet have three kittens?"

"Um, um, yes, certainly." Wisteria dropped her scoop in the bucket she was carrying and scanned the long narrow room carefully. Two kittens were all she saw. "Lobelia and Gentian…Foxglove is missing. Oh, dear me, where has that little scrap gotten to? What *is* this: run-away-from-home week??"

Beth gazed levelly at her friend, trying to calm herself. Kittens are always at risk—given their total lack of prudence. "Hawk and Bhu Fan are missing also."

She prowled around the room and quickly, from human height, spotted the warped baseboard. Silently, she knelt beside it, reached out and pulled it forward to where she could get a closer view of what was—and wasn't—behind it.

"I don't think we need Sherlock Holmes to figure this one out—" She peered up at Wisteria, who had come to stand behind her.

"I found Violet's door off the latch, although she and her two babies were inside. But there's something else."

Wisteria looked a question, her alarm growing.

"Hawk and Bhu, that pair of feline magicians: Hawk can open doors as well as we can. Bhu is about the nosiest cat on the planet. And I know sure as I'm standing here that cats talk to each other." She sucked in a breath. "I'll bet you anything you care to name that Foxglove went out that hole…because if there's trouble, kittens will surely find it…and when Violet realized he was missing, well, somehow, some way, she sent that intrepid duo of mine looking for him."

Wisteria stood there nodding her head, her lips tight. "Having seen that pair in action, I'd certainly attest to that." Wisteria squatted down, looked at the hole and then stood up again peering out the window on the back wall over Violet's cat flap to her outside run. "Let's go outside and see if we can find where that little tunnel opens up." She added in self-disgust, "I had no idea there was a hole like that in Violet's flat." The woman threw up her hands in despair. "I don't *need* this all over again! How have I come to be so careless? What is wrong with me???"

Beth attempted to calm her friend. She leaned over and hugged her shoulder. "Wisteria, dear heart, things happen. Particularly with cats. The truth of it is they-just-don't-mind-well. C'mon, let's go outside and see if we can figure out where they went."

Seeing Angel in front of Freddie's quarters where the two of them were evidently bringing each other up to date, Beth stopped in her tracks. "Uh, oh," she muttered. The two women left the cattery, carefully latching Violet's room as they went.

"What?" Wisteria asked, still in a dither, as the cattery door closed behind them.

"Starry's not here either." Beth shook her head. *What could possibly go wrong next?*

Wisteria let out a breath explosively. "What am I going to have to do, Beth, hire out that boy as a private eye? Or put a collar on him with a GPS unit on it? Come to that, maybe I should just take up golf and forget about cats..."

Beth Merryman smiled in spite of herself. "I'd say either might not be a bad idea—for somebody else...but a set of stud quarters with a stout padlock on the door might do in the meantime."

She followed Wisteria out into her garden. The two of them stood still for a long moment, looking sharply in all directions, calling out the names of the missing. Nothing. Wherever the cats were, it wasn't among the roses, foxglove, delphinium, lupine, hortensia and borders of bright blue lobelia. Beth couldn't resist naming them off as she hunted. If she could only grow flowers like this at home! She brought her wandering attention back to bear on their lost cats. So much was happening that her concentration was splintering in all directions.

Nevertheless, they searched carefully among all the raised beds and borders, coming at last to the back fence of woven willow wands and gazed out over the meadow. As Wisteria raised one hand to shade her eyes, Beth cried, "Look!" and reached out her hand to the top of one of the stakes to which the willow was attached. A tuft of white hair was caught there. She pulled it away from its snare. "Sure as God made little brown meerkats, this came from one of Hawkeye's big hairy white paws."

"Um, yes, I do believe you're right." Wisteria turned and faced Beth. "But Foxglove certainly couldn't jump that high."

"At eight weeks of age? No, he can't, but I wouldn't be surprised if he pulled a Peter Rabbit on us."

She squatted down and parted a tangle of sweet peas gracing the fence. "Uh, huh," she exclaimed, "this hole is certainly big enough for that little devil to squeeze through." She stood up and sighed, scanning the landscape.

"That little rascal went chasing after some will-o'-the-wisp right out into the meadow and then couldn't figure out how to get home. Hawk and Star and Bhu Fan have gone looking for him—I'd bet on it." She smacked her hands together for emphasis.

"How in the world, Beth, could they know to *do* that? Without us directing them like we did up on the fells when we were hunting Angel?"

"If I knew that, my fortune would be made." Beth paused and then turned on her heel. "I'm going to go get Chad. The more searchers the better."

Shere Khan had never been a cat to be confined. One way or another, he had always escaped any confinement, no matter how comfortable. Unless of course, it was a matter of his own choosing. Like his recent stint as headmaster of the Merry Maines gaggle at Chad's camp. But Gaston had taken over that chore, along with Martha, so The Great One felt it no dereliction of duty to sneak out of Bethmom's cattery to check on things now that everybody was back in their usual haunts. If his thumbs be furry, it was no matter. He still felt them pricking.

There was great unrest and apprehension among the felines, both homed and feral, of Penobscot County. Even Riddle, the monarch of Singletary Farm's pride, had heard whisperings of it. When he'd visited Shere Khan's charges at Chad's camp, he'd warned Khan, Smudge and Sweeper about it as Wulf had gone home with Cheryl. Sweeper had not been particularly distressed. Even though he'd been gravely injured in their escape from the New York City gang of thieves, he'd led too sheltered a life to be wary of humankind.

Smudge, on the other hand, pressed Riddle for everything he knew about untoward incidents out there which were proving so great a danger to the countryside's feline population. Deaths and disappearances. Smudge had seen a great deal more of mantoms' cruelty and indifference than any other member of the clan. When Shere Khan discussed the facts with him, Smudge confessed he felt the pricking of his thumbs as well, never mind his were a normal complement of feline digits.

When Khan managed to sneak out of the cattery while Martha was going about her chores, Smudge was right behind him. Khan merely looked over his shoulder and smiled. If he couldn't have Hawkeye as his lieutenant, Smudge would do very well. The two of them trotted across the pasture past the cedar swamp (where Shaggy, the bull moose, was dining at his ease) and through Ketler's orchard. From there, it was some little distance across the secondary road to Schultzburg not far from Muller's barn.

"Where we headed, Khan?"

"Miz Yoder's store. If there's any information to be had, that's where we'll hear it." Khan paused to peer all around, the tip of his tail making lazy circles. He sniffed the air. Beside him, the old street cat frowned. They had reached a vacant lot next to where an empty house sat back from an old gravel road, the big yard around it awash in tall grass, weeds and scraggly saplings. Light traffic on a nearby highway to the interstate cornered it with more abandoned buildings. A loud reverberating crack! rent the air and echoed away in the distance.

"I don't like the sound of that!" cried Smudge. 'I know gunfire when I hear it." The big white cat, a silver striped saddle across his back and the top of his head like a baseball cap on backwards, reared up on his hind legs and leaped to the top of an ancient automobile hood, a rusted-out, tireless coupe in the tall grass beside them, Shere Khan right behind him.

The empty farmhouse close by stood boarded up, forlorn and forgotten, no doubt the long-ago residence of that antique Dodge coupe's owners. In the distance, they saw a mantom running, rifle in hand. He leaped into a vehicle that roared into life. But then the vehicle suddenly stopped and the rifle poked out the passenger side window. The two cats crouched down and looked at each other.

"What do you think he was shooting at? It's not moose season, is it, Khan?"

"No," Shere Khan replied, his interest drawn somewhere else. He'd seen something moving toward them in the weedy grass. "No hunting season's open right now."

The wily old tom suddenly flattened himself and slid down under the crumpled fender of the canted car body. "Down, Smudge! Make yourself scarce!"

The old street cat didn't need any further warning. He'd dodged more than one bullet in his time. That noisy vehicle was now coming down a dirt track in their direction. The two of them watched warily from behind the wheel rim of their hiding place.

The old jeep, its paint spattered with mud, its fenders caked with more, slowed. A passenger, gun at the ready, peered from the interior. Occasionally he made comments to his driver, although Khan could not make out the words. It was enough, though, that the old tom recognized him.

"Styles!" he whispered. "Bastet help us all!"

"Who?"

"The poacher trapper. Remember that day at the beaver pond?"

Smudge growled in his throat. "I do indeed."

As they watched, the mantom swiveled the gun, it would seem, right at them. A feline voice cried out. "Khan!"

The gun exploded. A muffled howl of pain ensued.

"Got him!" yelled Styles and turned to his driver. "That's two we've got rid of this morning." Laughing derisively, he added, "Let's go the hell out and go get some coffee."

With that, the vehicle picked up speed and shot down the road out of sight trailing dust behind it.

Smudge and Khan were on their feet immediately and out from under the old derelict vehicle.

"Who called you, Khan?"

"Ah So," he replied. "I'd know that raucous rusty-hinge of an Oriental voice anywhere."

"Ah So?"

"A Siamese. Belongs to Miz Chase at the motel. Old acquaintance."

By now, Shere Khan was searching the tall grass around them in a rush, quartering back and forth.

"Here he is!" Smudge called as he'd nosed into a patch of weeds behind their hiding place.

Shere Khan was there in an instant.

Ah So lay on the ground, his eyes closed, blood seeping from a wound in his hind leg. Shere Khan touched his nose gently.

The big Siamese opened his eyes. His breathing was labored, his pain obviously intense. But he hadn't lost his wits.

"I was coming to warn you, Khan. That dogdung got Gandy just now...We were hunting mice out behind that old house." The big cat closed his eyes, his pain now more of regret. "Killed him dead. And it looked like—" He faltered—"Styles. Looked like he was headed your way. I saw you on the hood of that old car."

"Just lay still, old friend. Smudge will stay with you. I'll go get Miz Chase."

What sounded like a cross between a cough and a laugh emanated from the big cat lying in front of them. "Now how you gonna do that, Khan?" The dun-colored neuter with the chocolate brown mask wheezed, trying to get to his feet.

"She'll understand well enough, Ah So." With that, he quickly jerked the Siamese's collar right over his head before he collapsed back on the ground in a heap. "Don't you move...Smudge, sit on the old rascal if you have to."

The street cat nodded and gave the old Siamese a lick across his jaw. "I'll stun him with my war stories."

Khan laughed in spite of himself, picked up Ah So's collar in his teeth and took off past the deserted clapboard house at a gallop. The motel, he knew, wasn't far. Everything, though, depended on how busy Miz Chase might be with customers or her cleaning crew. And he had to cross a busy highway to get there. Shortly, he skidded to a stop, looked in both directions and seeing no speeding cars close enough to delay him, skittered across the road, bushy tail streaming behind him.

He prayed she'd be outside supervising her maids. It was that time of day certainly. If she was in the motel office, that would be bad news. It would take more time than he felt Ah So *had* to get at her if he had to wait for some tourist to open that heavy door for him. Khan tried not to think about his nephew, Gandy. He'd had no idea the two cats were in that field hunting. But Bastet willing, he'd get help in time for Ah So.

Luck was with him. Miz Chase was walking down the row of motel rooms, her cell phone to her ear, a concerned look on her face as Shere Khan barreled up to her. Upon seeing the big Coon, the woman quickened her pace, put her cell phone in her pocket and quickly, knelt down in front of him.

"Eeeeow!" he cried through clinched teeth and dropped Ah So's collar at her feet.

Foxy stood up, stretched and looked out from his makeshift lair in the tall grass. He scanned the sky. No ravens in sight. "Mee-Ooow!" he cried, "Where are you, mum? I want to come hooommme!"

No reassuring reply came from Violet. Only the sound of wind and distant bird chatter. The small kitten picked his way through the grass, not an easy task for one who weighed no more than a big ball of yarn.

Presently, fortune smiled on him. Or so he thought. A puddle appeared before him. A groundwater seep probably. A drink might fool his empty stomach. He approached warily, put down his head and lapped at the clear water. Something jiggled in the puddle. He drew back in alarm.

No! Not *in* the water. *Over* the water. The reflection of a very large round-faced, silent-feathered bird with huge claws was coming straight at him. Crying in fright, he tried to run away but there was no cover. The air gusted around him.

Suddenly, the puddle erupted in splashes of water flying in all directions and the plummeting owl was both very wet and stuck, its talons having penetrated deep into the soft mud at the bottom of the puddle. And it had no prey for its pains. For once, the distortion of the reflective water's surface misled its remarkable eyesight and it missed its target. The big raptor swiveled its head, its malevolent glare catching sight of the tiny feline crouched in the thick grass, ignoring the mud that gave his face a raccoon's mask. The white-faced barn owl struggled to get up. Just as it appeared to have succeeded, spewing water and mud everywhere, its eyes targeted on Foxy, a loud bark and a deep growl drew its attention in another direction.

A huge dog, shaggy golden coat dancing around it, leaped forward, snapping playfully at the raptor. The owl, renewing its efforts to get safely airborne, now became the hunted instead of the hunter. With great effort, it managed to flap up out of the dog's reach and fly away, calling down dire imprecations on its attacker as it went.

Foxy, having witnessed this uneven encounter, sat hunched in the weeds, frozen with fascination. The kitten had never seen a dog in all his short life, but somehow, he didn't fear it either. Once again, he simply waited. What to do?

The big canine, feathery tail wagging joyously as the owl flew away, sat down, looked at the puddle, took a few laps and only then spotted Foxy. With a happy leap, he shook his head, got to his feet and brought his huge nose down to the level of the kitten and paused, sniffing loudly.

Before Foxy could react, he found himself picked up in a very slobbery but soft mouth and carried away.

"Mum!" he cried. But in vain.

CHAPTER TWENTY-ONE

A S THEY STOOD MOTIONLESS behind Wisteria's garden in the open meadow, Chad, the tallest of the three, spotted Hawkeye first. He was leaping up and down, bounding as he was over the tall grass to have a better chance at spotting anything so small as a kitten. He could hear chatter among the three cats, although he could not see Star and Bhu Fan. But it was a relief to know that those three, at least, had not gotten all that far away. He clapped his hands loudly and shouted to get their attention.

"Hawk! You fat rascal, get your butt over here!"

Wisteria and Beth, who had spread out perhaps some fifty feet to either side of the game warden, stopped dead at the sound of his call. And then they, too, gave a sigh of relief. There was much movement and thrashing around in front of them. Two other heads popped up from the tall grass at the sound of Chad's voice, looked toward their humans and came loping like gazelles toward them. But Hawk stood his ground. He did, however, rear up on his hind legs and roar.

"Rhiooow!" The big neuter hollered at the top of his lungs. *Over here!*

Chad's relief was short lived as he came up to where Hawkeye was standing. He looked carefully at the ground and then he glanced at Beth and Wisteria as they converged on him. Beth bent down to pick up Bhu Fan while Star twined around her feet, complaining loudly. *We can't find him, Bethmom. That tiny blue devil has disappeared.* "Rhiooow!" The little Korat clung to her shoulder dejected, breathing hard. Star's posture indicated he didn't feel much better. Wisteria hefted him and the two women moved to where Chad was motioning to them.

Hawkeye had found the puddle, now almost dried up, having been emptied by the unintentional swan dive of the swooping barn owl, whose feathers were scattered about here and there, in the mud and stuck on tall grass stems, waving in the breeze. The raptor's talons had also left their marks in the soft ground. Beth scowled while Wisteria, her characteristic um, um, giving her time to think, knelt beside Chad and hugged Star under her chin for solace.

It was all there. Chad, who was quite accustomed to interpreting such signs in his occupation as game warden, had no difficulty reading what had happened here. The tiny blurred feline paw prints, the owl feathers…Obviously, the kitten had paused to drink and got snatched up by a hunting owl—of whatever variety was native here. From the feathers, he surmised it was a barn owl… No, maybe the raptor didn't get him. It could be much, much worse. There was something that drew the game warden's attention beside the puddle. But he didn't mention his guess to Beth and Wisteria, who were both trying their best to hold back tears.

Foxglove, he thought unhappily, had not been snatched up by the barn owl. He'd bet on it—though that had certainly been the raptor's intent. Too many feathers were scattered about as if the owl had been plucked like a chicken. No, a second villain had entered the fray. And judging by the size of his paw prints, it was a very large dog who had de-feathered the rampaging owl and then made a meal of Violet's little blue grey kitten.

Beth was sucking in her breath, trying to keep from crying. She and Wisteria had seen the big paw prints now. Chad pulled his wife to him in a hug and looped his other arm over a distraught Wisteria. Star and Hawkeye were peering about, sniffing at the feathers and the huge dog prints.

Ah, Hah! Cried Bhu Fan, leaping from Beth's grasp. *Hawk, Star, Let's go!*

To the amazement of their three humans, Hawk, Star and Bhu sprinted away from them in a southerly direction, easily choosing the clearest path across the meadow toward the farm and kennels of Wisteria's neighbors.

Chad, Beth and Wisteria all looked at each other and Beth made as if to call out for the cats to come back.

'Don't!" Chad cautioned, his hand out. "Let's go see what they're up to...Wisteria, who lives down there?"

Wisteria gave Chad a look that indicated they just might be leaping out of the frying pan into the fire. "Alex and Ginger Zart....nice people." She gazed straight ahead as they marched quickly along in the wake of the three cats. "They raise border collies."

The game warden pursed his lips in a wry expression. "Surely a border collie would be unlikely to show any interest in a small kitten—and surely they don't run loose."

Wisteria's voice cracked. "I daresay." She turned her head to glance at the game warden. "But they also have two house dogs— and they do occasionally get loose. I've seen them out in the meadow hunting."

"Oh? What kind of house dogs?" He hesitated, not sure he really wanted to know.

"Golden retrievers."

There was no response to that. Silently, the three of them made their way to the house now in front of them at some little distance, Chad and Wisteria glum and fearful. But Beth held hope quietly to her breast. She knew Hawkeye and Bhu Fan. If Foxglove had been killed—well, it didn't bear thinking about. But she wasn't going to holler, as her old nanny used to say, until she was hurt. And that pair of feline sorcerers of hers wouldn't have brought them here to find a dead kitten. Or so she hoped.

The three of them stopped as Chad paused to open the front gate to Wisteria's neighbor's garden. His wife couldn't help but smile. Hawk, Bhu and Star hadn't bothered. She didn't doubt for a moment that Hawk could have opened that gate all by himself. But in their excitement, they'd gone over it like three steeplechasers racing down the stretch. And this gave substance to her hope. They knew something she didn't—as her cats had proved time and again.

They were now waiting for their humans, jumping around in excited circles at the door, making enough noise to raise the dead.

Well, the noise was certainly enough to bring somebody forth. As Wisteria and her companions got to the little porch, the door opened. A petite brunette, glasses perched low on her nose, about Beth's age, wearing a voluminous silky teal colored caftan, looked down at her catly callers in a somewhat disconcerted state. The two goldens crowded behind her somewhat bewildered because the cats weren't paying them the slightest bit of attention.

"Eeoow!" Cried Bhu Fan, at which point, Ginger Zart looked up, saw her more likely visitors and smiled broadly.

"Wisteria, love, I was just about to call you! I think I have something here that belongs to you. And I must say, he's eating me out of house and home--"

While Wisteria Cate and her two Americans stood anxiously on the Zarts' front stoop, their hostess pulled forth from the depths of her silky sleeves, a small blue bright-eyed kitten. "Me-uuw!" he cried, *oh, wistymum, please carry me home!* The kitten tried to wiggle free of his rescuer's grasp as she laughed and reached out toward Wisteria. *Please, please, please!*

"Oh, oh, um, um," cried an inarticulate almost certainly speechless Wisteria, her face bright with relief, as she reached for the peripatetic tiny Foxglove.

Chad opened the door to the cattery with a big grin on his face. In trooped Bhu Fan like a prancing pony, tall high, green eyes bright with self assurance. Behind her came Hawkeye, his tail to the perpendicular, just as delighted as his dusty sidekick. Behind them, Star, sleek as a raven's wing—if also coated with the powder they'd stirred up in their race across the meadow—came in, tail high, trotting along. And in the rear, doing his best to keep up, scampered a small blue grey kitten, his tiny tail also straight up, a look in his eye that said he wasn't sure whether his mum was going to be pleased about his homecoming or dust his britches for him. But whatever his reception, he'd take it like a tom. He was too grateful to be safely back among his own kind to worry about the consequences.

Wisteria walked over and unlatched Violet's enclosure. But the blue queen was paying no attention to her at all, her eyes fixated on her wandering offspring. Violet hit her screen door with a thump and trotted across the common room, growling and crying and singing praises to Bastet and making a bee-line for the luckless Foxy.

Aw, mum, don't lick me so hard—I won't have any fur left if you don't let up!

Don't be cheeky, young sir! I'll do much worse if you ever pull a stunt like that again…We didn't know what had happened to you. Scared us out of half our nine lives!

With that, Violet picked up her errant kitten by the scruff of his neck and carried him back into her enclosure, gathered in her two other kitlings, who were making much over their sibling's return, and settled down in her nest box where she pulled Foxy close to her belly's warm fur. Purring reverberated through the cattery loudly enough to shake the rafters.

The three grownups watched this scenario play out, smiling broadly to themselves. This homecoming was a vast relief to all concerned.

"No time for tea now. We need something a bit more restorative," declared Wisteria as she led her guests across her garden and into her kitchen. She reached into the cabinet for a squat brown bottle. "A wee drop of Bailey's Irish Crème in some good hot coffee ought to do the trick, what?"

Bhu Fan, Hawkeye and Star, having refreshed themselves with a bowl of the quintessentially English feline fare "Felix Marinades", sat among the other cats at CumbriaCoons: Freddie, Countess Cottia, who had come from the house to see what all the excitement was about, Chrysanthemum and Wisteria's half-grown queens, Iris and Lily. Angel, who kept herself curled up at a short distance away, was close enough to hear what had transpired out in the meadow, yet far enough to be separate. This shunning of the group didn't go unnoticed.

While Hawkeye told everybody about the owl and the dogs, Bhu Fan got up and walked over to Angel. This self-imposed distancing would not do. Cats need to be all in one clan in a cattery. She'd had to learn this the hard way, being royalty, but she'd knuckled under to it all the same—not that she was about to admit to it to anybody. The little Korat, however, wasn't sure whether Angel's reserve was because her erstwhile traveling buddy was now so enamored of the lovely Chrysie or if there was some other cause. Perhaps she'd had a real bad experience up in the fells...

"Angel, I think you're feeling badly; something wrong for you? Would you like to tell me about it?"

The silver torbie gave Bhu Fan a wan smile as the little Korat settled down next to her and curled up in a ball. "No," she admitted, "I'm all right. I just don't seem to be able to, to *belong* any more." She turned big green-gold eyes on the perceptive Bhu Fan. "I've lived in two worlds and maybe it was bloody awful, as Derryth would say, up there where loose dogs and eagles and other strange creatures live, with nothing to eat but what one killed and de-furred...I was, it was, oh, I don't know. He was just so, so...lordly." Angel heaved a deep sigh. "It's warm here, the food is good—I don't have to work for it and I don't have to be concerned with where I'm going to sleep tonight and is it going to be safe and—" the young queen sniffed and put her head down between her paws. "What am I going *to do*, Boo?"

"Derryth, eh?"

"Oh, yes, Lord Derryth—of the fells and forest. I've never met a tom like him, Boo...but he wouldn't let me stay. He said I, I didn't belong in the wild...Well, I know I could have *learned*..."

Young, lovesick queens, I ask you! Bhu Fan mused to herself. But she knew better than to take that approach with the grieving Angel.

"He was right, you know...and yes, I don't doubt you could have learned, Angel, but he was really being unselfish—can't you see? He didn't want danger and deprivation for you. And all who live in the wild suffer such. He wanted you to be safe and happy—"

"I'm not sure I can be, Boo, without him, happy, that is."

Bhu Fan sighed. She was going to have to try a different tack. "Well, Angel kitling, think about this—you've seen how Violet has suffered when young Foxy went adventuring...and would you like any kittens of *yours* to suffer, be deprived, hungry, cold, scared—in danger all time? "

Angel lifted her head and thought about what Bhu Fan said. She *had* seen how poor Violet had worried and grieved, not knowing what had happened to her littlest tom…And what must it have been like for *him*, the little scrap; he could have been killed easily, too young to save himself…And while she chewed on a toe with a broken claw, she had to admit, now that she was no longer a flighty kitling—or so she told herself—she was just going to have to keep her memories and take what Bastet handed out and not look back. Angel heaved a great sigh.

Bhu Fan waited.

The young queen looked her in the eye, nodded, got up and walked across the floor to where Starry was stretched out between Hawkeye and Chrysanthemum, boxed his ear and said facetiously, "and just where were you, my black scamp in shiny armor, when that awful mantom threw a blanket over me???"

Wisteria Cate, her American guests and Paul Mellish, sat around the big oak round table in her kitchen in the evening a few days later, having a farewell dinner for Beth and Chad who would be catching a plane for Boston the next day. Beth was looking at the water pipes which came down the wall over the sink on this side of the walls. It had piqued her curiosity before and she'd contained herself. Now she took a bite of biscuit and murmured, "Why, Wisteria, did they put the water pipes where they are?" She cocked her head. "Instead of inside the walls where they'd be invisible?"

Wisteria laughed. "I asked that when I first moved here. The plumber told me they did that so they could get to them easier when they froze up." Her hostess laughed along with everybody else. "This cottage was built when 'central heating' meant you had a heated towel rack in the bathroom. And of course, during the war—it was just about that time—coal was rationed and I wouldn't doubt that whoever lived here, made do with great fortitude and little else."

"Speaking of building houses and such, Wisteria," Paul spoke up. "I was wondering if you might let me restore your old barn out there and fix it up for Sir Francis, Maid Marion, Tatty Bumpkin and all the rest?" At this question, not only did everybody seated around the table look at him, but Centurion, Lady Lucy's blue kitten, stirred in his lap as well.

Paul blushed. "We're, ah, all about to become homeless."

"*What*?"

"Well, the powers-that-be, to use an American expression, are moving faster than I thought possible. They are so stirred up about those old coins you found that they're going to let the university archeologists have a go at digging up the place, use my farm for their inside work with the eye toward turning it into a museum eventually... they might even build a complex like the one up in Rheged—you know it? Where they've built all those shops into the cliff?—Well, they're planning on doing the same thing here: turn that old ruin into a tourist attraction with a cliff-climbing site, shops and, even, if I'm understanding them, they're going to rebuild the old fort as well and—taking a page out of your American theme park book, Chad—stocking it with re-enactors, if that's the word..." He chuckled to himself, "that is—if they can raise the funds."

His audience sat there in stunned silence. Wisteria was the first to find her tongue. "You're welcome to turn my old barn into whatever you please for the cats, Paul—but *you* can't *live* there.

"Er, you don't want me around, Wisty?"

"Of course not. I mean, yes, I most certainly do want you around—but not living in the barn! That's just not *on*. No, there's plenty of room here...upstairs—" When she realized what she'd said, Wisteria yelped, turned beet red and put her hands to her face. Beth bit her lip and tried not to grin; Chad hid behind his teacup.

Paul fixed Wisteria with a stern visage and, handing Centurion to a bemused Beth, drew himself up, a decidedly mischievous glint in his eye. "Wisteria, darling. It's quite all right for our children to live in sin—but they're not about to let us do it!

"We're going to have to get married!"

✡ ✡ ✡

CHAPTER TWENTY-TWO

N OW, SIRE, WHAT'S ALL this about near misses and missing cats and—" Bhu Fan shuddered. "—*Death* while we've been gone?"

The little Korat looked inquiringly at Shere Khan as she cosseted small Centurion from where he watched the proceedings, eyes wide with wonder, between her front paws. His journey across the big ocean sharing a carrier with Her Royal Highness had imprinted him closely (to his mind anyway) with his new foster mom. Had Bhu been aware of this, it would have no doubt surprised *her*, motherhood never having been something she aspired to. However, Bhu was intent at this moment on finding out what had befallen her shaggy locals in her absence, never mind that it was Shere Khan's kingdom in which she was a mere Johnny-come-lately. Khan, however, being the gentleman he was, would never remind her of this. Like Hawkeye, he had a soft spot for the skinny little shorthair and would never put her in her place. She'd certainly made her contribution to the health and welfare of the MerryMaines. And there was nothing skinny about her intelligence.

The old tom made himself comfortable. That the little Korat princess should intuit mayhem in her absence didn't surprise him, knowing of her sorcerer's inclinations as he did. But he wanted to get everything that had happened in its proper sequence as the cat killer was still out there. And it was this conference of Penobscot County felines' elite who were best equipped to deal with bringing him to ground ("justice" was a concept cats found lacking; their goal was merely ridding themselves of a threat). But first, Khan felt, a little light comedy was in order.

"We need to back up a bit further—to the exodus from Merry-Maines to Chad's camp." He began, licking a paw. "Beowulf spotted that official van first." The old tom turned and looked at the big smoky neuter who had, before his abduction and return, been the cattery's senior tom and star attraction. And still a force to be reckoned with.

Wulf grinned and smoothed a patch of errant fur on one shoulder. "I was watching that cocky ole blue jay flitter about the maple outside Bethmom 'n Chad's bedroom upstairs. Wretched bag of tatty feathers." Beowulf shook his head in disgust. "But right then, I couldn't bring myself to snatch him off that limb…he was working like a momcat with ten kittens to feed, tryin' to fill a nestful of mouths bigger'n Posey's while his consort nattered at him, sitting there on her big fat butt…Anyway, I could see I was makin' *her* nervous so I went up on the roof to enjoy a bit of breeze 'n that's when I saw that white official lookin' vehicle with a truck behind it, turning onto our road." The big cat frowned and looked over his shoulder, his glance catching Bhu Fan. She'd certainly understand the hunch he'd had right then.

"Worried me. Martha had just come home. Khan 'n Smudge were downstairs somewhere. Sweeper was with her…I felt like I better alert the cattery crew that we were having visitors—and not happy, helpful ones either, it didn't seem like. I zipped downstairs, through the shed (where I ran into the bushel of apples and overturned it, spooking old Shaggy) and out to the barn, got everybody front and center in their enclosures when Khan, Smudge, 'n Sweeper dashed in like the fox raiding the henhouse. Khan started opening latches 'n explaining what was happenin' 'n the four of us quickly herded everybody out." Wulf stared heavenward. "Thank Bastet we had no kitlings right then so young they couldn't keep up."

The big neuter, his mouth dry at the recollection, looked to Shere Khan who took up the tale, laughing. Well, he *could* laugh about it *now*.

"It didn't take much to spook ol' Shaggy. He knew he wasn't supposed to be in Bethmom's shed, (she'd run him off more'n once with her broom) helpin' himself to her apples as he was....We could hear that old moose rousting those two mantoms, scatterin' 'em like a covey of ground birds. It musta been a hoot to see.

"By then, we had the queens and kitlings, Simon and Rio out of the cattery and down the hill toward the Moosery, everybody low to the ground." He measured his audience. They were certainly not bored at the telling.

"It was a good thing the hay in the meadow hadn't been cut yet. If those mantoms had looked in our direction, they'd have seen us for sure if it hadda been. But the hay was high enough that we were able to sneak off unseen."

"But, but, sire," interrupted Hawkeye, "I thought you herded everybody off to Chad's camp in the woods out near the beaver pond."

"We did. Eventually. But the first night we paused at the old barn, the kitlings, you know, not having any experience at hoofin' it—well, to make a long story short—"

"Yeah," injected, Smudge, "no kibble in the Moosery. 'N too likely for somebody, like guests or hikers or such to come waltzin' in...We weren't takin' any chances. Felt like with the door locked and the curtains drawn 'n a big bag of kibble Chad keeps out there, the crew was safer in the deep woods." Smudge's countenance grew dark. "I know about dog pounds and catchers with long poles—"

Little Centurion, now called 'Turey by the cattery's kits, spoke up. Hawkeye had to chuckle at what he asked. Some of the Korat's penchant for dotting all the I's and crossing all the T's had obviously rubbed off on him during their long journey home.

"If the door was locked at this hiding place in the woods, Sire, how did you get everybody inside?"

Shere Khan turned his head toward the small newcomer and smiled. This little tom would go far; he already wanted to know things. The Great One explained about the wood box outside behind the chimney, a large contraption that had a lid to keep the stored wood dry and another opening on the inside of the cabin for extracting it without having to brave any unkind elements of weather outside.

The little blue tom nodded sagely. It was all Shere Khan and the other elders could do to keep from laughing out loud. Such response was not to be made fun of, however. A knowing look passed between Khan and Hawkeye. Centurion was going to be a wise and worldly tom someday soon when Simon retired and went to live with Mrs. Brannigan. Khan ducked his head sadly. Poor Gandy. Miz. Brannigan was still angry and sad and grieving for her Gandalf. He had no doubt that if she had any idea that dogdung, Styles had shot him for sheer vindictiveness, she'd go after *him* with a rifle. He sighed. The time had come to get down to the meat of the matter: what to do about that vicious sorry mantom.

Shere Khan and Smudge related to the gathering the sad story of death and near-death in the tall weeds outside the old house not far from Schultzburg.

"Ah So will make it." Shere Khan looked over his conferees. "He may lose a leg but Miz Chase got him to Doc Watts before he bled to death…" The old tom heaved a great sigh. "But Gandy, well, Smudge and I were too late for Gandy." He looked over at the old silver tom, Simon, who was sitting tall and solemn at the door of his enclosure. Simon gazed at Shere Khan and nodded his head. He'd miss the cattery crew but he was ready for his life to turn in a new direction. And by all accounts, Miz Brannigan was a kind and loving ladyqueen. He'd do what he could to make her laugh again, not in any way deterred by a life-style change with a trip to the vet beforehand.

"So what can we do, Sire?" Hawkeye did not want to dwell on what had already happened. He wanted to know what they could do to prevent anything else dire from coming to pass.

"I'm going to leave you for awhile—" Khan began.

The cats let out a collective howl of protest. "No, sire, no. You mustn't go after that mantom alone."

"Oh," he reassured them, "I'm not foolish enough to do *that*. I need to warn Minstrel, although I think he's safe enough in Muller's barn…That old farmer catch Styles in there, he'd take a pitchfork to him. No, I need to warn Riddle and his son, Whistle, and Big Al and Woozy 'n, well, there are cats all over the county loosely attached to farmsteads…cats who live solitary. They might not know just *who's* the maniac out there with a gun who likes to use our kind for target practice…Miz Daphne at The Red Moose has a new Coon, one she brought from out west when she moved here to take over the Emporium. I wouldn't put it past that killer to snatch that cat right off the counter by the cash register. If he thought he could catch that ladyqueen looking in the other direction—"

"I'll go with you, Khan," spoke a solemn voice. "You'll need someone to watch your back." The old street cat smiled wickedly. "And who better than me? If it's anything I know about, it's mantoms with guns—"

The old Maine Coon turned to face Smudge. He could see Hawkeye fidgeting out of the corner of his eye.

"Sire, I—"

"Yes, I know, my son. You would gladly be my backup as you have done in the past so well and so often." Shere Khan went over and gave his eldest a head butt. "But someone needs to be here who can take charge and get everyone to safety if needs be…and you've the quick mind 'n talented thumbs for it. With Chad home, I daresay there's danger here. But if he and Bethmom went off together even for one of their musical evenings, Styles, I think would like nothing better than to get even with the game warden, once and for all. And what better way, than heisting his bride's cats and doing away with them?"

A collective shudder passed through all the cats as The Great One, out of breath from such a long speech, gazed thoughtfully at Hawk. "This is your domain, my son, and it needs you to guard it." He looked toward the stud pens. "You can always deputize Rio and Simon —we've run off a few villains together, haven't we?" The two big toms peered back at Shere Khan and nodded affirmatively without speaking. "And Wulf is a powerful deterrent as well…"

Hawkeye looked at his sire. Then he looked around the cats all gathered there watching him. He knew, well as if Bhu Fan was turning her subliminal orders on him, that they counted on him as they did his sire. He gazed at the floor and nodded his head. Duty was duty and not always one's druthers.

"Hawkeye will take care of things here, Sire." Bhu Fan stood four square in the middle of the room, her head high, ears forward, tail moving in lazy circles. "Wulf and Sweeper, Simon and Rio are right here to back him up." She looked significantly all around the room. "Lyric, Gracie, Sonnet, Gremmie, Rain, Madame, Magic and Moonrise…" She swung her head as all the queens returned her fierce stare, nodding their agreement. "That misbegotten lesser humanoid walk in here, he won't walk out again."

Shere Khan was mesmerized on that moment, realizing he wasn't seeing a skinny little blue "domestic feline" not much bigger than a loaf of bread: he was looking at a huge shimmering, consummate blue panther. He shook his head and blinked. Well, hadn't they all sprung from such ferocious ancient stock?

Shere Khan and Smudge paused at the edge of the cedar swamp to catch their breath and a few fish fry at the same time before heading back to work. In their endeavors to warn the local feline population about the mantom with the gun, they had been fairly successful. Either the cats who lived feral headed for new territory or had gone to ground. Cats attached to families spent more time snoozing on the sofa than on the hood of their owner's pickup truck.

But for all their efforts to protect felinekind, Khan and Smudge were themselves still out there at risk, for the cause of all their consternation was still at large with his rifle at the ready, his cousin Pierre heretofore too intimidated to refuse Styles his role as chauffeur. It wasn't that Pierre LeFaux had any principles about killing pets—or rutting moose, for that matter. His only concern was steering clear of his cousin's violent temper by doing his bidding. For all that, LeFaux had found it prudent recently to take a job cutting timber upstate at Houlton on the Canadian border just about the time Khan and Smudge were making Styles' targets scarce.

Thus it was that Styles found himself on foot and hunting fewer quarry. Well, actually, that was nothing new. Poaching was hardly something accomplished on wheels. It might annoy Styles that until he had a chance at bigger game, his drive-by shooting had been curtailed. He'd just take his pleasure as he tramped through the woods while he checked his traps. And if he happened to chance across a tame puss when he went to town, well, he kept carriers in his van for just such opportunities. After all, he felt he was doing Patten, Gilby, Stacyville and Schultzburg a favor, keeping them free of vermin-ridden strays. He was no bleeding heart like Harry Armstrong. If people didn't know (or care) what he did after he trapped wandering felines, well, they wouldn't care either if he took them out in the woods, turned them loose and used them for target practice. That most of the town cats he came across weren't vermin-ridden strays but beloved house pets never occurred to him. Although, he had found it prudent to keep clear of Barney Branni-gan and Duncan Chase, a henpecked pair if he ever met 'em. And as soon as prey became scarce and cover reduced by cold weather, he'd go after those vicious rogue lynx, game warden or no. It had become all the same to Gary Styles. As long as he had ammo, he was in business. One way or the other, whichever species he found in his gun sights.

The pristine white Maine Coon was stretched out in the front window of the Red Moose next to a collection of dolls, teddy bears and antique toys. She was, by all accounts, a beautiful cat and a great advertisement for her mistress' store, which sold everything from books and bedding to quilts and candy.

Having just moved to Gilby with her human family, she'd not yet gotten acquainted with any of the locals, although being a gre-garious soul, she had every intention of doing so. She'd noticed from her window an occasional sighting of a very large and handsome brown tabby tom who to her great puzzlement, seemed to be sneak-ing around in a most furtive manner. Further, he had a confederate shorthair and whenever they'd cross paths with another cat sunning on a stoop or prowling about the grocery stores, meetings would take place and then everyone would slink away. Most peculiar. The white cat had never in her life been menaced and observing her kind behaving in such a watchful distrusting state was disturbing.

Feeling a familiar urge, the white cat jumped down from the window and went in search of her litter tray which Miz Daphne had placed in the storeroom at the back of the store. She noticed that her mistress was off-loading merchandise from her station wagon and the store's big rear door was open. The cat looked outside but had no desire to go out herself. She moved to the corner where her litterbox sat. The phone rang just then and her mistress put down the box she'd been bringing inside and went to the front of the store to answer it.

The white cat had just stepped out of her box when everything went dark and she found herself enveloped in a fuzzy wrap of some kind. It was dirty and dusty and she began to sneeze as she struggled to get free. The next thing she knew, she'd been thrust into a small carrier, thrown into the back of some sort of vehicle and was being carried away. Totally confused and frightened, she crouched in the furthest corner—and waited, all her ancestors' instincts coming to the fore.

CHAPTER TWENTY-THREE

S MUDGE GAZED AROUND AT the woods, the meadow, the beaver pond. The trees were all in the process of putting on their autumn raiment of golds, russets and reds. Nothing moved that Smudge could see. The only unusual things he spotted were the huge smelly tree-eating monsters parked close by. But they were idle at the moment so didn't make much of an impression on the old street cat. Bastet knew he'd seen plenty of mechanical monsters in his time. It was quiet. Too quiet. His thumbs began to prickle.

"What are we doing here, Khan?"

"This is where Loki and Crya hang out. I need to warn them."

"About that mantom and his gun, you mean?"

"That, too, but no; about all the traps he's set around the pond." Khan scanned the meadow. All he saw was a "V" of geese in the distance winging south, gossiping as they went.

"Wouldn't Styles shoot them, too?"

"He might. More likely he'd prefer them stuck in one of his traps."

Smudge looked a question.

"It's Loki's pelt he wants. Without the blemish of a bullet hole in it."

"Oh," responded, Smudge, his brow furrowed.

"Isn't that him—over there? Looking around the old logging track Chad uses when he comes this way?"

Shere Khan leaped up on a fallen log some four feet off the ground where it rested against a stump. He gazed in the direction Smudge indicated as the old street cat sprang up beside him, scrabbling at the bark. He was still learning, more used to brick and concrete than tree bark.

"Yep. That's him." The old tom let out a howl and waited.

Presently, Loki came loping toward the two cats perched on their lookout. Apparently he was alone.

"Where's Crya and the kits, Loki?"

"Up on the ridge. That bunch of knuckleheads still haven't got a clue about hunting...they think that's what *we're* for—"

Loki stopped and turned his head toward the meadow.

"What you up to, Khan?" He said abstractly. Lynx, like all wild creatures are very wary, always checking their surroundings.

"Wanted to warn you about the clearing here by the beaver pond. It's full of leg traps. You know—those steel-jawed contraptions with sharp teeth."

"Ugh!"

"Yeah. I think I know how to spring them. But I need a little help. I'm not as tall as you." He motioned to a long stout stick in front of him on the ground, beaver-chewed to a rough point on one end.

"Okay. Sure." Loki peered at the stick, picked it up in his jaws, one end still dragging the ground. "Yeah," he repeated, nodding his head. "I can do that—"

"What's that I hear?" exclaimed Smudge, who was also by nature wary of his surroundings. His ears swiveled.

Khan and Loki stood motionless.

"Noisy, smelly moving-monster."

"Yes," Khan agreed, swiftly scrambling upward to where his fallen log blended in with the painted leaves. "You guys get down. Maybe I can get above him for a better look-see."

As the three felines watched, the two on the ground peering out from behind the fallen log, a rust-spotted decrepit van stopped a few yards away at the edge of the trees. The driver got out, gazed at the timber cutting machines for a moment, then reached back across his seat for his rifle. He walked around to the vehicle's rear doors, pulled out more traps which he dropped clanking on the uneven ruts his vehicle had made. Turning back to its interior, he extracted a large pet carrier which he dropped carelessly to the ground. A terrified squeak emanated from inside the crate. Smudge and Khan looked at each other and the old street cat, belly to the ground moved off in the direction of the vehicle and its involuntary passenger.

The man then picked up the traps and walking over, dropped them beside Khan's fallen tree. He then returned to his vehicle, took a pair of cartridges from his vest pocket, snicked back the bolt on his thirty-ought-six and inserted the shells. Shere Khan shuddered at the sound as the breech was closed and slowly backed down the tree to cover underneath while the mantom peered off in the opposite direction.

About that time, Crya and the kits, not seeing the dark colored van partly obscured by the timber trucks, loped out of the woods on the other side of the meadow, coming in their direction.

"No, Crya!" howled, Loki and sprinted across the ground toward his family, hoping to draw the gunner's attention.

Styles, who had just released the catch on the pet taxi, straightened up and swung around, a gleeful expression on his face. Forgetting the tame cat in the carrier, he scurried for a small rise in the meadow where he could get a better shot at the fleeing lynx, his concern for unblemished pelts forgotten.

But the lynx had disappeared. He thought that they couldn't have gotten far as their kits couldn't move all that fast. And he was sure they wouldn't leave them behind.

Stealthily, he approached the trees around the clearing beside the beaver pond. Holding his rifle at the ready, his gloved finger on the trigger, he scanned the woods, intent on his quarry. If they broke cover, he was certain he would spot them quickly enough to get a shot off.

Behind him, Smudge had reached the pet crate. As Khan watched from under the fallen log, ready to provide another diversion if need be, Smudge led the white cat away from her prison. Unfortunately, if Styles turned around he couldn't have missed them.

That white-coated Maine Coon queen stood out like the headlamp on a logging train. With Smudge almost as obvious.

Being a cat himself, Shere Khan could see Loki better than the hunter. The Great One realized Loki was torn between leading his family off to safety and finishing up what he'd started last spring when this same mantom had trapped Crya in that cage.

Off in the middle distance behind him, Khan heard another angry roar that set the hair on his back straight up. The woods had suddenly come alive. *Bast Bespoke, I'd forgotten*, he muttered to himself. *It's the time of the rut.* He turned back to where Styles was standing, his search intent on the lynx pair, which he presumed were out in the meadow.

Quickly, mistress, roll in this mud—like I'm doing—see?

The white cat looked at Smudge, a startled fearful expression on her face. *Why would I do that??* She whispered. *I'd ruin my coat—*

The gunner isn't as likely to see us, that's why. You want him to spot that lovely white coat and shoot you?

As if to make his point, the rifle fired. The white cat jumped and complied, although she'd never heard gunfire before. Then, dripping with water, her pelt a muddy brown mass of dreadlocks, she followed Smudge, who had also rolled in the mud. The two of them quickly melted into the underbrush, the old street cat calling down unpleasant curses on the mantom with the gun.

It was suddenly quiet. "Missed!" Cried the poacher, angry now and no longer a disciplined shooter. His emotions had gotten the better of him. The lynx had vanished again. He turned around and kicked the crate, intent on flushing the game he'd brought with him. But the carrier was empty. He cursed, pulled the bolt, inserted another cartridge and looked around. That white cat had to be close. She couldn't have gotten far—and with that brilliant coat of hers, she should be easy pickings.

Styles peered down the length of the creek below the beaver pond. When he'd shot at the lynx, he'd heard another noise in the distance. But he hadn't been paying attention. Then it penetrated his brain. It was a bull moose bugling. Styles smiled. An old hand at poaching moose during the rut, he knew that big beast was probably too pre-occupied with some great ugly cow to pay any attention to him.

And suddenly there he was! Only it wasn't a great ugly cow he was intent on—but another, younger, more agile bull. The bigger moose clearly showed an old wound on one shoulder and he wasn't as quick as his adversary. But he was older and wiser. The two were locked in combat some few yards away along the meandering creek.

Styles raised his rifle and fired again. The bullet ricocheted off a tree between the two fighting behemoths, sending splinters flying in all directions. The gunner swore and, intent on the two, moved toward the beaver pond to get a better shot through the trees. When he stepped sideways, he heard a loud thunk! and felt a fearsome sharp pain in his shin as one of his forgotten trapsets grabbed his boot. He yelled in surprise as it threw him off balance. In a frenzy from the pain, seeing the old moose turn his attention in his direction, all of which happened in mere seconds, Styles attempted to stop himself from falling. He had to get out of the way of the wretched beast. He put out his hands to break his fall, dropping his rifle in doing so, his glove still caught in the trigger guard. The stock of his weapon hit the ground—discharging as it landed butt first.

The noise so close suddenly galvanized the charging bull moose who turned from his rival and, covering the short distance smartly, lowered his huge head and tossed the prone figure of the mantom high in the air, leg trap, stake and all. The man landed in a limp heap on his rifle and didn't move. Satisfied he'd neutralized his two-legged opponent, the big bull turned and galloped back toward his own kind. He still had another fight to finish.

The woods were suddenly silent again. Shere Khan did hear the two moose retreating in the distance. He looked toward where Styles had fallen. A bloody, trampled mess with one leg still caught in the trap. The mantom wasn't moving.

"Khan?"

The old tom looked toward the bushes edging the clearing.

"You okay, Smudge? The white cat?"

"Yeah, we're okay. But she's a little miffed at me for getting her coat all muddy for nothing."

"Well, better dirty than dead…like Styles." Smudge had started across the clearing.

"Watch! Old friend. There are still loaded traps about…"

As Smudge and the white cat stepped around along the edges warily, Khan looked up to see Loki and Crya galloping toward them.

"All of you okay, Loki?"

"Yeah. We stashed the kits up on the ridge….You okay?"

"Yep. But we need to spring all the traps, Loki, before the beavers come looking for new building stuff—like that chewed-off stick."

"No problem, Khan…at least that worthless mantom took out one of the traps for us."

CHAPTER TWENTY-FOUR

C HAD MERRYMAN SAT ACROSS the lunch table from a very distracted wife. Beth had put his ham sandwich, baked beans and deviled eggs in front of him and said nothing about his muddy boots on her shiny kitchen floor. He had left the house at daybreak, taking Khan and Smudge with him and looked decidedly grim when he got home. He glanced at Beth, who for some reason, seemed to be at sixes and sevens about something— and it couldn't be the row of cats lined up on the counter. A bit distracted himself, he decided he'd get to Beth's news all in good time. He ran his hands through his hair, looked down at his plate. And ate. Silently.

Bhu Fan squirmed. Beth might as well have. Chad shook his head, put down his fork, gathering his thoughts. He gazed fondly at his wife. She could certainly take the sting out of a lot of misery. And she was very good at containing her curiosity. The little blue Korat was not. And why did he think that small cat was waiting just like his wife for him to explain everything—or was Bhu Fan waiting for Beth to explain something to him? He sighed, sipping his coffee.

"I think we know pretty much what happened down at the beaver pond after Khan brought us that white cat and a shell casing." He frowned. "Well, given the state of Smudge and the white Coon, it had to have happened close by the beaver pond…But won't anybody ever know for sure the details. Khan and Smudge sure can't tell us."

"Chad, darn it! What happened? I know when Khan dropped that shell at your feet yesterday afternoon, *he* certainly hadn't shot anybody—who did??"

"Actually, it was Gary Styles…and I think the sorry bastard shot himself."

Beth turned white. It wasn't like Chad to swear. "Suicide? I find that hard—"

"No, not that." He paused, picked up his mug and gazed at the bottom of it, handed it to Beth to refill for him and looked back up at her.

"Not suicide; stupidity."

The game warden shook his head and dropped one hand to scratch Smudge between his ears where the old boy sat beside his chair.

"This is the way I see it—as does the Sheriff—from the signs." He chewed on his lower lip.

"Styles kidnapped Mrs. Grayson's white Coon right out of the back of her shop. One of the rural route carriers at the Post Office next block over saw him speeding away down the alley at the time in question. We're guessing, of course, but there was Styles' van and an empty pet carrier down by the beaver pond…" Chad sighed. "There were enough paw prints and tracks down there to write a wildlife manual, and what Khan's and Smudge's were doing there beggars the imagination. There was also a dead body with a thirty-ought-six under it, a bunch of illegal traps—all sprung—shell casings and bullet holes ever which way." He lifted his head to gaze at Beth, although, somehow, she didn't think he could see her.

"Jim Proudfoot and I think he intended to use the little cat for target practice after he checked his traps and set more in position. But somehow, he seems to have found himself hip deep in more game than he knew what to shoot first. There were lynx prints and beaver tail-trails and a pair of bull moose chewing up the scenery who probably didn't take kindly to his riflery. And the only game bagged was—himself!"

Beth Merryman looked at her husband in horror. "—While somehow Khan, Smudge and Divinity looked on!"

"Divinity?" Chad sputtered and gave his wife a questioning smile.

"Yes. That's Daphne Grayson's white girl. And I can tell you, she was one happy, very relieved soul when I told her she was here!"

Her husband shook his head again, glad to change the direction of the conversation. "Why would anybody name a cat 'Divinity'?"

It was Beth's turn to laugh. "Divinity is the name of white fudge—haven't you ever had any? 'Tastes divine'... Well, chalk it up to Coon breeders who have a weakness for word games. Daph bought her from a cattery in Colorado called Candy'sCoons, the breeder being a rather famous cat show contender named Candy Piper...and like many another, she kept to her theme." Beth giggled. "Divinity is already a cat show Grand and I understand she came from a litter with kittens named O. Henry, Ghirardelli, Godiva and—oh the pain of it: Snickers!" She brought the conversation back to its more grim aspects.

"So how did stupidity kill Gary Styles?"

"Our guess is he was attempting to shoot a moose—or lynx or beaver—but in the doing he stepped on one of his own traps which caught his leg and threw him off balance. The moose—obviously not a lynx—charged, he dropped his rifle, the gun misfired and that was the end of Penobscot County's last overgrown juvenile delinquent." He paused. "Well, it's pretty certain one of the moose charged him as it was fairly obvious he'd been pitched up in the air, leg trap and all but the moose surely didn't shoot him as well...He wasn't a pretty sight."

Chad Merryman ran his hand through his hair again, pushed back from the table and stood up.

"And if truth be known," he added as he reached for his cap and kissed his wife, "I find that poetic justice."

Before Chad Merryman could reach the door, however, Beth cried, "Oh!" and motioned him back. "In all this—horror—about Styles, I forgot something and it's really very important. Sit down, sweetheart, while I go get something."

Puzzled, the game warden pulled out his chair and sat as ordered.

Beth came back into the kitchen, smiling, the poacher momentarily forgotten. She laid a handful of papers on the table in front of her husband; very old papers, some near to crumbling, but all readable and intact. "There," she cried with vindication, "take these to your dad!"

Chad carefully gathered up the papers, reading each one and laying it carefully aside. "How in the world, honey, did you come by these? Where in hell did you *find* them? This will set my folks to dancing a merry jig, I can tell you that!" He reached for Beth and pulled her down on his lap and gave her a hug, while Hawkeye and Bhu Fan, along with a puzzled Madame and offspring looked on, Her Royal Highness smugly wafting her whippy tail around her paws.

Beth looked over at the haughty Korat. "Long story."

"I've got time," Chad said, a twinkle in his eye.

Beth sighed, again looking at the cats. "The little madame there: Bhu Fan...I was showing Cheryl the quilt I brought home from Kendal this morning—remember?"

Her husband nodded his head.

"Well, I was steamed! When Cheryl and I went up to my workroom, Bhu Fan was in there—and I can only guess that her chief pick-pocket-and-door-opener let her in—Anyway, there she was in solitary splendor, stretched out on my antique quilt like the Queen of Sheba..." Again Beth gazed at the little Korat who gazed back quite unperturbed.

"I was giving her what-for for getting into my loft, with a few well-chosen words for her henchman, when Bhu extended a paw, extending a claw—and pulled up the corner of the quilt where that little patch was attached to the back. Then, before I could stop her, she started picking at it and pulling it off!

"Well, I grabbed her and shoved her aside and looked at the damage. Then...well, Cheryl and I couldn't believe it. Under the little nursery rhyme patch was a piece of paper—a very old envelope. Well, that really aroused our curiosity. So we set about opening up the back of that part of the quilt, knowing then why it was 'tied' instead of quilted there." Beth heaved a great sigh. "Well, to make a long story short, there were all these papers: old letters dating from the early 19th century and this document, which I think is a charter or patent or whatever it's known as, stating that the parcel of land grant marked off by such-and-such dimensions: old tree so many cubits or feet or meters (I'm not up on a surveyor's nomenclature)—from tall stone to creek—you'd know better than I—" Beth had become so excited after the damper of this morning's horror, that she was rapidly having trouble articulating her news. "Well, there it is anyway; what I think your dad needs to hold off the timber wolves."

Chad looked at her and then the "reprieve" he held in his hands. "Just one question, Honey." He cocked his head. "How the devil did all this documentation get stowed away inside a quilt and then travel all the way to England? Or better yet: Why?"

Beth smiled. "Well—and I know you think the 'wells' have got to run dry sooner or later—the young Merryman who in the early 1800s occupied the property had evidently gone off to the British Isles to try to free a brother or cousin—some relative—who'd been conscripted into the British navy in the War of 1812. His bride, who'd been left to mind the store, as it were, was being threatened by another Britisher, some English peer with a Spanish name—if you can believe that—who coveted their land tract, farm and forest. She was afraid if he got his hands on the title or deed or whatever they called it then, her husband would come home to a nasty mess and family evicted. So she stuck it all inside her wedding quilt along with letters of explanation, some from other family members and, entrusting it to her youngest brother-in-law, sent it off to England—so that whatever happened to *her*, he'd still have a place to come home to." Beth peered down at the assortment of letters. "A very brave young bride, she was..." Again she sighed. "Whatever happened after that we have no way of knowing. Nobody has bothered to record that."

Chad Merryman shook his head in wonder, carefully gathered up all the papers and once again, started for the door. "I'll give all these to Dad—after getting everything copied—and then you and I can go over everything and write it all up so Mom can add it to the family history." He shook his head again. "It's like finding the pot of gold at the end of the rainbow."

Beth nodded her head as her husband went out the back door, happy that his grim mood had lifted. And what a relief it was going to prove for his folks. She couldn't work up any sympathy for the late Gary Styles. Momentarily, she thought about his wife Mona and her daughter, little Annie. Gary had not been her real father, only her step-father, thank goodness. Hopefully her grandfather, Mr. Singletary, would take up the slack for both of them, bring them home and find Annie a new kitten. She shuddered, trying not to think how close Shere Khan, Smudge and Divinity had come to being more of that rapacious man's victims. She refused to even contemplate how many close calls Chad had had!

The phone's insistent ringing interrupted her thoughts. Bhu Fan leaped to her desk and put one paw on the instrument as Beth crossed the room to answer, pressing the speaker-phone button as she did so.

Hawkeye looked at Boo shrewdly. What was that cat up to now? He shook his shaggy head in exasperation.

"Beth! I know there's a five-hour time difference. I hope I haven't caught you too early?"

"Oh, hey, Wisteria, No, no, of course not. We just had lunch. How are you?"

Beth smiled at her cats, who seemed to be very intent, lined up listening like the FBI on a wiretap between Madonna and J. Edgar Hoover, looking for a little racy diversion. Bhu and Hawk, of course, knew Wisteria's voice. But the others: Magic, Moonrise, Madame, Sweeper and Smudge looked on just as keenly. They had heard Hawkeye's version of what-I-did-on-my-summer-vacation…

"Um, um. Well, first I wanted to tell you Paul and I got married—"

Beth erupted happily; she could almost see her friend blushing.

"Congratulations, Wisteria, Can the two of you come for Christmas?"

"Um, yes, probably…but that's not the important news."

Trust a cat breeder to not think getting married was the important news. She grinned at the telephone. "So what's the important news?'

"Angel had her kittens! Four of the wee mites: three little females and one strapping tom."

Beth's mouth dropped open "That was fast work. Star?"

"Oh, no, no. Not Star...the wild tom, the one who brought her home to Sir Francis. Remember Paul's story about how she got to Fellshadow Farm?"

Beth paused. She did indeed remember. They'd all been a bit awed by the obvious certainty that a Scottish wildcat was now lurking about in Cumbria's fells. "Yes, now that you mention it, I do recall—but, Wisteria, dear heart, how can you be sure?"

"Oh, not so difficult. You know little Centurion and how plush his coat is and how Paul thought one of Lady Lucy's ancestors up in Scotland—" she laughed conspiratorially—"had an affair with one in their captive breeding program? Which DNA proved to be correct?"

"Well, yes I do, but—"

"No buts this time and no doubts. This little chap not only has the plush coat—well, most all kittens do—but he also has the coloring. If you didn't know his dam was a Maine Coon, you'd think he'd stepped right out of the Highlands. We'll do the DNA test, though, just to be sure."

Beth smiled at the mental image this brought forth unconsciously. She stroked Bhu Fan, who was all but sitting on her head. "Have you got a name for him?"

"No. I've named the little queens: Thistle, Rose and Heather. But I just haven't come up with any good—"

"How about...Derryth, Wisteria? Name him Derryth, do!"

"Well, of course. That's a good Celtic name. Means 'oak', I think. Capital! How did you come up with that?"

Beth frowned, staring unseeing at Bhu Fan. "Well, to tell the truth, Wisteria, I don't know. It just popped into my mind."

CHAPTER TWENTY-FIVE

TWILIGHT WAS PUSHING LONG shadows across the cattery floor. Chad had not yet returned home but like the newly conscientious husband he was, had called to say he'd be there for supper. And Beth, adjusting to her new way of life with a hungry man to feed, was busy about her kitchen, an aromatic casserole in the oven. Looking forward to hearing about his folks' reaction to the old documents she and Cheryl had found.

The cats were adjusting, too. And felt themselves lucky. Beth-mom's new consort had blended right in. It was a marriage—if not made in heaven—at least earthbound in a manner that suited everyone.

Shere Khan, as was expected, held the floor out in the cattery, his audience mesmerized. What had transpired down at the beaver pond gripped every one of them. But felines are a pragmatic species. Que será será. They thanked Bastet that Gary Styles was no long a terrifying menace. They were glad Shaggy had dodged another bullet to fight another day. They hoped they might someday catch a glimpse of the elusive Loki and Crya, who now, it seemed, would not have to worry about "moving house" as Hawkeye had called it: they were safe on the Merryman preserve. They were amused at Bhu Fan's tale of Angel's newborns and the marriage of Beth's old friends.

At the moment, however, the happening that stuck in the mind was the actual arrival of Shere Khan, Smudge and the really weird-looking smutty colored Coon with dreadlocks.

When they burst into the cattery as Beth and Chad were changing litter boxes, the event had to be as exciting as Peary's return from the North Pole. Certainly two of the trio were garbed like woolly Eskimos.

Beth quickly turned as welcoming howls, chirps and trills—with a few derisive cat calls—ushered the returnees into their domain.

"What?" exclaimed Bethmom as she spied the three muddy cats, one of whom was a stranger. "Who have you brought home *this* time, Khan?"

The Great One ignored her and dropped the shell casing he carried in his teeth at Chad's feet. The game warden frowned as he knelt down and picked it up. It puzzled him... Well, the cats already knew *that* story.

They were still chuckling over Beth's reaction to the blinking, dun-colored creature in the lumpy overcoat. Without even thinking about it, she had swooped up the cat, set her down beside the sink and set about filling it with warm water and suds. The cat, for her part, showed not the slightest revulsion to what she had to know was about to happen to her. Well, of course, she wouldn't. Divinity had been handled by groomers and show judges from A to izzard. She simply looked very uncomfortable in her quickly-hardening shell of mud. What happened next, Beth would have sworn set all the cats laughing and whistling, bunny thumping the floor as they did so.

The ugly creature sitting on the counter beside the sink made a flying leap and dived head first into the warm, reviving, sudsy water, rolling around, upending herself, shaking vigorously and then sitting down, still flicking her head clear of the awful dreadlocks, purring like a rusty chainsaw, a mobcap of suds on top of her crown. It was obvious she was in no hurry to leave the bath water which was divesting her of that awful mud. And as it left her now slowly emerging pristine white fur, she burbled and sang and swam.

"Ah, hah!' cried Bethmom, who had stood back in wonder at this exhibition. "Now I know who you are." She dried her hands promptly, walked across the floor, slung a towel over her shoulder and grabbed the telephone.

Simon broke their collective reverie. "Dya' think, guys, she'll come back—like soon? Like before I go to Miz Brannigan's?" That the big silver tom had been immediately smitten with the heavenly Divinity was all too evident.

"Dunno, Simon. But I did notice how her owner looked you over when she came for her cat…"

"You want one last fling, do you, old man?" Shere Khan smiled wickedly.

"Um, maybe," muttered Bhu Fan, who was sitting outside the circle cleaning her whiskers.

"It's worth a try, I s'pose." She cocked her head thoughtfully.

"No, Boo!"

"*What*?"

"You gotta quit *doing* that!" Hawkeye admonished, sending an apologetic look toward Simon.

"Doing what?" The little Korat asked innocently, ignoring the stern look on her favorite servant's face.

"Gettin' in people's heads; you know what I'm talkin' about— like putting the thought on Bethmom so she'd know what to name that little tom of Angel's—"

Bhu Fan raised her eyebrows and looked offended.

"And you sure got my tail in a crack when you ripped open that quilt—and how did you know anyway, where to open it up? Was it that old patch tipped you off?"

Bhu nodded her head, still a bit resentful at Hawkeye's tirade.

"Was it something embroidered on that patch? I saw lots of tiny stitches in it. Looked like words."

"Bhu Fan drew herself up and bristled.

"I can't read. You know that, Hawkeye-my-peasant."

The big brown tabby scowled and showed his teeth.

She gave him a playful look, relenting. "But I'd seen that rhyme before in very old picture book at Rose Cottage…Remember?

Catemom said she'd had it when she was small girl-child. She sang it, saying it was one of her favorites…"

"So--?"

"It seemed like quilt maker was trying to secretly tell somebody something and so I thought that's where treasure was hidden."

Hawkeye looked skeptical which annoyed Bhu Fan. When she merely gazed at him with her eyes half closed, he added, "Okay, I'll bite: what did it say?"

Looking very smug, Bhu Fan stood up straight, like the school boy on the stage for his first recitation, and sang forth.

"Now isn't this a dainty dish to set before a king…?"

The End

Readers are welcome to visit and learn more about the Scottish Wildcat at www.garnetquinn.com or query author at garnetquinn@comcast.net

10179200R0

Made in the USA
Lexington, KY
01 July 2011